PRAISE FOR
JAIMIE ENGLE
AND
JME BOOKS

l. Ron Hubbard Writers of the Future Award
BRAG Medallion Honoree Award
Top Ten Book of 2014 Kid Lit Reviews

"...the world Engle has created in this novel is an intriguing one, equal
parts familiar and fantastic." *Kirkus Reviews*

"...belongs on your bookshelf - young or old - right along with
Tolkien and Grimm." –Amazon.com

"I did not want to leave until the last page was turned." –Kid Lit
Reviews

"...the same kind of universe you might meet Captain Malcolm
Reynolds or Luke Skywalker in." –The Story Sanctuary Reviews

"Jaimie Engle brings "The Dredge" to an exciting, unexpected,
and ultimately satisfying ending." –Third Flatiron Editor

INSPIRE. EMPOWER. EDUCATE
WWW.JAIMIENGLE.COM

BOOKS BY JAIMIE ENGLE

Clifton Chase and the Arrow of Light
A boy is chosen to change the past by a magic arrow

The Dredge
Supernatural gifts are sought through deception in a future world

Clifton Chase and the Arrow of Light:
the Coloring Book
Condensed version of the novel with pictures to color

Visit the author at jaimiengle.com and facebook.com/jaimiengleauthor

Dreadlands
Wolf Moon

Jaimie Engle

JME BOOKS

Text copyright © 2016 Jaimie Engle
Cover design © 2016 Philip Benjamin of Benjamin Studios
Interior illustrations © 2016 Debbie Johnson
Edited by A Writer For Life
The text for this book is set in Fairfield

Published in the United States by JME Books,
a division of A Writer For Life, LLC,
Melbourne, FL 32935.

Visit us on the Web: jaimiengle.com

Educators and librarians, for an author visit
or bulk order discounts, visit us at
jaimiengle.com or email jaimiengle@gmail.com.

Summary: With a grandmother who is unnatural, an anxious mother, and
a missing father, Arud's family tree is rooted in secrets.

ISBN: 10 0997170905 (tr. pbk.)
ISBN-13:978-0997170900
ISBN-13: 978-0-9971709-1-7 (eBook)

10 9 8 7 6 5 4 3 2

JME Books are meant to empower, inspire, and educate readers.

For Jason.
Without you I'd have titled this book after baitfish.

Nina,

Believe in the

impossible!

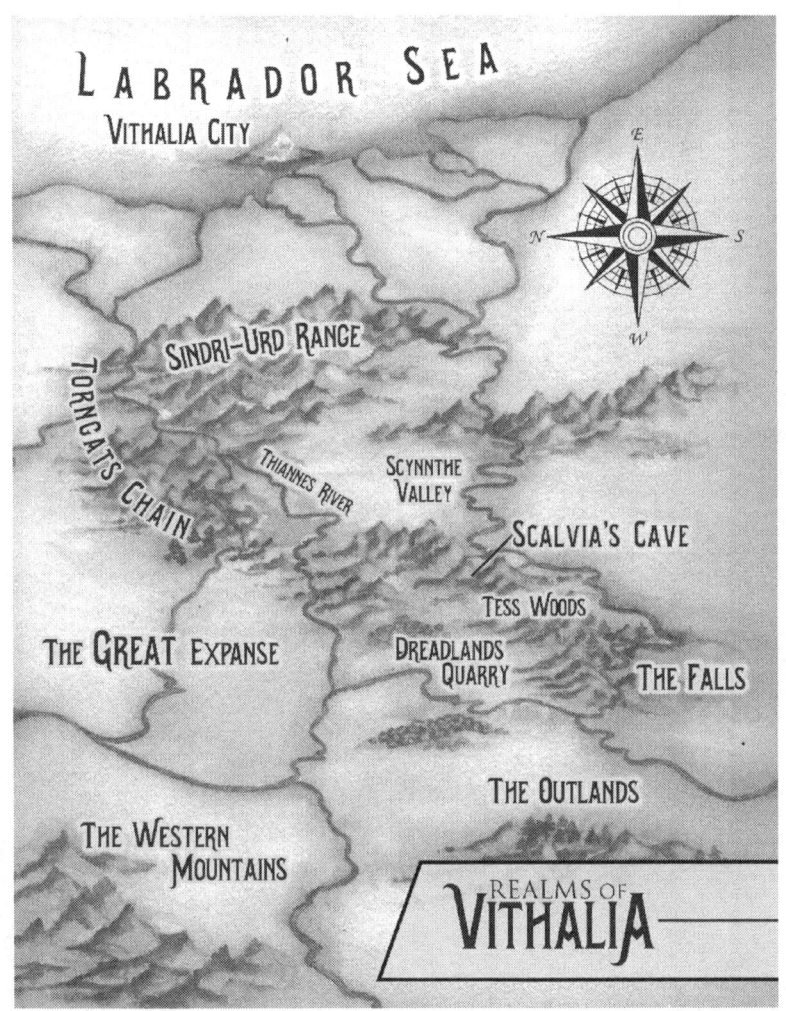

Jaimie Engle

Ψ ONE Ψ

Arud Bergson crept out of his house before dawn, his sleep cut short by nightmares of the ferine hunting him in broad daylight. Darkness clung to the remnant of night sky while cool air washed over his pale skin. As he slipped through his front yard and into the surrounding woods, he thought of the deer he would catch for his mother to make bruukish. The traditional stew induced a deep sleep in most, though Arud found sleep impossible, no matter how much he ate.

Not when creatures rose from the shadows.

As he trekked deeper into the woods, Arud's quiver bounced with dull taps against his back, while his crossbow stayed readied in hand. His grip was strengthened by a pair of hide gloves, like the ones gifted by his father prior to their first hunt. "The smell of man is the strongest one in the woods," his father had said that day. "Every branch and weed you brush against catches your scent. There it can linger for days. The deer will know where you are long before you know of its whereabouts."

"How do I catch one, Father?"

"Hunters don't catch deer, Arud. They hunt them. They wait for them."

"But for how long?"

"I cannot say. Each deer follows its own instinct. What I can tell you is that you must be still. Be at one with your surroundings. Allow the deer to sense a false security in your field of view and then, when the moment feels proper, that is when you strike."

"And how do I do that?"

"Forcefully, but with great reverence. And remember, the best way to hunt your prey is when they don't know they are being hunted."

"Yes, Father."

Arud had been a boy then. His arms no longer trembled when he took aim, though his belly still knotted up. He had accepted his place in the circle, where the lives of the innocent sustained the rest. Hunting was necessary for survival in the Outlands. Not to mention the utter displeasure he would face from his grandmother if he didn't return home with meat for supper.

After an hour, Arud reached his favorite hunting ground, a natural embankment near a spring-fed lake. He crouched in the trench he had carved out over the years and laid his bolts on the moist earth. His hand reached tenderly for one bolt in particular. It was the last one his father had carved before his two-day trip to market for supplies. More than a week later, he hadn't returned.

What could have happened to him? Arud's mouth went dry thinking of the unpleasant possibilities as he methodically rolled the ash wood bolt between his fingers. He dreaded the thought that his father wouldn't make it home before nightfall.

Before the creatures broke their bonds to the Dreadlands.

Late afternoon sunlight filtered through the branches. Cautiously, a spotted deer emerged off the embankment. Arud raised his crossbow. She reached the lake and lowered her slender neck to drink as he took aim and released the shaft.

The bodkin tip sliced into the deer's chest. She jerked up and sprinted to the woods. Arud swore as he grabbed another bolt and darted after her, over the drifts and around the fallen trees. Droplets of blood marked her path. His lungs burned as he chased her a quarter mile north of the lake, where she collapsed in a clearing, panting. Her blood pooled beneath her. She was not a large doe, no more than a hundred pounds, but heavier than sixteen-year-old Arud could handle without help.

He knelt beside her and unsheathed his knife. "I'm sorry," he whispered. The doe's black eyes stared ahead. He plunged his blade deep into her throat. "Thank you for giving your life so that I might sustain my own." Her head went limp and Arud stroked her soft fur until her spirit left her.

He set his crossbow beside the deer and searched the forest for a large stick to tie a drag rope around. He found one quickly and was carrying it back when his blood chilled. White orbs stared out from the dense woods no more than a tree length away. Pointed ears on top of the animal's head twisted. Its canine muzzle rippled into a growl showing pink gums. A ferine, Arud was certain, from the stories he'd been told all his life.

But it wasn't possible. It was too early for the ferine to hunt. How was this one here?

He rose slowly to his feet. His crossbow lay several yards behind him, beside the dead deer. He stepped back. Twigs snapped beneath his boots. His body trembled as the monster edged closer on all fours, maneuvering its massive body across the uneven terrain. It stared icily at Arud, who bumped the deer's hind legs as he back-stepped, taking his focus off the ferine long enough to retrieve his crossbow, but not long enough to locate his bolt.

Useless, he thought.

Muscles rippled through the ferine's smoky-gray pelt. It crouched on its strong hind legs as it prepared to strike. Saliva dripped from its sharp yellowed fangs. Froth covered its jowls.

"She's all yours." Arud said, as he backed closer to the birch groves. "I will not fight you for her."

The ferine growled louder as it neared Arud's kill. He continued to broaden the distance between them. As he reached the tree line, half a dozen yards away, the snarling ferine stood over the deer. His deer. With a quick jerk, it sunk its serrated teeth into the doe's soft flesh and ripped out mouthfuls of meat, which stained its muzzle and broad chest a deep shade of crimson. With the beast preoccupied, Arud seized the opportunity.

And fled.

His breath came out in sharp spurts as he crossed beneath limbs and over piles of fallen leaves, between logs and through the shallow stream, before he rested. The ferine would not go this far when it had food to eat, would it? It didn't appear to be following him, but Arud was taking no chances. He reached the embankment where he hastily packed his bolts and other supplies before continuing home at a near sprint.

Finally, Arud plowed out of the copse and entered the safety of his home. His father had filed pines into spears that bordered the property, the trunks jutting out of the earth at various angles ready to waste any creature that attacked their home. Arud doubled over to catch his breath. He searched the woods for movement, but found none. The distant mountains and valley spread as a rolling canvas to the north, and Arud wondered why they lived in the Outlands far from the other villages. Secluded and alone. Wearily, he trudged over to the well and brought up the bucket, gulping down mouthfuls of water before coming up for air.

What would they do if his father didn't return in time? What could he do if that ferine followed him? He had never heard of such a thing, a ferine out in broad daylight prowling without a full moon. His recurring nightmare flooded his mind. He searched the dense trees again while wiping his mouth with the sleeve of his cloak, expecting to see the ferine stalking him like in his dreams. But after a while and still no sight of it, he assumed the deer had sufficed, and let out a deep, tired sigh.

The blood-red sky of twilight covered the horizon, spanning from the Outlands to the Great Expanse beyond and into the distant unseen waters of the Labrador Sea. He knew this would be his last sunset before the fierce ferine pack surged with power from the full moon.

His thirst quenched, Arud crossed the threshold into the stacked stone house. The door creaked closed on rusty hinges. Darkness filled the hall. Arud felt his way past his mother's open door into the living room. His grandmother's chair sat empty. His sister's sweet laughter carried through the opened back door. He followed her voice to the meadow in the backyard where she lay with their mother in the grass.

"And what does that one look like, Lykke?" Arud's mother pointed to a rather large, dumpy cloud beside a squat, rectangular one.

"A goat running from its bath," Lykke said with a giggle.

"It looks more like you running from a bath," Arud said as he stepped through the grass.

"Arud!" Lykke rushed into her brothers arms. He lifted her with ease. "How was your day? Did you see any rabbits? I saw two, and—"

"Lykke, please," their mother said. "Let your brother settle before drowning him in questions."

"Arud doesn't mind. Do you?" Lykke's eyes glimmered, the brown marbled with green like grass in honey, and she grinned.

He kissed her forehead. "I have something for you."

Lykke jumped on bare feet, her curls bouncing off her shoulders, her hands clapping like hummingbird wings before her chest. He removed a small triangular stone from his pocket and knelt before her. "What is it?" Lykke asked, reaching for the object.

"An arrowhead." Arud grinned. "An ancient one, from the people who lived here before us. But you must be very careful not to lose it." Arud closed

Lykke's hand around the stone.

"Why?"

He paused, drawing out his sister's curiosity until she looked as if she would burst. "Because it's enchanted."

She slowly opened her hand as if afraid the arrowhead might try to escape.

"It's blessed with a protection charm. As long as you carry it, no harm will come to you."

She wrapped around him. "I won't lose it. Ever!"

"Didn't you hunt any meat?" his mother asked.

Lykke pulled away, her gaze fixed upon Arud's. "No."

"You have to make the kill. It is your job now." His mother's voice pinched. "Until your father returns."

Arud ran a jerky hand through his dark hair. "You mean *if* father returns."

His mother gaped at him, opened and closed her mouth, then looked away. Arud's hands dropped to his sides. Why had he said that?

Lykke lifted her chin. "I think it's good that Arud didn't kill any animals today. Who cares if we have no meat for the stew?"

Arud remained silent about the deer in the woods.

"Your grandmother will care," their mother coarsely whispered.

"Then, I will go out and find something…a rabbit at least."

"No," Lykke whined, reaching for Arud's leg.

"Lykke, I have to," he said, shaking her off.

"I have last night's stew simmering. I had hoped for fresh meat to add, but we will survive."

Arud and his mother each held their secrets; eventually he would have to tell her about the ferine, but not in front of Lykke.

"Sit with us, Arud. Mother and I were cloud-gazing."

Arud looked once over his shoulder at the trees before taking a seat beside his sister. He could feel his mother's stare boring into him. "Where's Grandmother?"

His mother snapped her head back with a disgusted snort. "Toov left early. And I hope she stays away all night."

"But Mother, the full moon will bring out the monsters tonight."

Their mother smoothed out her skirts. "I didn't mean anything by it, Lykke. Besides, it wouldn't be your grandmother who I would fear for."

Arud let out a laugh, his hands forming a steeple in his lap, until a sensation, like icy fingertips, crept across the nape of his neck. He turned. Toov stood in the doorway wearing an ugly twist to her mouth.

"Grandmother." Arud stood, his limbs shaking.

His mother jumped up too, her face ashen. "Mother. I didn't hear you return."

"It seems not, Vinter," Toov said. She faced Arud. "Why are you not hunting, child? Is it the practice of the men in this family to spend their days at play?"

Arud's ears burned. "I left early to hunt and took a deer with no trouble." He paused for too long.

"Well, where is it," asked Toov in a voice trembling on the verge of laughter, "this deer you hunted so easily?"

"It was stolen from me. By a ferine."

Toov's mouth spread in a wry grin.

Vinter's fear showed. "A ferine? But it is too early."

"The poor deer." Lykke began to whimper.

"It's not possible," Vinter said.

"I know," Arud whispered.

Toov turned toward Lykke. "Stop your crying. You will soon understand the necessity of the kill, young Lykke. The want for meat is unequalled."

"Not everyone has your insatiable hunger." Vinter's ashen face flushed red. "Well, it is time for the rest of us to resume work." She disappeared around the side of the house.

Immediately Arud gathered an armful of wood from the pile and headed toward the back door. When he passed Toov, she clamped her bony hand like a vise around his wrist. "Why did you not fight this ferine you claim you saw?"

"What makes you so sure I didn't?" He avoided her calculating glare by staring at her cracked, yellowed nails. Dirt clumped beneath the tips. He wondered why, since the old woman only sat in her rocker and knitted.

"You'd better board up early, boy," she continued. Arud looked up into her cloudy grey eyes as she said, "The full moon will be strong tonight."

Ψ TWO Ψ

Arud entered the house with an armful of wood, piled it near the hearth, and began adding tinder to the fireplace.

"I saw the trinket you gave Lykke," Toov said. She sat in her chair knitting, not bothering to look up as she spoke.

Arud's pulse raced as he continued to feed the flames.

"Is this how you spend your time when you say you're working? Digging in the dirt like a child? Why do you fill Lykke's head with such superstitious nonsense?"

Arud turned. Lykke stood behind him holding the arrowhead, a single tear streaming along her cheek. He rose and knelt before her placing a tender kiss on her forehead. "Go and play," he whispered, folding her hand around the trinket.

She offered a half-smile and hurried out of the room. Arud waited for her door to close before he faced Toov. "I wasn't playing. I told you, a ferine stole my kill."

She snorted. "So you say. No son of mine would be—"

"He isn't your son, Mother," Vinter interrupted from the kitchen. "So you have nothing to worry about."

Toov slowly lifted her head. "No—No, he isn't."

Her eyes reflected the firelight, then dimmed as she returned to her knitting. "He is his father's son, of that I am certain."

Vinter barreled forward, as if to attack, stopping inches from Toov. "Do not dare speak ill of Berg when he is unable to defend himself."

Toov twisted the knitting needles in and out of the yarn, her smirk lingering like a foul odor. "I only speak the truth, Vinter. There's no need for your animosity."

Vinter stood frozen.

Arud opened his mouth, hoping words would pour out of it in defense of his father, but instead it produced nothing. Only silence.

He told himself to stand up to her, to tell the old witch to leave them alone.

But he couldn't.

His mother shuffled back to the kitchen, stirring all the things she couldn't say into the black kettle. "Supper is ready," she stated before heading to her bedroom.

"I find no desire for last night's food any more than I desire the company of incompetent hunters." Toov stood and left the home.

Arud's lip trembled as he ladled hot stew into two clay bowls for him and his sister, wondering again when—or if—his father was ever coming home.

Ψ THREE Ψ

Arud bolted the front door and latched the windows tightly. The full moon crawled out from behind the clouds, bathing the meadow in a cold white light. Vinter cooled a tonic of boiled herbs, mixed the tea with honey, and her daughter reluctantly drank. Lykke had been born with the illness, a fever with hallucinations that sent her into fits of rage. Vinter's remedy curbed the symptoms, though Arud imagined Lykke would need the monthly tonic throughout her life.

A light burned in Toov's detached cottage. Arud never understood how the old hag could stand to sleep alone, but he figured she was vile enough to keep anything away, even those creatures that lurked in the darkness.

Vinter sat silently at the kitchen table, her hands clasped before her. Arud knew her heaviness. This was the night the ferine crawled freely throughout the realm of Vithalia, creatures who fed on the flesh of men before disappearing into the shadows till their next awakening. And Arud's father still hadn't returned home.

"Your father will make his way," Vinter said, staring at the table.

Arud said nothing in reply, feeling childish for not having soothing words for his mother.

"He is strong, Arud. And you carry his strength." She faced her son. "He will return to us."

But Arud saw she doubted her own words.

He forced a halfhearted smile, the best he could muster, and walked down the hall to the room he shared with Lykke. After closing the door behind him, he grabbed the planks leaning against the wall and nailed them across the frame. He sat on the edge of his cot gripping his crossbow.

There would be no sleeping tonight.

Ψ   Ψ   Ψ

Arud opened his eyes to a quiet room. He must have dozed briefly, but something had awakened him. A sliver of moonlight stretched across the pine floor. Lykke's chest lifted and lowered rhythmically. What had pulled him from sleep?

A howl rang through the air, lifting the tiny hairs on the back of his neck. A second howl answered the first. He forced his legs over the edge of the cot; his heart raced. He slid against the wall beside the boarded window and carefully peered between the slats.

White moonlight covered the ground like winter's first snowfall. Darkness plagued the dense forest bordering the property. No movement. He wished he could remove the slats to see clearer, but he didn't dare.

A shadow peeled back from the distant woods; a ferine with black fur gleaming as if obsidian. Silver strands wound throughout the dark fur; shimmering veins pulsating with power from the moonlight. It was more than double the size of the ferine Arud had seen in the woods earlier that day.

He collapsed to the floor. Where was Father? He

had never been gone this long before. Something terrible must have happened. If it hadn't yet, it surely would tonight with each village locked down, and each home boarded up. He hoped his father had found shelter in time.

"Arud?" Lykke's voice cracked through sleep. "Arud?"

"I'm here, Lykke."

"Is Father okay?"

Arud sat beside her on the cot. "I hope so."

"I dreamt that he—" Her hazel eyes filled with tears. "Is he ever coming home?"

Arud pulled his sister into his chest. "Shhh. Father is strong." He rocked her back and forth, stroking her hair. "He will come home." Arud repeated his mother's words with the same lingering doubt.

Pebbles crunched in the bed outside their window. A panicked chill swept down Arud's back. His body tensed, and Lykke immediately quieted.

He pushed off the cot and, with unsteady legs, walked swiftly back to the side of the window. He wiped sweat off his brow. Crossbow in hand, he slowly slid until he could peer through the space between the slats.

The black ferine stared back at him.

He gasped and jumped away. "Lykke, hide! Now!"

Lykke darted beneath the cot. Arud paced in panic. What was he supposed to do? He held his bolt in one clammy hand. If that ferine wanted to get through his window, could he even stop it? He forced his feet to the floor and readied his crossbow with shaking hands.

Then waited.

The creature's piercing shriek filled the air and Arud dropped his weapon to cover his ears. Then, as suddenly as it had begun, the ferine's howl silenced and the room fell still as death.

"Arud?" Lykke's shrill voice rattled beneath the cot. "What's happening?"

Arud lifted his crossbow from the floor and glanced through the slatted window.

The ferine was gone.

Ψ FOUR Ψ

Arud slipped in and out of a sleep broken by night terrors. Amber-eyed creatures, like the one outside his window, surrounded him, their serrated teeth dripping with blood. They howled and shrieked, hiding in the dark shadows of his mind. And no matter how fast he ran, their jaws snapped at his heels.

His racing heart forced his eyes opened.

Lykke lay in his lap asleep. Sunlight sifted through the slats covering the window. They had survived another Wolf Moon. Carefully, Arud lifted Lykke's head and set a pillow beneath it. She shifted, but quickly stilled without waking. He placed his ear against the plank-covered door, and although he didn't hear anything, he listened a few extra minutes before deciding the house was safe and removing the boards.

He opened the door to a still house.

"Mother?"

"In here," Vinter replied.

Arud ruffled his hair as he crossed the hallway to the living area where his mother sat by the fireplace. Her hand touched the stone mantle. Her bare feet rested on the hearth. Arud sat beside her. Dark circles framed her tired eyes, fixated on the flames burning in the firebox. Had she slept at all?

"A ferine came close last night," Vinter said.

"Yes, even to my window."

Vinter turned sharply, her brow furrowed, before looking away. "Then, it is time for you and Lykke to leave this place." She moved to the cedar trunk pressed against the stone wall.

"Leave? Why?"

"It's no longer safe here." She dug through the trunk, removing stale-scented traveling cloaks and bags. "Your father's brother lives in Vithalia City. You will lead your sister there."

Arud opened his mouth to speak, and then closed it. What was she talking about? Leave home for Vithalia City? To meet an uncle he had never heard of? "For how long?"

"For as long as it is necessary." Vinter rummaged through the trunk. Arud crouched beside her and placed his hand on her shoulder. She stopped, buried her face in her hands, and shook her head. "I can't lose all of you."

Arud leaned forward, his voice softening. "I don't understand, Mother. Why do we have to go?"

"You just must trust me. I know it is unclear, but soon you will understand. Now go wake your sister and pack your bags. It will take nearly three weeks to reach the city and you must arrive before the end of this lunar cycle."

"What about you? And father?"

"I'll wait here for your father's return, and then we will meet you and Lykke. Please, Arud. Do as I've asked."

Arud nodded obediently, though his mind raced, searching for answers he knew would not be given. His mother's skin had turned sallow. Her once strong hands appeared brittle. Vinter had always been beautiful with delicate features and a slim figure, but since Berg's recent disappearance, she seemed frail and fragile.

"I'll go pack."

Vinter nodded approvingly as Arud left the room.

Ψ Ψ Ψ

After twenty minutes, the bedroom door flung open. Vinter flew into the room, her skin layered in a fine sweat. "Hurry, Arud."

He looked up. "What's the matter?"

"Your grandmother is coming soon. You must leave before she can prevent it."

Arud quickened his pace, tossing the rest of his and Lykke's clothes into their bags.

"What's happening?" Lykke asked, rubbing her eyes. Noticing Arud packing, she added, "Where's Arud going?"

Vinter knelt beside the cot, brushing a strand of curls behind Lykke's ear. "You and Arud are going on a journey."

Lykke yawned. "A journey?"

"Yes."

Lykke reached for her mother's hand. "Are you coming with us?"

Vinter shook her head. "No, *lovell*. I am waiting for your father. But when he returns, we will meet you and Arud in Vithalia City."

Lykke's face lit up. "The city?"

"It is beautiful beyond your wildest imaginations. You will have so much to occupy your time, you'll hardly notice my absence."

Arud strapped the first bag closed, then handed a

clean slip and dress to his sister. Lykke lifted her nightgown over her head and changed into an ankle-length linen slip. "Of course I will notice." She raised her arms for Vinter to put on her dress. "When will you be coming?"

Vinter slid Lykke's shoulder straps into place, attaching a bronze brooch to each side. "I will come with your father once he arrives home."

Lykke's face turned down. "But what if he doesn't come?"

Vinter's eyes faltered, but then her mouth curled into a smile as she reworked the already placed brooches. "Of course he will come."

"It isn't your job to worry about Father," Arud said. "Now, finish getting dressed."

"Here." Vinter unhitched the beaded necklace from around her neck. "Take this."

Lykke traced her finger across the smooth glass and amber beads, twirling them to scatter the light. She looked up. "But Father made this for you. I've never seen you without it."

Vinter took the necklace and clasped it around Lykke's neck. "Yes, and I will expect it returned when we meet again." She grinned and Lykke smiled back.

Arud dropped a bag at Lykke's feet. "Lift this. Is it too heavy?"

She picked up the sheepskin bag then shook her head. "No. It's fine."

"Good. Strap on your boots."

Vinter stood. "Arud, bring your bag with you into the kitchen."

She left the room and he followed, leaving Lykke to finish getting ready. His stomach wrung in knots.

Any moment his grandmother could appear, and nothing good would come from it.

Vinter removed herbs from a row of tins descending in height beneath the kitchen window. Meticulously and with practiced hands, she measured the herbs by sight, combined them, and placed the blend into a small decorated tin. "This is the mix for Lykke's tonic. You'll need her to drink it once before the you reach the city."

Arud placed the tin into his bag. "How will I know when?"

Vinter packed dried meat and vegetables into various sized drawstring pouches, along with loaves of dark bread, hard cheese, and dried fruit. She passed them to Arud, along with two sheep bladder waterskins. "When you see Lykke's symptoms surface, prepare her tonic. The fever precedes the rage. Any abnormalities in her body or behavior indicate her sickness is flaring, and you must give her the tea at once. Do not wait long after she shows these signs, or it could be too late."

"What if I have no way to make a fire? Or no water to boil? What if I—"

Vinter placed her hands on Arud's shoulders. He stood nearly a foot taller than her, with a lean build like his father; broad shoulders to carry heavy loads, long legs and arms with muscles defined by many years working in the fields. "You will do fine, my love. And your father and I will see you soon."

Arud stared into her blue eyes, trying to decide if what Vinter said was true.

"The animal you saw in the woods, the one that stole your kill, you are certain it was a ferine?"

He nodded. "Yes, but I don't want to believe it."

"Nor do I. Something strange is happening to the creatures. Somehow, they have managed to crawl without the full moon. I hope you will remember that as you travel."

"Yes, Mother."

"Do you know the way to the city?"

"I've heard from Father," Arud said, attaching his rolled blanket to the base of his pack. "The Tess Woods cover the realm from the Outlands to the Scynnthe Valley. The Thiannes River courses through the realm to the Labrador Sea where Vithalia City lies. I know my way to the river. Beyond that...I don't know the way."

Vinter gleamed, her head turned ever so slightly to the side. "I'm glad to hear that you have minded your father's words. At the river's bend where the bank lies the widest, you will wade through the shallow water to the Scynnthe Valley. Two mountain chains tower at the valley's edge. The Torngats wind toward the Great Expanse, long and wide, but the pass is full of hidden dangers. The Sindri-Urd Range is jagged and steep, and although its pass leads more directly to the city gates, it is less frequented. Many find they are not able to survive the climb. But don't worry. Each will eventually lead to Vithalia City. When you arrive, you will know which pass to take. Do you understand?"

"No. I do not understand. Why would you send Lykke and me away when there are ferine hunting in daylight? How could that ever be a solution I would understand?"

"Are you questioning my decision?"

"I am questioning your sanity."

Vinter turned her focus back to the work of her hands. Arud's heart pounded as his anger fed him courage. "What would Father say?"

Vinter slammed her hands on the counter. "Your Father would not question me. If he were here, he would be the one telling you to go. It is not always necessary for you to know the details, Arud. You and Lykke are no longer safe here. You will take her to Vithalia City and make haste. Do you understand?"

"As much as I am able."

"Good. When the time comes, everything will be clear. But now you must leave." She called out toward the bedroom. "Lykke?"

Lykke appeared in the doorway, wearing a black travel cloak. Blonde curls popped out from the bottom of a tan handkerchief drawn in a knot at the nape of her neck. "Is it time to go?"

"Yes. And quickly."

Arud followed his mother to the door. Lykke walked with him, hand in hand. "I still don't understand why we are going without you," Lykke said.

"I've already told you. I am waiting for your father."

Vinter scanned the yard before leaving the threshold, scampering quickly to the edge of the surrounding woods. Arud stayed close to her heels and Lykke pattered in hurried steps to keep pace. The grass bent beneath their boots. Arud watched as a flock of geese headed south across the clear blue sky. When they reached the woods, Vinter turned.

Lykke's lower lip trembled. "Must we go?"

Vinter bent low, taking Lykke into her arms. "It

isn't safe here anymore. I have kept you in the Outlands too long."

Lykke wrapped her stiff body around her mother's waist.

"Then come with us," Arud pleaded. "If it isn't safe here."

Vinter brushed the backs of her fingers down his cheek. "I cannot leave without knowing your father is safe." She shook her head. "But you and Lykke must. That ferine will return for you at the next full moon. They seldom change their minds once they have found a scent they desire." She grasped Arud's hand with her cold palm. "That ferine won't stop looking for you until you are caught."

Ψ FIVE Ψ

They had hiked for several hours before Lykke finally stopped crying. The dense woodlands spanned thick with pine and birch trees packed tightly together. Sap perfumed the clean air. Fallen logs and hidden burrows littered the leaf-covered earth. Arud helped Lykke over small drifts and held back low branches so she could cross more easily through the trees. By midday, the forest began to thin out; limbs spread as if the boughs grasped for one another. The brisk autumn weather faded quickly as winter stretched from its three seasons of slumber. Arud pulled his cloak tighter.

"Look, Lykke," he said in a hush. "A hare."

She looked with reddened eyes to where Arud pointed. "It looks scared."

"It should be."

"Why?" She faced her brother who held his crossbow trained on the small animal. The bolt shot out striking the hare before neither it nor Lykke could protest. Lykke gasped, covering her mouth as the hare slumped over, dead.

"Go gather branches." Arud snickered.

She moved off into the woods as Arud lifted the hare by its hind legs to retrieve his bolt. He frowned, reminded of the bolt he had abandoned beside the deer; the last one Berg had built. He found level ground between two trees and scattered fallen leaves to reveal the earth. Arud removed his knife from a deep leather sheathe, and with the straight edge, sliced down the midsection of the hare. As warm blood poured out, he removed the innards and flattened the carcass. Using the tip of his knife, he cut a slit, then ripped the fur off the meat as easily as taking off a coat.

Lykke appeared with an armful of branches, bracken, and dry leaves. She grimaced, looked away from the naked hare and dropped the wood. She set a tinder bundle on a small piece of bark curled and frayed at the edges. One by one, she leaned the branches in a triangular formation while Arud finished preparing the game.

"It's ready," she said, admiring her work. "Father taught me how."

Arud smiled. "That looks like the perfect fire lay." He wedged a long stick through the hare lengthwise and balanced the spit on his and Lykke's bags. Arud clashed pieces of birch bark against the flint rock he carried, until the resinous shavings of wood sparked, and finally lit the tinder. He blew gently, watching the flame catch and spread to the brittle wood.

"Is there anything to drink?" Lykke asked.

Arud passed Lykke a waterskin. The redness in her eyes had dulled to a pale pink. After she drank a few sips, she handed the skin back to Arud. Very soon, the smell of roast hare filled the air as the dripping fat popped and sizzled in the flame. Arud's stomach grumbled.

"Do you know the way?" Lykke asked.

"I think so, though I'm not sure which mountain we cross. Mother wasn't clear which to take."

Lykke nodded, drawing in the dirt with her fingertips. "What do you think is happening back home?"

Arud breathed deeply, imagining the punishment Vinter would face by Toov for their disappearance. Arud never understood why his grandmother kept them under such tight scrutiny, especially Lykke, who was never allowed to roam the woods unaccompanied. "I don't know. I'm certain Grandmother didn't approve of Mother's decision."

"Why?"

"Who will she have to hunt for her meat if I'm not there?" Arud answered. He wished he could take his words back after seeing Lykke's forehead scrunch in worry. "And no one but you is able to disarm Grandmother once she gets into one of her moods."

Lykke grinned, still staring at the dirt before snapping her head up sharply. "Do you think Mother will be all right?"

"Of course. Mother is cunning and wise. She knows how to handle Grandmother. Don't you worry."

Seeming satisfied, Lykke turned her attention back to her drawing. "What did Mother mean when she said the ferine would be back for you?"

Arud recalled the image burned in his mind of the amber eyes staring at him through the window, although this time he also envisioned the ferine's snarling muzzle and sharp fangs beneath. He shrugged, trying to hide the memory. "I don't know."

But he did know.

"Well, at least we won't have to worry about seeing any creatures again until after we reach Vithalia City," Lykke said.

Fear's fingers gripped his chest. The ferine only crawled with the full moon's light; it had always been so. But the ferine in the woods that stole his kill spoke otherwise.

It had crawled during the day.

Ψ SIX Ψ

Arud licked his greasy fingers while Lykke picked sinewy meat off the bones. A northwesterly breeze had picked up, blowing a crescendo of cold, dry air through the trees. Half a day's sunlight remained. Arud stomped out the small fire and handed Lykke her pack.

For hours, they pressed through the birch trees in silence, the steadily growing wind pushing dead leaves off weak branches. The Thiannes River coursed in the distance, and Arud hoped he wasn't walking them in circles.

As the sun lowered in the west, light filtered through tall crowns of clustered spruce, oak, and pines. Pools of light spotted the dull browns and greens of the flora and fallen leaves. Arud pulled his cloak tighter as a chill swept past him. Lykke shivered. Very soon they would need to build a fire.

The churning river resounded as they reached the edge of a steep hill, where trees grew in a sloping line; a jagged rock wall stretched up from the riverbank several hundred feet parallel to Arud and Lykke. Large stepping stones pushed through the water's surface like the capped heads of tiny gnomes. Whitewater rushed past in waves.

"Let me go first." Arud bent his knees taking cautious steps. The sharp angle pulled him into a jog, but he slipped on slime coated leaves, landed hard on his rear, and tumbled the whole way down.

Lykke burst into laughter.

Arud's gaze flicked upward. "That was funny, was it? Let's see how you do."

Lykke curtsied and sat. She pulled her cloak into a careful knot before her chest and scooted to the edge. Leaning back, she yelled, "Here I come!" She launched down the hill, gliding across the leaves, using the knot as a rudder. She skidded to a stop beside Arud, a wide grin spread into her flush cheeks. "Maybe next time I should go first."

"Let's just set up." Arud pointed to a sandy embankment where the river branched into a shallow pool. Fragments of leaves and bark had matted to the back of his hair and cloak. Lykke tried brushing them off, but Arud pushed her hand away and told her, in a thickening voice, "Get the fire ready. I'll catch us dinner."

Lykke gathered wood and tinder while Arud unpacked a small fishing rod. He strung the line using his cloak pin as a lure and pierced it through a piece of hare he'd saved from lunch. Barefooted, he walked to the pool and peered into the crystal water. Trout swam in schools nibbling on insects and small fish. He cuffed his pants and stepped into the ankle deep water. The cold snatched his breath away. The fish scattered as he waded deeper.

He wondered about his mother. Was she all right? Had Toov punished her for their disappearance? If only Berg had arrived on time. Arud had so many questions for his father that he feared would remain unanswered.

A twig snapped.

Arud spun around. The woods lay still. Squirrels chattered and birds called. Leaves rolled in the breeze.

He listened for the source, until satisfied that he and Lykke were alone.

Why had no one ever told him the creatures were capable of daywalking? Was it because he had been the first to ever witness it. Arud shivered.

After some time, the curious trout moved closer, taking cautious bites. Arud watched, waiting for the biggest trout to forego its better instinct and latch onto the free meal. The trout took the bait. Arud waited until the fish had eaten most of the meat before yanking on the line. The pin tip slashed through the trout's mouth and he pulled the flopping fish out of the river.

Lykke had fallen asleep on the shore, but opened her eyes when she heard the commotion. "You caught the big one. How?"

"Patience." Arud set the trout on a tree stump to clean it. "If you wait long enough, the fish eventually come to you." He sliced the trout and dunked it in the river to clean out the blood and guts. "If it doesn't know it's being hunted, then it won't be prepared to fight." He raked off the scales with his blade.

Lykke squatted beside Arud, hugging her legs to her chest. "So the fish stood no chance of escape. You had it hooked before the metal even entered its mouth."

A tentative smile built across Arud's face. "Well, that's a grown up thing to say."

"I am nearly ten, Arud. Hardly a little girl."

"Then how come I'm the one doing all the work?"

Lykke's fingers fanned out against her breastbone as her mouth hung opened. "I'm working. I gathered all the wood, and the leaves, and set up everything for you. All you did was catch a stupid fish."

Arud tilted his head and paused. "I see. Then I bet it would be no trouble for you to make the fire."

Lykke glared at him, her lips pencil thin.

"Go on," he said. "Take the birch bark and a stone from my bag and get started."

With a loud huff, she turned and stomped back to Arud's bag. She removed his flint stone and bark in big, exaggerated motions, not hiding her agitation. She smacked the birch against the flint, and he smirked, knowing that before their meal, Lykke would be eating her own words.

Ψ SEVEN Ψ

Arud opened his eyes to darkness. He thought he'd heard something, though the stagnant forest was still all around him. Lykke slept soundly cocooned in the blanket beside him. Arud's eyes adjusted, and he scanned the basin. A raccoon scurried past, leading a pack of rodent thieves toward the water to steal fish.

A bat crossed overhead.

An owl hooted.

Nothing seemed out of place, yet the gnawing sensation in his stomach told him otherwise. He lowered his head to the ground and stared into the star-strewn sky. Was his father doing the same thing? Arud imagined his father had returned home right after he left. He smiled as he pictured Berg and Vinter traveling in their wake, each step bringing them closer to reunion. But his smile quickly faded. He and Lykke were alone.

A distant howl echoed through the trees. Arud's heart hammered in his chest.

"That ferine will return looking for you."

He shuddered, picturing the amber-eyed ferine as it wandered the hills. Was it searching for him? He had never heard of such a thing, a ferine stalking outside a full moon. What could this mean? Everything he had been told about the creatures since he was a boy was being shaken. Every story and lure, every warning and precaution proved unreliable, even false, against this new reality, as if the very laws of nature were being broken and there was nothing anyone could do to stop it. Especially not him, Arud Bergson, a boy from the Outlands, an outcast of the realm. What could he possibly do against a ferine out in the open?

Arud listened to the woods for a long time: the chirping cicadas, the whirring wind, the rushing river. But no ferine. It had howled only once. Clouds drifted in long mists high above the treetops. He knew those clouds. They preceded the cold of early winter snowstorms. He hoped otherwise.

What would his father say? *"Arud, those clouds mean to warn of winter's lashing. Heeding the warnings of nature will keep you alive."*

In the morning, he would have to make different preparations. Otherwise, they might not make it to Vithalia City.

Ψ Ψ Ψ

The morning came, prickling with cold, and Arud immediately built a fire. For breakfast, he broke off pieces of dried meat and bread Vinter had packed, careful to ration it for the journey. They ate silently. Though wrapped in a blanket, Lykke still shivered.

"How are you feeling?" Arud asked.

"Cold."

"I know. It seems winter is sending its first storm early this season."

Arud poured mint tea into mugs and handed one to Lykke. Her eyes closed as she cupped her tea beneath her nose. Steam brushed her cheeks.

"After breakfast, we need to get moving."

"Because of the ferine?" Lykke asked.

Arud faced her, his lips pressed in a fine line. "You heard it, too?"

She nodded. "Was it the one Mother said would come looking for you?"

Arud paused. He couldn't tell her the truth. "No, of course not. That couldn't happen until the next full moon. It must have been something else. A mountain lion."

"It was no lion, Arud. I heard the howl as plain as you."

Arud breathed deeply as Lykke sipped her tea. Her gaze drilled into him, but he did not meet it.

"Is it going to follow us the whole way?"

"I don't know," he said, resigned. What was the point in lying when she knew the truth?

Her hands trembled. Arud placed his arm around her shaking body. "I wish Mother was here. I don't understand why she sent us away."

"I don't either. All I know is Mother wouldn't have done this if there were another way." He pulled back from Lykke. "You have to believe Mother did what she felt was best for us. And she will meet us in the city with Father. You do believe this, don't you?"

She nodded as tears seeped from the edges of her eyes, the hazel darkening into a deep-algae green.

"Then focus on those thoughts, on seeing Mother and Father again." He kissed her forehead. "Let me deal with the ferine while you worry about packing."

Lykke rolled her blanket to fit beneath her bag. She polished off her tea, rinsed the mug in the pool, and tied it to the string on her strap. She laced her boots, the soft leather still warm from the fire. Arud packed their gear into his bag. His crossbow hung from a twine rope latched to the strap. His bolts poked out the top. In three motions, he grabbed a bolt, readied his crossbow, and took aim on a squirrel several yards away. He released. The bolt stuck into the trunk inches above the squirrel's head.

"What are you doing?" Lykke covered her mouth as the squirrel darted away.

"Testing my speed, and the squirrel's." He approached the tree and pulled out his bolt. "Let's get moving."

They followed the river. The rising sun melted the thin clouds. The spreading heat warmed the air. By late afternoon, they had stripped out of their traveling cloaks. They coursed up tree-covered hills, the river flowing far beneath them. The hills hardened into rock from where the Thiannes had carved her path over the centuries.

As the trail wound away from the river, Arud helped Lykke avoid the jagged edges of sharp flint stones. He broke off several pieces and slipped them into his pocket. They would come in handy on the many cold nights, Arud imagined, ahead. The river, barely visible, remained within earshot as the rock ledge softened to dirt, then evolved to an open meadow covered in lush green grass.

They rested in the meadow, munching on dried berries from Arud's pack. Lykke rubbed her shoulders. Arud knew the pack bore down on her, but he had already taken most of the load on his own aching back and was unable to withstand anything more.

"What do you think the city will be like?" Lykke asked, biting into a gooseberry.

"Like nothing we've ever seen." Arud popped a handful into his mouth.

"Please tell me," Lykke begged. "What do you think?"

Arud shrugged. "Father has told me they have lights in the city which never go out."

"Like candles?"

"Kind of. But they burn in oil sconces, thousands of them. And there are people whose only job is to fill the vats with oil to keep the city lit."

"The people must be wonderful. I bet they wear clothes that feel like clouds against their skin, and have soaps that smell like springtime."

Arud smiled.

"And I bet they never have dirt beneath their nails or calluses on their hands, because they have servants to do the hard work for them."

Arud nodded. "You're probably right. But who would they find to do their work?"

Lykke shrugged. "I don't know. Maybe they have elves. Or trolls they've captured from the mountains." She began to laugh.

Arud laughed with her. "I guess we'll have to wait and see."

"And what of our uncle?"

"That I don't know. Father never spoke of him."

"I wonder why."

They sat in silence, Arud completely lost in thought. Why had no one ever spoken of this uncle they were being sent to stay with? Would he even know who they were?

Lykke sat up. Her vision focused on the meadow. "We have to leave. Now!"

"Why?" Arud squinted searching for the impendency. "What do you see?"

"We aren't alone." She swung her pack onto her back and broke into a run.

Arud quickly packed what remained and ran to catch up. "I don't see anything. What makes you so sure?"

She kept going, without so much as a glance back. "Because, Arud, I can smell them."

Ψ EIGHT Ψ

"**H**urry!" Lykke raced across the meadow, her black cloak rising like a fleeting shadow behind her.

Arud's muscles tensed as he bolted after her, peering over his shoulder as he ran. What did she mean, she could smell them? He flared his nostrils and inhaled only the musk of the trees. Lykke had already cleared half the meadow, and Arud watched in bewilderment as she lengthened the gap between them. He ran at full speed, yet somehow she continued to gain. There was no time to think about it now.

"Run, Arud. Run!"

She abruptly veered toward the river on a diagonal. Arud grimaced as his bag slammed against his back and his bolts rattled in their quiver. Still Lykke moved farther and farther ahead.

The ferine roared from deep within its throat. Arud gawked as the black beast charged on all fours, pounding across the meadow, its sights set on him. He quickened his pace, but the ferine raced closer, its speed unnatural. It would catch up to him long before he could reach the woods on the other side.

Lykke screamed and lurched to a stop where the meadow seemed to drop off. Arud found his second wind, running to catch up to her and see what could possibly be worse than the bulking ferine gaining on them. He came to a sudden stop beside her. The long drop ended in a hungry river with rocks like jagged teeth. Arud looked back. The ferine had cleared the halfway mark in the meadow and would be on top of them in seconds. He had time to notch a bolt and shoot, but would need to wait for the ferine to move closer. What if one bolt wasn't enough? He couldn't take that risk, not when he had Lykke to look after.

"We have to jump," he said.

"I can't," Lykke cried, shaking her head rapidly.

"You have to or that ferine will kill us."

She stepped away from the ledge, still shaking her head. "No."

Arud grabbed her hand tightly pulling her to his side. "There's no time for this," he said sternly. "On three you jump or I'm pulling you with me."

"I'm scared."

"Trust me. Our fate will be worse if we don't jump."

"All right." She placed her hand in Arud's.

"On three."

Lykke closed her eyes.

"One."

The ferine closed the distance between them, its black paws striking the grass.

"Two."

The beast drew nearer, its pants rasping thick as sap on the back of Arud's neck.

"Three."

His heart lodged in his throat as the river moved closer and closer. Lykke screamed. Even as they hit the icy cold rapids, he did not let go of her. They sliced through the pounding water until Arud overpowered their momentum and pulled them to the surface, where they emerged, gasping. Arud faced Lykke. "Are you all right?"

"I think so."

The massive black ferine paced at the top; silver strands pumped through its fur like a pulse. Its amber eyes locked on Arud's. Chills prickled up his spine. The current swept them through the curving fjord away from the meadow and the woodlands, and out of the ferine's sight. The monster couldn't possibly follow them.

Could it?

Arud swam one-armed through the churning river, his muscles strained as he searched for an inviting shore. The river widened to parallel banks of rapids. With each dip and drop, both Arud and Lykke fought to keep their heads above water. Arud navigated through the swelling white waters, avoiding the rocks. The banks taunted a safe haven on either side as the current wrestled them downstream.

"Lykke, can you swim over there?" He pointed to the high wall on the far shore, where roots stuck out of the bank like thick arms. It would be at least a foot and half climb out of the water.

"I, I don't know. I can try."

Her teeth chattered, her lips shaded a pale blue. He had to get them out of the cold. But the swelling rapids were picking up speed, the shoreline fading farther and farther out of their reach. They cut across the current, swimming toward the bank, but the river surged, carrying them downstream against their will.

"This isn't working," Arud said in frustration.

"Why is the water moving so quickly?" Lykke asked.

Arud's eyes widened. He knew exactly why.

"Swim harder," he shouted, dragging Lykke

toward the bank. But it was no use. The river overpowered them. The initial purr of the Thiannes had grown into a growl, its deafening rush like a stampede of wild animals thundering through the air. Frantically, Arud searched for a fallen trunk or a rock bed to catch hold. Overhanging branches teased with limbs lying outside his grasp.

There was nothing to save them.

"Hold on to me," he said. "Do not let go."

"Why? What's happening?"

He didn't have to answer. Less than one-hundred yards ahead, the river dropped off and out of sight.

"Arud," Lykke's voice quavered.

"I've got you," he said. "I won't let anything happen to you."

With a final race of momentum, the hands of the river pushed them over the edge with a heinous surge of water. It happened so fast, the air left Arud's lungs. He had no idea how far they dropped, plunging down the waterfall to the large basin beneath. He lost his grip on Lykke's hand. The scenery blurred. His heart threatened to burst in his throat. Hitting the basin, Arud fought against tons of water pummeling him as he swam away from the plunge pool. With a gasp, he surfaced in the waterfall's lake. He didn't see Lykke anywhere.

"Lykke!"

She did not answer.

He waded, spinning in circles. Where was she? He dove under and opened his eyes but could not see through the murky water. Reluctantly, he surfaced.

"Lykke!"

Silence.

In a panic, he swam back toward the waterfall and dove through to the other side. He wiped his eyes clear while catching his breath. Something thrashed against the rocks. He didn't need to move any closer to know it was Lykke's pack, which had pushed into the cove without her.

Ψ NINE Ψ

The mist from the waterfall covered Arud's skin like a fine sweat. He pushed Lykke's pack onto the rock ledge and set his own beside it, then dove beneath the falls, back to the lake, swimming out until the surge silenced. The current stirred up loose plants that floated to the surface. He took a death breath and dove deeper.

Using the bank as a guide, he ran his hand against the smooth rock wall. The current picked up, and Arud worried it would get worse, as the rocks abruptly sank back and the water tugged, pulling him beneath the bank. Flailing for control, he swirled in darkness, desperate for air, until finally, the surge broke, pushed him out a spout, and flung him onto the hard stone wall of the cave he had been treading beneath.

He coughed out the water he had swallowed, retching on all fours, until he could breathe again. Exhausted, he looked around. It was very dark, and he found it hard to focus. He wondered if Lykke had been pushed inside as well, when her cough echoed through the cave.

"Lykke?" he called out, his voice hoarse from retching.

"Over here," she replied faintly.

Arud stood, his hands outstretched, as he felt his way through the darkness. "Where are you?"

"Here," she managed, followed by several deep coughs.

He could just make out her shadowy silhouette sitting on a rock. "I see you." He ran over and crouched, wiping strands of wet hair off her face. "Are you all right?"

She forced a smile. "I think so. But next time you say jump, I may not listen."

He let out a deep breath and hugged her tight against his chest. "You scared me to death! I thought I'd lost you."

"But you didn't."

"Can you walk?"

"I can try."

He helped her to her feet. Arud looked around the cave. Water trickled down the walls onto a glittering stone floor forming small puddles. The ceiling hung with stalactites. The wall near Lykke emitted a faint glow. Arud looked closer. "Glow worms. We can use these."

He searched the floor for a stick but found nothing. He looked back at the ceiling. Carefully, he pushed the stalactites until he found one, like a loose tooth in a monster's mouth, that he could wiggle free. With a crack, the mineralized icicle dislodged, and he carried it over to the worm-covered wall. "Help me put worms on this. We can use them as a torch."

They gathered as many of the glowing worms as they could fit on the jagged rock. The mock torch glowed enough to light their path. "Let's get out of here," Arud said.

Lykke grabbed ahold of her brother's wet cloak as it dripped water in a patter on the stones beneath him. He led them through the sloping cave going up, then down, as he followed the rumble of the waterfall, though it drifted louder and softer as he crept, proving unreliable. The path eventually opened into a large chamber in the heart of the mountain. The Thiannes River churned above them. The mouths of many carved pathways, the same as the one they had exited, lined the chamber in a ring resembling the hollowed out legs of a monstrous spider. A rock fell from the abyss above them. Arud swept around, pushing Lykke behind him as the sound echoed throughout the chamber.

"What was that?" Lykke whispered, tightening her grip on Arud.

He twisted the torch around, the light from the glow worms too dim to illuminate the dome. Another rock bounced off the shimmering floor, rolling to their feet.

"I have a bad feeling about this," Arud said.

A rumble shook the sides of the high walled ceiling. Rocks hailed to the ground. A funnel of black creatures, moving as one, poured down the tube into the large cavern, heading right toward them.

"Run!" Arud yelled, pushing Lykke toward the closest opening.

She ran hard, her boots catching on the grooves in the rocks as Arud plowed behind her, pushing her to move faster. The fuming black shadow edged closer. A chord of shrill pitches shrieked through the air. The cramped tunnel narrowed as Arud and Lykke plowed through. The light from the glow worms barely showed the curves in the pathway and Arud had seconds to change their direction before slamming them into the wall. Air fanned behind them as the dark army gained. Shrieks mixed with Lykke's cries intensified as they bounced off the smooth walls.

The creatures were right on their heels. Arud slammed into Lykke and pushed her to the cave floor, his body covering hers as the swarm of assaulting bats filled the empty space in the tunnel. Lykke screamed. Arud covered his head.

The last of the bats straggled past and Arud lifted off his sister. "Are you okay?"

"No," she said, through her tears. "What was that?"

"Bats," Arud said while standing.

"Disgusting."

"Actually, it's a good thing." Arud helped Lykke to her feet. "They'll show us the way out."

He led her by the hand down the tunnel following the diminishing bluster of bats. "That arrowhead I gave you must have protected us," Arud said.

Lykke tilted her head. "Go on."

"The people of this land fought creatures long ago, much like the ferine, only they were bats led by a god named Camazotz."

Lykke shuddered. "I would rather face wolves than bats any day."

"Be careful what you wish for. Neither are enemies you ever want to face. And at least the ferine are bound to the Dreadlands. The werebats of Camazotz have no bounds, until they were trapped in the Torngatd hundreds of years before our people ever set foot in Vithalia."

"So you believe in them? And you think they are trapped in the mountains?"

The wail of the waterfall grew louder. The floor ramped up and the smallest fraction of light shone in from up ahead, glinting off the minerals in the tunnel walls.

"I am no longer sure of many things I once believed with certainty." Arud quickened his pace, climbing the incline toward the light. The opening came into view, and he threw down the stalactite. "But I am certain we have found the way out." He and Lykke exited the tunnel, arriving on the ledge behind the waterfall where Arud had left their bags. His eyebrows and mouth turned down.

"What is it?" Lykke asked.

"Someone has taken our bags."

"Who?"

"How should I know? But they have my crossbow. We won't survive without it."

Lykke's shoulders crumpled forward, and she sat on the wet rocks. "What do we do now?"

Arud paced, running his fingers through his thick hair, muttering to himself. With a sigh, he threw his arms up. "We press on. We have no other choice."

"But we have nothing."

"And we will die with nothing."

Lykke's eyes constricted, then she looked away. "You sound just like Father."

"Good."

She looked back at her brother, his smile large, his muscular frame pressing through his wet clothes.

"We need wood and tinder. We make camp here."

"Behind the falls?" Lykke asked. "But everything will be wet, and there isn't enough time for the wood to dry out. We won't be able to make a fire."

"Then we'd better move quickly so the wood can dry before sundown."

Lykke huffed loudly as Arud dove into the cold water, under the pounding falls, to the lake. She plunged in after him. "It is so....c...cold," she chattered, surfacing.

Arud swam in long strokes to the bank and pushed himself ashore. The falls were framed with varying shades of greens and browns from a variety of trees and bushes. With skepticism, Arud eyed the foliage cramping the basin. Someone else was there with them, hiding behind the bramble or in the trees, and he meant to discover them first. A lookout of flat rock extended from near the top of the falls. Arud grabbed hold of a knotted tree root and climbed, using the indents in the rock to leverage his feet and hands.

"Arud," Lykke called. "What are you doing?"

He continued climbing until he reached the lookout. The valley stretched on for miles, the river disappearing beneath the forest far in the distance. He couldn't see Vithalia City or any nearby village. Nor could he see any person lurking beneath the camouflage of treetops.

Carefully, he climbed back down with a little more difficulty as gravity helped him across the slippery slope. Lykke piled gathered sticks and moss. Arud pressed through the trees, looking for birch wood. He found a white birch tree without much trying and used his fingers to peel back the loose bark.

He felt the prick in his back before he even heard a branch snap.

"Don't move," the girl said. "Or I shall strike."

Ψ TEN Ψ

Arud stood still. The pointed tip of something hard pressed between his shoulder blades. "What do you want? I have nothing to take," he said. "My gear's already been stolen from me."

"I don't want your gear," the girl said.

"Because you're the one who took it?"

She didn't respond.

"What is it you want then?"

"That is my business," she said.

"Really? Because it feels like it's become my business, with whatever it is you've got shoved in my back." She breathed heavily, and he waited for her to falter. "Why don't you lower the weapon and we'll talk." He peeled off bark in small slivers as he scanned the ground for something to club her with. He didn't see anything.

"Why don't you shut up, or I'll stick this bolt through your back." She stepped closer.

Arud could almost pinpoint her exact proximity, how close her legs were, the precise angle of her bolt. "So you did steal my gear," Arud said, keeping her distracted.

In one fluid motion, he flung the slivers of bark over his shoulder and into her face. He swept his right leg back and caught her square in the calf. Arching his back, he pushed his chest forward and away from the bodkin tip. His leg caught her while he swiveled around, pushed through with his momentum, and knocked her legs out from under her. She slammed to the ground before she knew what hit her. As he clamped his hands around her wrists, she kicked him hard in the groin. Arud grimaced as she broke free. He grabbed her by the legs as she crawled away, flipped her onto her back and squatted on her chest, pinning her down with his weight. Panting, he snatched the bolt, *his* bolt, out of her hand and pressed the bodkin tip into her neck.

"Get off me!" She writhed beneath him.

He fought back a smile. He was intrigued by this feisty girl who was much stronger than she looked. After several moments of hard struggle, she finally succumbed, though her breaths still came in angry rants. Her round eyes shone gray with yellow along the edges, resembling a double eclipse. "You want to kill me?"

"Only if I have to," he lied, tightening his grip on the bolt. "Who are you?"

"My name—is Scalvia."

"Why are you here?"

She wriggled to break free again. Arud pricked her skin with the tip of the bolt drawing a trickle of blood. "I said, 'why are you here'?"

"I live here. This is my home." Her lips were stained red like the wings of a cardinal.

Arud regretted pricking her. He'd only meant to scare her. He withdrew the bolt. "No one lives between Vithalia and the Outlands except in the outposts. Why did you steal from me?"

"I only wanted to talk."

"You're lying. You don't even know me. How'd you even know I was here?"

"Please let me up so I can explain."

Arud stared into her eyes, her bright glaring eyes, with thick black lashes fanning out like peacock plumes.

"Please."

He slid off her, feeling foolish for pinning her. She turned her head away and rubbed her neck where the bolt had pricked. Her hair fell down her back in long black waves. "I saw you go over the falls," she whispered. "I thought you might need help." Turning to Arud, she asked, "Where's the girl? Is she all right?"

"Lykke," Arud said. He jumped up and sprinted back through the trees to the lake, completely forgetting about the strange girl with the gray eyes and black hair. He knew it could be a trap. After all, the girl had tried to kill him only moments before. Lykke could have already been captured. This girl was very cunning, and Arud would need to be more careful in the future. If he made it out of there alive.

"Lykke!" He plowed out of the tree line.

She was sitting near a pile of wood, waiting patiently. "There you are. I was wondering if you had left me..." Her eyebrows lifted as she looked past Arud. He turned hastily. Scalvia was walking up beside him. "Who are you?" Lykke asked.

"My name is Scalvia."

"You are very beautiful."

Scalvia's cheeks tinted rose and she smiled. "And what is your name?"

"Lykke," she said. "It means happy. And that's my brother, Arud, if you haven't already met."

"We have," Scalvia said, facing Arud, a wry look

on her face.

Arud cleared his throat. "Where are our things?"

"They are secure. I can take you to them, if you'd like." Standing on the bank, Scalvia's slip dress neared the ground, her pale skin reminding Arud of goat's milk.

"This way." She turned, exposing the laces of her black bodice, climbing up her bare back like clinging ivy.

Lykke leaned close to Arud. "What should we do?"

Arud's gaze trailed Scalvia as she disappeared through the trees. "I can't do much with this bolt. I need my crossbow." And your tonic, he thought. "We have little choice but to follow her."

"I like her," Lykke said.

"You would." Arud shook his head. "Come on. She's already got a head start." Arud took Lykke by the hand and they stepped into the woods.

Ψ   Ψ   Ψ

The forest thickened, and the falls quieted the farther they traveled. The limbs' green leaves contrasted brightly against the dark backdrop Scalvia created. Arud and Lykke stayed close, avoiding fallen trees and moss-covered rocks till the sloping forest floor opened to a large rock hill topped with more trees. Scalvia stood at the entrance to a cave at the base of the hill. She looked over her shoulder. A smile lifted her red lips, and she motioned them to follow her inside. The entryway was narrow and led into near darkness.

Lykke stopped short and pulled against Arud's hand.

He bent down. "What is it?"

"I don't like this," Lykke said.

"This way." Scalvia's voice echoed off the rock walls and floor.

"You said you liked her."

Lykke stared ahead with scrutinizing eyes. "She isn't what makes me uncomfortable."

Arud felt warmth press out the cave entrance. He was ready to get out of the cold, even for a few moments. "We won't stay long. We need our things, or we can't continue. You understand?"

She slowly nodded.

"Good. Then let's get this over with." He squeezed her hand and they stepped inside, following the shuffles of Scalvia's boots on the hard stone. Up ahead, a flickering light pierced the darkness, and shadows touched the walls. Their path curved, and the light played tricks on Arud's eyes as the girl's shadow grew larger, then bent and arched like the four-legged ferine hunting him in the hills. His palms became clammy. Where was she leading them?

After the curve, the cave opened into a den with walls draped in tapestries. Heavy rugs covered the floor. Wood chairs were set around a table in the center, and a clay stove burned a small fire. The smoke billowed up through a fissure acting as a flue in the rock ceiling. Three others stood beside Scalvia.

Arud protectively guarded his sister with his body as he pushed her behind and reached for his bolt. He wished he had never followed the beautiful girl through the woods. "What is this?" he seethed. "A trap?"

"No," Scalvia said. "This is my family."

A man with dark hair, a trim beard, and the same striking features as Scalvia motioned welcome to his guests. "I am Ek and this is my wife, Ahlgren." A small-framed woman, with eyes reflecting the firelight, nodded toward Arud and Lykke.

Arud did not move. He caught a glimpse of his and Lykke's bags against the far wall, near a hutch. He didn't see his crossbow. He hoped it was wedged beneath his bag. At least if he had his bow he could try shooting his way out, although he wasn't sure how easy that would be.

A boy who appeared to be his age stepped out of the shadows. He resembled Ek, same dark eyes and hair, and the same stocky build. "We are not safe with them here," the boy said as he crept closer to the fire. Arud could now see his eyes, green as sea foam. "They cannot stay."

"That is enough, Vang," said Ek, glaring at his son.

"He's right," Arud said. "We're not staying. We only came to retrieve what was taken from us." He glared at Scalvia, who lowered her head.

"Please," Ahlgren said. "You must be hungry. At least eat before you continue your journey. You need nourishment."

With a sideways glance, Arud looked down at Lykke. Her eyes did not hide her hunger.

"Thank you. My sister needs food and rest."

Ahlgren moved back to the stove to finish preparing the meal.

"Are you thirsty?" Ek asked.

"Yes, please," Lykke said.

Ek took mugs from the hutch and filled them from the pitcher on the table. He handed one each to Arud and Lykke. Arud had tasted this drink before, the sweet syrup with a hint of flowers. His mother made the fermented drink for festivals in the Outlands, or at least a variation of the elderflower mead he was drinking.

Vang glared with cold flat eyes, and Arud's mouth went suddenly dry. He gulped down more mead trying to coat his throat and calm his nerves.

"Scalvia will take you to change clothes before supper," Ek said. "Your belongings are over there. Please, take them with you."

Scalvia turned toward an opening behind her. Lykke followed without hesitation, though Arud moved cautiously throughout the room. His eyes locked with Vang's. He lifted his bag, and anger flooded him.

"I'm missing my crossbow—"

"In good time," Ek interrupted without looking up, in a tone implying there was no need for further discussion.

With clenched fists, Arud yanked his bag and stepped through the corridor, heading down another narrow hallway. He couldn't leave without his bow and would need to placate these people until he could figure out an escape. The cave curved in a maze of chambers, lit by burning pitch hung from the walls.

Scalvia waited for him before a door. "You may change in here."

"And Lykke?"

"She is across the hall."

Scalvia stared into Arud's face, her pupils wide, her smile relaxed. His stomach tensed as he shoved quickly into the small room, closing the door behind him. Sunlight filtered in through a long fissure in the rock wall. In the corner, a large burlap blanket covered a mattress of leaves and moss. Arud sat on the bed and opened his bag, shuffling through the contents. His quiver and bolts were also missing, but he found Lykke's tonic and let out a sigh of relief.

He changed into clean clothes, now knowing how the rats felt in his traps back home. Where was he? Who were these people? And what did they want with him and Lykke? With his bag slung over his shoulder, he opened the door.

Scalvia stood waiting in the hall. She grinned.

Lykke exited her room, wearing only her linen slip, and Scalvia's attention shifted. "Let me help you." She took the outer dress from Lykke's hands and slipped it over her outstretched arms. "There you are. Just like a beautiful skjaldmaer."

Lykke giggled and Scalvia smiled, turning round eyes upon Arud. He gave a half-smile, trying desperately not to get lost in her beauty.

"This way," she said.

Arud followed her down the hall, back into the main room. On the table, plates surrounded two large crisped ducks garnished with onions and cabbage. Arud's mouth watered at the scent, the hints of dill and coriander infused in the fowl's skin.

"Ah, you look much better," Ek said from the dining table where he sat beside Ahlgren. "Have a seat."

Arud, Lykke, and Scalvia sat at the table followed by Vang, who slipped out from the shadows, his face like stone; eyes fixated on the strangers.

"Let us pray." Ek bowed his head and the others followed suit.

Arud lowered his head. He could feel Vang's glare. He wanted to reach across the table and slam Vang's head into the crisp ducks. Maybe that would break his stare.

"Lord Odin and Lady Freya, we give our greetings to thee," Ek solemnly prayed. "Please Bless this bounty set here before us and enjoy this good food with us, as we do enjoy it. Hail and love to Thee…"

Arud lifted his head as they spoke in unison "Hail and love to Thee." A bone-chilling fear spread down his spine, as he caught them all staring at Lykke, whose head remained bowed.

Eyes closed.

Ψ ELEVEN Ψ

They ate quietly, as if they hadn't all been staring at Lykke moments before. This had all been a trap. Arud pushed his food around on his plate, no longer hungry. He had to get them out of there. But how?

He caught Lykke's smile out his peripheral, her face beaming as if she were having supper at a friend's or a relative's house, and not in this unknown den, which kept Arud's stomach twisted in knots.

Finally, Ahlgren broke the silence. "You are not from here. Where are you traveling to?"

"Vithalia City," Lykke said between chews. "To meet our uncle."

Arud glared at her, wishing his sister had not shared their plans with these strangers.

"Is that right?" Ahlgren said. "You seem quite young to be making this trip alone. How old are you, Lykke?"

"Nearly ten, Ma'am."

"My, my, almost a woman."

Lykke giggled.

"And you are traveling alone?"

"Mm-hmm," Lykke said, her mouth full.

Arud set his fork down heavy. "We are followed by our father and our mother." He admonished Lykke with a stern look that she met with a slight frown. "They are no more than a day behind us, due to my father's business taking more time than he'd expected."

"And why are your travels bringing you to the city?" Ek asked, gnawing on a duck wing. "Just to meet an uncle?"

"That is our business, sir," Arud said, staring up at him.

A large smile crossed Ek's lips. "Very well."

They quieted again, their cold conversation replaced with the lifeless sounds of meat ripping off bones. Sips filled the still air, mixed with the rich scent of duck.

"I understand you went over the falls," Ek pressed.

Neither Lykke nor Arud answered.

"Must have been quite a scare."

Lykke looked at Arud, who shook his head slightly, before she lowered her stare back upon her plate. Scalvia turned sharply, her cheeks ruddy. "Perhaps you didn't hear my father addressing you?"

"That's enough, Scalvia. I'm certain Arud has his reasons for keeping silent."

Arud's shoulders relaxed, sensing the questioning would cease, when Ek took a big bite of cabbage and asked, "Where were you coming from, anyway?"

Arud pounded his fists, rattling the mugs on the table. "We wish to keep our business our own."

Everyone stared at him: Ek's lips tight, Vang's eyes squinting, Scalvia's face washed in disdain, Lykke's mouth gaped in disbelief. Only Ahlgren refrained from revealing her disapproval, her lips curled in a peculiar smile, and somehow her expression made Arud the most uncomfortable. Tears sprung to Lykke's eyes, and Scalvia placed a protective arm around her shoulder. Around *his* sister's shoulders, as if Lykke needed protection from her own brother. Vang cracked his knuckles and shook his head in reproach.

"I see," Ek said, returning to his meal.

Arud could stand for no more. "My crossbow was not with my things. I wish it returned."

"Of course," Ek said, cleaning the wing bone. "All in good time."

"Are we not free to leave?" Arud asked, his pulse rising. "Are we prisoners here?"

Ek set down the wing, licking his fingers one by one with a loud slurp. He and Ahlgren exchanged a glance before Ek leaned his elbows on the table and stared directly into Arud's eyes. "Arud, we know a ferine follows you."

Arud leaned far back in his seat. He thought he might pop out of his skin, a sense of claustrophobia strangling him. "How could you know?"

"We heard her howling last night. We are too far from the Dreadlands to hear such things." Ek's forehead creased, his eyebrows and mouth turned down. "Only a powerful ferine could crawl without the moon's light. And it is only through mythology that we read of such possibilities. I'm not aware of a single soul who has seen one outside a Wolf Moon."

But Arud had.

"Ahlgren insisted Scalvia search the woods for the ferine's prey. We expected to find no one. Especially not two unaccompanied children."

Arud gulped hard.

"Scalvia has a nose for hunting," Ahlgren said, beaming. "Since she was a little girl."

Scalvia's face reddened.

"Why does the ferine hunt you?" asked Ek. "How

does it leave the Dreadlands?"

Arud shrugged. "How should I know? How it is even possible outside a full moon?"

"Nothing stays the same forever," Ek said, stroking his beard. He looked as though he considered telling Arud more, but held back.

Ahlgren watched Ek in silence. Turning to Arud she said, "We do not wish for you to feel imprisoned. We only offer protection."

Arud felt the room spin. He was afraid he would be sick. How could this be possible, any of it? Why had his mother sent them out into the open? They would surely be caught and killed by this ferine.

"Which is why you are not welcome," Vang said, his eyes constricted. "You have brought your scent, and the creature hunting you will come here looking for you."

"Vang, that is enough," Scalvia screamed. "You selfish brute!"

"Quiet," Ek said. "Your brother speaks truth, but it is of no consequence." Facing Arud he said, "We offer you a safe haven for the night if you will accept it."

Arud looked from Ek to Vang. At least this explained his aggression. He presumed it was already near sunset, much too late to make camp. He turned to Lykke, her moist eyes pleading with him to stay. Reluctantly, he nodded. "Thank you for your hospitality. We will burden you for only this night and leave after first light."

Ek smiled broadly. "Good. Then it is settled. And tomorrow, Scalvia will lead you through the Tess Woods. No one knows them better than she."

"But father," she said in protest, her lilt wavering.

"I cannot go alone."

"Scal-vi-a."

She lowered her head. "Yes, Father."

Ek turned to Ahlgren. "Woman, you prepared a fine meal. Thank you."

Ahlgren smiled, then stood to clear the table.

"Arud, join me outdoors while the women clean up," Ek said.

Arud looked to Lykke.

"Go on," Scalvia said. "She will be fine with me."

Arud reluctantly followed Ek and Vang to the cave entrance. The air had cooled drastically as the sun set behind the mountain. Trails of light bounced off the trees as night squeezed in. Vang stood with Ek, whispering something that Ek shook his head at.

"Arud," Ek said. "Join us."

Arud plodded over and Vang drifted to the side. An owl hooted in the distance while a few bats flew overhead. Rustling wind swept through the leaves in small currents that dropped off. Arud took a seat on the boulder beside Ek, his palms sweating, his mouth suddenly bone dry.

"Arud, what do you know of the ferine?"

Arud shrugged. "I'm not sure now. It seems everything I was ever told is being proved otherwise."

Ek smiled. "Yes, it seems that way to all of us." He turned to Vang. "Leave us."

"What? Father, you can't be—"

Ek's lips pressed into a white line and his clenching jaw pulsed. Vang's face tightened. His ears reddened. He turned on the balls of his feet and stormed into the cave.

"He will be fine," Ek said, more to himself as he

faced Arud. "My family has lived in this region of Vithalia since Leif the son of Eric the Red came ashore hundreds of years ago."

Arud fiddled with a weed that had cracked through the rock.

"There were creatures in Vithalia then, too, plundering the territories of our ancestors from Vineland up through Labrador to the northernmost point of Mark Land, driving most of the Vikings back to Greenland. For centuries, the creatures have plagued Vithalia every twenty-eight days, as I'm sure you've been taught, when the full moon's power surges."

"Yes, that much I know." Arud stared at Ek's profile.

"Do you know some can shift into other forms?" Ek faced Arud.

"What do you mean 'other forms'?" Arud asked.

"It is said that the oldest can shift into human form. But it is believed to be a myth, one that I am not sure I fully accept."

Arud's skin crawled and he shuddered. "So how would you know if you saw one?"

"Most likely you wouldn't," Ek said, taking out a rolled leaf packed with herb. "But things seem to be changing as of late, don't they?" His broad smile was warm, though Arud felt chills cross his bones. "This ferine chasing after you without the full moon is an anomaly. There is no recording of it, or mention of it in any of the stories passed down through the generations that I've heard." He clashed a piece of birch bark from his pocket against a flint rock until a spark caught on the end of the leaf. He primed the herb through deep breaths.

"So, why do you think it is happening now?"

Ek exhaled a cloud of smoke. "There is the legend of the Great Mother to consider. If she has been awakened, then the creatures would become more powerful, finding strength in her sorcery without the moon."

He blew out heavy smoke and offered the rolled leaf to Arud.

Arud waved it off.

"You know not all creatures of ferine blood have evil intentions." Ek puffed deeper. His shoulders and face relaxed.

"The one I've seen have showed nothing but evil intentions."

They both fell quiet as Arud considered Ek's implication. Finally, he asked, "What is the legend of the Great Mother? I've never heard of it."

"The ferine legend speaks of the awakening of the Great Mother once the chosen one is of age."

"The chosen one?"

"A human child of ferine blood who will rise up against this evil and bring healing to these lands. But if the legend comes to pass, if it is more than words on a page, we must not allow the Great Mother to take hold of this child."

"Why?"

"If she does, then the creatures will roam freely when there is no full moon. Mankind will be enslaved, if the creatures deem their lives of any worth at all. More likely, this region will be overtaken by the ferine, spreading throughout all the realm until there is nothing left."

"What happens if she doesn't reach the child?"

"Then balance will be restored in Vithalia between ferine and man. The people will be at peace, which is why I believe the ferine stalks you."

Arud let out a nervous laugh. "I'm not religious. I don't believe in prophecies and I hope you're not implying that this legend has something to do with me. As if *I'm* that child. Trust me, I have no ferine blood."

Ek faced Arud with dark, focused eyes, his mouth stretched in a fine line. "I do not mean to imply anything, Arud. I only know that there is a ferine roaming in wolf form without a full moon, and you seem to be its target."

Arud swallowed hard. The sun had almost set, and he shivered from a cold fear.

Ek snuffed out his rolled leaf upon the boulder and set the rest in his pocket for later. Methodically, he removed a sack from around his waist and opened it. "It is time to move inside." He pinched into the sack and took out a handful of shimmering granules that he scattered over the boulder and on the ground in front of the cave as he backed toward the entrance.

Arud watched from the cave mouth. The grains caught the poor light of dusk and twinkled. "What are you doing?"

"Protecting us by covering our scent."

"What are you using?"

"Powdered silver."

"How does it work?"

"It is a repellent against the ferine. Not a guarantee in this consistency, but it should pack enough pain to deter the one hunting you." Ek reached the entrance and dumped a generous heaping of silver granules on the ground, which he rubbed in with the heel of his boot. "Help with the door."

Arud grabbed one end of the heavy stone boulder and Ek grabbed the other. From inside the cave, Ek nailed a plank across the stone, sealing off the only way in or out. Arud felt like he had sealed them inside a tomb, knowing there would be no way to escape if the ferine found him.

Ψ TWELVE Ψ

Arud lay on the burlap mattress unable to sleep. The night grew longer as he stared at the stars through the split in the cave wall. He trembled. What would he do if the ferine found him? What could he do? He never should have followed Scalvia, nor accepted her father's hospitality. He was not thinking clearly. With twenty-six days till the next full moon, they still had almost three weeks journey before reaching Vithalia City. There was little room for error. The closing of his door pulled him from his thoughts.

Lykke stood barefoot in the entryway, her shoulders hunched. Her chest heaved. In the darkness, he couldn't make out her face, but he knew her expression wasn't right. She lurched forward in long strides. What was she doing? Arud perched on his elbows, wondering for a moment if it were even Lykke.

"Arud," she whispered. "Are you sleeping?"

He pushed the strange thoughts away as her imaged returned to normal. "What is it?"

"I had nightmares."

"Come here."

She crawled into Arud's bed, and curled beneath the fur blanket.

"Do you want to share your dreams?" he asked, stroking her soft hair.

Lykke shook her head. "They were too horrible to speak aloud."

"Well, it was simply a dream. And dreams aren't real."

Lykke sat up. Starlight fell across her wide eyes casting the rest of her face in eerie shadows. Her irises were changing, growing a deeper shade of brown. "But this one was so real. How can you be sure it won't come to pass?"

"Because it was just a dream." He kissed her forehead. "Now, try and get some sleep."

Lykke put her head down and closed her eyes. Rubbing her back, Arud sang Vinter's lullaby, which she always sang to Lykke when she had nightmares back home.

> *Baru, baru, sleep quietly.*
> *Let fear far from you lie.*
> *Baru, baru, fall fast asleep,*
> *for I will stay nearby.*
>
> *The night is long, but day will break.*
> *Tomorrow's light will shine.*
> *So hush, my lovell, don't you cry.*
> *Just lay your head 'gainst mine.*
>
> *Baru, baru, sleep quietly.*
> *Baru, baru, sleep tight.*
> *The darkness won't stay long, my love.*
> *Soon you'll walk in the light.*

Lykke snored softly. Arud leaned his head against the cold stone and stared out the window for some time before a dreamless sleep fell heavy upon him.

Ψ Ψ Ψ

A shiver forced Arud from slumber. Cool air had filled his room. Lykke lay curled in a ball beside him, her cheeks cold to the touch. He draped the animal fur over her small frame, but she did not stir.

"Lykke." Arud shook her gently.

"Hm?"

"It's first light. Time to go."

Lykke snuggled deeper beneath the fur. "But it's so cold. Do we have to leave so early?"

Arud grinned. "I'm afraid so. We mustn't overstay our welcome."

She opened her eyes, and Arud's mouth turned down in a frown. A green ring ran around her irises, the centers now a dark chocolate. "Do you feel all right?" he asked.

Lykke nodded. "Just cold."

"Go get dressed, then meet me in the den."

Lykke peered through the small fissure in the cave wall. "The sky looks gray. Do you think it might snow?"

Arud stared out. "I hope not." He turned to Lykke. "Come on, now. Go get ready." He scooted her up and out the door.

After dressing, Arud shuffled down the hall, carrying his belongings. The pitch on the walls still burned to light the way. He reached the main room, where Ek and Vang sat at the table.

"Good morrow," said Ek. "Did you sleep comfortably?"

Arud ran his fingers through his hair. "Yes, thank

you. Now, I think we should be going."

"Will you be staying for breakfast?" Ahlgren asked.

"No, Ma'am. I want to get moving as soon as—"

"Nonsense," Ek interrupted. "Ahlgren will serve hot porridge. Then you may take your sister and go."

Arud forced a smile as his hands clenched and unclenched at his sides. "Thank you again, sir." Now he really wanted to get out of there. Still, he knew Lykke would need a good breakfast to stay moving through the woods.

Ek leaned back in his chair at ease and in control. "Take a seat. Scalvia will attend to your sister."

"Perfect," he answered in a sharp tone. He sat beside Vang, who seemed to have calmed from the night before, though he still kept one eye locked on Arud.

"It seems early winter pushed through during the night," Ek said. "The ground is covered in frost. Have you any warmer clothing?"

"No, sir," Arud said. "We hadn't planned for an early winter."

Ek motioned toward Vang. "Bring one of your furs for Arud."

Vang acknowledged his father's command, glared at Arud as he stood, and disappeared down the hall. Ahlgren set a bowl of white grains before Arud, the steam piping. He blew on a spoonful and sank his teeth into the porridge. The heat warmed him, and he was grateful Ek had insisted they stay for breakfast.

Lykke appeared in the hallway, clothed in her wardrobe from home, aided by Scalvia, who stood beside her. His sister sat quietly, said nothing more than thank you for her food, and ate the porridge as quickly as the heat would allow for, washing it down with warm tea. Scalvia sat across from him. She was not smiling. Arud remembered Ek's words that she must accompany them through the Tess Woods, and how displeased she had seemed. He wasn't too happy about the situation himself. She had been easy to take down in the woods and would probably prove to be another girl to look after. Just what he didn't need.

Vang returned carrying a chestnut-colored fur with deep brown swirls resembling that of a fox. He tossed it on the floor next to Arud. Ahlgren left the room, then reappeared with two furs draped over her arm. One was pure white, perhaps from snow rabbits, the other a smaller version of Arud's. She handed one each to Scalvia and Lykke.

"These will keep you warm for the journey," Ahlgren said. "They did a good enough job for the animals Freya put them on." She smiled, though Lykke's face blanched.

After breakfast, dressed in traveling cloaks and furs, Lykke and Arud gathered their bags. Ek held out Arud's crossbow and bolts. "I have modified your weapon."

Arud's face flushed and his eyes narrowed. "My bolts didn't need modifying. My father showed me in great detail how to build strong bolts." He mulled over the shaft that appeared untouched, then to the bodkin tip Ek had replaced with wielded silver.

Ek let out a hearty laugh. "It is not your craftsmanship, nor your father's, upon which I am offering improvement." He placed his large hand upon Arud's shoulder. "Do not be so against help when it freely comes. Not everyone is your enemy."

Arud looked upon his face and saw many of the same qualities in Ek that he knew in his own father: joy and strength, intelligence and love. Yet, Arud was angered with his father for his disappearance, for leaving him alone, for never speaking of a brother in Vithalia City, for many things.

"Forgive me." Arud dropped his chin to his chest. "You have been nothing but kind and helpful."

Ek slapped Arud hard on the back making him jump. "It is now in the past."

He led them through the hallway to the cave entrance, followed by Vang, Ahlgren, Lykke, and Scalvia. Arud trailed behind. He exited the cave mouth to bright sunshine, though the air had barely warmed. The silver dust on the ground had been disturbed. Fragmented track marks weaved through in a circular pattern.

"Why do those tracks look that way?" Arud asked.

"The ferine," Vang said. "It paced before the cave until it could take no more. See?"

Vang pointed away from the cave and Arud noticed the prints were stained black. He crouched to the ground. "Is it blood?"

"Yes," Vang said. "The silver makes their pads bleed. I think it's safe to say a ferine stalks you regardless of what the moon says."

Arud's knees weakened. He felt lightheaded.

That ferine won't stop looking for you until you are caught.

"You will find silver powder in your gear," Ek said. "Be certain to surround your camp with it each night."

Arud swallowed hard. "What happens if the ferine is not affected by it?"

Ek's face turned grave and he said, in a deep voice, "You run. You run, and you pray. A ferine without reaction to silver is a demon you do not wish to face." He stared at Arud a second longer until Arud nodded his understanding.

He wanted to go back to his room, to crawl beneath the covers and hide away from all of the fear and uncertainty surrounding him. It was inescapable, a heavy cloud he could barely breathe beneath. But he knew he couldn't hide. He had to get Lykke safely to the city. He had promised his mother as much. And even if her word hadn't been truthful, he would not fall short on his promise to her.

Scalvia hugged her mother and her father good-bye, then Vang, his forehead creased with worry.

"You be safe," Ek told Scalvia. "Don't be foolish or let your guard down for even one moment." He looked to Arud. "Be wary of whom you trust till you reach the safety of the city walls."

Arud turned grimly. He wondered if he was ready to make this trek. He wondered if he would be capable of protecting Lykke when the time came. He hoped he would, but he wondered.

Ψ THIRTEEN Ψ

Scalvia led Arud and Lykke through the Tess Woods. Arud watched as she swatted away low limbs with the gleaming blade of her sword and helped Lykke through the broken foliage. She seemed fixated with his sister, checking constantly to see if Lykke needed rest. A wood bow was slung across Scalvia's chest and a quiver hung from her back, filled with two dozen arrows made of what looked like solid silver from shaft to tip. As Lykke sipped water from Scalvia's waterskin, her eyes caught Arud's. Gray eyes filled with secrets. They stared at each other for the briefest moment. Arud was determined to discover her secrets before they went their separate ways.

By midday, the sun had completely disappeared behind dark clouds. Scalvia made small talk with Arud and showed different plant varieties and bird species to Lykke. More than once, Lykke grabbed Scalvia's hand. Arud frowned. She must miss their mother terribly.

They camped at the top of a large hill. The thick green of the trees spreading in every direction had dwindled to sparse patches of spruce and fir. The air filled with songbirds and the scent of sap. From there, Arud glimpsed the Thiannes River churning in the distant east. To the west, the rocky terrain sloped in a downward curve into The Great Expanse. The northland spread with high mountains capped with the whitest snow. The peaks soared into the clouds like icebergs breaking the surface of the ocean. Arud wondered if that was the point where the winding river crossed the Scynnthe Valley. There Scalvia's guidance would no longer be needed. The thought brought Arud unease.

"Who's hungry?" Scalvia took a loaf of bread from her large pack. She broke it and passed pieces to Lykke and Arud.

"We need to build a fire," Arud said. "It's too cold to just sit here."

With her mouth full, Lykke stood, cramming in bites of food as she searched the grounds for tinder and small dry branches. Arud removed his knife and birch bark from his pack, noting a half dozen pieces of bark and two flint rocks were all that remained. He would need to find more birch before they left the woods.

In no time, the blaze warmed the air around the fire pit. A muted sun appeared as a cataract through thin clouds. Arud pointed. "It will be snowing in three days."

Scalvia shook her head. "Less. Those clouds warn by their size of tomorrow's storm."

Arud studied the sky. She could be right. "We need to find shelter. It will be too cold to sleep on bare ground tonight."

Nodding, Scalvia said, "The forest ends soon, and only a valley stretches to the next copse. We need to go if we hope to clear it by nightfall. Lykke, are you ready?"

She shook her head. "My bag is so heavy. May I rest a little longer?"

Arud nodded. "Only a little." He tramped away from the girls, scanning every edge of the hill as he ate an apple. He stopped and stared into the precipice of rocks and boulders to the west, jagged teeth in a wide-opened mouth waiting to swallow its prey whole.

"Don't get too close," Scalvia said, creeping silently from behind.

Arud inched closer to the edge.

"The Dreadlands," she said as her gaze fixed briefly upward. "Home of the ferine that cannot shift and where exiles are sent to be torn to pieces by wild animals."

Arud faced Scalvia. She sat on the grass and he sat beside her, leaving a space between them. From downwind, he could smell fragrant mint oil on her skin.

"Did you know the Purebloods can escape their animal form even outside a full moon?" she continued. "The ferine grow in strength with each new moon. The Purebloods have been around for centuries and they can travel in and out of form whenever they wish, but they are bound to the Dreadlands."

"How come I've never heard this before?"

Scalvia did not answer for some time. Arud stared at her profile, at her slightly upturned nose and dimpled cheeks. "I'm certain there is much about the ferine you have been sheltered from."

Arud believed her.

She faced him. "The Pureblood are cold. You can sense their presence and feel their thoughts." She looked down at the grass. "The Cur aren't so easy to spot."

"The Cur?"

She nodded. "It's the name given to the offspring of the ferine who have bred with humans."

Arud's face cringed in disgust. "Who would ever want to mate with such hideous creatures?"

Scalvia squinted her eyes and leaned away from him. "Not all of them are hideous, Arud. You know little of the ferine. Only the fear and fantasy you were taught as a boy."

"That fear and fantasy has kept me and my sister alive every moon cycle." His voice tightened. "Maybe you are the one who has been sheltered from the truth."

Scalvia turned upon Arud, showing the points of her canine teeth. "Me? You can't be serious."

"You're the one living in a fantasy. You're convinced the ferine are capable of something besides pure evil." He shook his head. "Nothing you say about them will change my mind."

Scalvia scowled. "Are you this pigheaded about everything? Or only things you know nothing about?"

"Everything!" Immediately, Arud wished he could take back his words.

A smile crept sideways across Scalvia's lips. "Well, at least you're honest."

Arud rolled his eyes. "You know what I meant."

"Oh, I know," Scalvia said grinning, "that your tongue is much quicker than your mind."

She laughed a songlike sound, forcing Arud to smile. How could he stay angry at her? At least they had ceased arguing. For the time, anyway.

"It hasn't always been this way, you know," Scalvia continued.

"What do you mean?"

"My father tells of days long gone when the ferine and humans coexisted." She let out a heavy breath.

"But not anymore."

An icy gust blew past. With a shiver, Arud said, "Well, maybe it's good—"

Scalvia's head shot up. Her nostrils flared; eyes widened.

"What is it?" he asked. Was she smelling something, the way Lykke had in the meadow? He moved his head, trying to catch the scent, but smelled nothing.

"The storm is moving in. We must leave now." Scalvia stood.

"Scalvia, wait."

She turned around.

"Thank you for guiding us. I know it isn't what you want to do."

"You're wrong. It's exactly what I want to do."

Arud's head leaned to the side. "Then why did you seem so upset when your father suggested it?"

"Because," she said. "I know I won't likely make it home." She trudged back to camp, her fishtail braid swinging behind her.

Arud stood alone, his half-eaten apple in his hand. He stared into the pit. The Dreadlands. Was a ferine down there right now, watching him? What else lived down there? The thoughts of Purebloods and Cur made his head spin, and though he hated to admit it, he thought Scalvia wasn't far off when she said he was sheltered from the reality of the ferine. He had been fed nothing but lies from his parents. A cold chill billowed inside him, matching the wind. Would it be the same, if he ever did see his parents again? He had so many questions. He worried he wouldn't find any forgiveness, no matter what they told him.

When he arrived back at camp, Lykke lay asleep near the fire, wrapped tightly in her fur cloak. Scalvia was putting out the fire. The swirling smoke blew west like an opaque wall. He moved alongside her and took her by the hand. "What makes you think you won't make it home?"

She pulled her hand away without reply and began packing her things.

Arud crouched next to her. "Scalvia. Talk to me."

She shrugged.

He grabbed her again by her arm. She tried to break free, but he tightened his grip. "What makes you believe you won't reach home?"

"I can't explain why. It's a premonition and nothing more."

"You're lying."

She glared at him coldly.

"How can you expect me to trust you when you don't trust me?"

"I do trust you, Arud. I just don't want to see you or Lykke get hurt." Her eyes lowered, and she shook her head. "I won't let anything happen to either of you."

"Nothing will happen to us, Scalvia. We need to stick together."

Her eyes moistened; her white skin like drifts of untouched snow. His heart pounded in his chest. "I trust you," he said. "And I believe you're going to lead us safely to where we need to go. But now is not the time for this. We have to keep moving if we're going to reach a safe haven by nightfall."

Scalvia nodded and finished gathering her gear. Arud watched, wanting to comfort her. Instead, he stirred Lykke from sleep and helped her with her cloak and bag.

"This way." Scalvia marched ahead.

As he followed, Scalvia's tears and her fear of never returning home irked him. Why did she claim they were grounded in some silly premonition? She knew. Why wasn't she telling him? And, more importantly, what exactly *was* she doing here?

Ψ FOURTEEN Ψ

A bitter-cold rain started in the late afternoon on the fifth day. Arud thought of his mother, of Toov, of his father, wondering when he would see any of them again, wondering if Toov would even let his parents come after them, that is, assuming his father had made his way home.

Despite the thick fur coat, Arud shivered. So much for keeping Freya's creatures warm. Scalvia had led for several hours with short periods of rest, mostly for Lykke's benefit, whose exhaustion showed in her hunched shoulders and splotched cheeks, even though she no longer carried her pack. Arud wondered if they could cross the valley in time for sunset, especially with the sleet falling heavily.

Scalvia favored the northeast side of the open field, hugging the river at a trot while Arud and Lykke followed blindly behind.

The nearest edge of the Tess Woods lay several hundred yards ahead. Arud kept one eye steadily on the woods, the other trained on Lykke, whose sweat rolled down her temples despite the cold.

With an hour, two at most, of sunlight left, they reentered the forest path, identical to the one prior, except instead of sloping upward, it angled downward. They plodded along. Lykke lagged and Arud grew tired as the weight of both their packs pressed on his already aching back and shoulders.

Finally, Scalvia stopped in the open woods. "We

make camp here."

Arud gave a silent look around. "You can't be serious."

Scalvia tilted her head. "Why not?"

"Why not? Because any number of things can attack us in the open like this."

She raised her eyebrows, placating him, and walked away. Arud's body tensed. Heat flushed through him. She was acting like he was making a big deal out of nothing. Didn't she realize a ferine followed him, one who moved among the shadows during all the moon's phases, and could be waiting in these woods to strike? "No," Arud said, shaking his head. "I won't allow Lykke to camp here. It isn't safe."

"And I suppose you know of a better spot," she asked, "with all your extensive knowledge of these woods?"

Arud's teeth clenched. What was the matter with her? He wanted to grab Lykke and go, leave this girl behind, and never look back. He could take better care of Lykke alone, anyway. But where would he go? He was already off course, he knew, from the one Vinter had instructed him to follow. No, he needed Scalvia to guide them, no matter how much the thought infuriated him. "It isn't that I know of a better place, I'm just unfamiliar with this one. And being out in the open doesn't strike me as a wise place to make camp."

"I wish you'd trust me. This is the safest place for your sister." Scalvia removed her pack. "Remove your burden and then we can set up camp." With an elated groan she stretched. Her back arched. Her arms spread like the boughs of a tree.

Arud stared openly, but he forced himself to

rummage through his bag until he found his waterskin. He took a long drink. He wanted to hate her, but found he couldn't. Deep down, he did trust her for some unknown reason. It made him feel weak and powerless, but his feelings couldn't be helped.

Scalvia sat on a rock, unpacking her knife, a roll of twine, and several small hooks.

"What are you doing with those?" Arud asked.

"Making traps." She fumbled silently in her pack.

Arud rubbed the back of his neck. "What are you planning to catch?"

"Hares mostly. And squirrels. This part of the woods is full of them. We should be able to snare a few for supper."

Arud watched her fingers dance across the twine, weaving it between sticks and hooks until she created a solid trap. Then she started on the next one, working in silence, staring down at the earth. Arud turned to check on Lykke.

"How're you doing, skjaldmaer?" he asked, touching her forehead. "You feel warm."

She sighed heavily. "I'm tired of walking. This is much harder than I expected."

"You're much stronger than you know. How about I make you up a little bed? You can rest until dinner."

She grinned, flopping down on her back. "That would be wonderful. Thank you, Arud."

He gathered several pine branches laden with needles and layered them against a felled oak. Lykke quickly moved inside the burrow and lay down. Her eyes closed, and sleep overtook her before Arud had even finished with the outer branches. He frowned. Lykke seemed to be acting differently, seemed to be showing signs of the sickness—sweaty skin, exhaustion, eyes glazed over and changing color. Maybe he was overreacting, and the tonic Vinter had given was working fine. The journey had been physically grueling for both of them, though Arud was used to laboring in the fields. Lykke rarely did more than help with household chores, or sort through the crates of apples he gathered searching for rotten fruit. That must account for her fatigue, he decided. Although it did not justify her shifting irises.

Arud ambled over to Scalvia who had produced four more traps. "Is there water nearby?" he asked.

"Yes." Looking up, she softly said, "Walk with me. There's a creek not far off. We can lay these traps along the way."

Arud grabbed his and Lykke's waterskins and half the traps. He followed Scalvia through the woods. Peering back, he asked, "Will Lykke be all right alone?"

"Yes. These woods are fairly safe, most of the time. Except, of course, for the occasional snow leopard."

Arud paused, searching Scalvia's face. "Are you serious?"

She smiled. "I am, but we have nothing to fear in daylight."

"You aren't funny."

"Then, why are you smiling?" Scalvia trotted past, not waiting for a response.

Arud watched Lykke's burrow over his shoulder until it fell out of sight. He hated having no knowledge of this place, of having to trust this girl who he knew was hiding things.

Like I am.

"So, why are you really headed to Vithalia City?" she asked, as they worked in a large circle away from camp toward the creek.

Arud debated if he should tell her the truth. Why should he? She wasn't being upfront and honest with him. But maybe if he gave her a little information, it would prompt her to do the same. "To stay with an uncle. My mother insisted our home in the Outlands was no longer safe."

"Why is that?" Scalvia asked, wedging a trap beneath some bramble, then baiting it with a small piece of dried meat.

"She didn't say."

Scalvia stared up, almost through Arud, and he absentmindedly rubbed the trap between his fingers. "What?" he finally asked.

"I don't believe you. There's more to this story."

He withheld revealing more, but her smile intoxicated him, and he found the desire to please her overcame his better judgment. And why shouldn't he tell her? Maybe if she understood the dire straights they were in she would be more willing to hear him out the next time he disagreed with her. "A ferine appeared near my window the night of the Wolf Moon." The memory of the ferine broke out a cold sweat across his skin.

Scalvia's countenance faded. "I see." She finished with the trap and took several strides with Arud walking silently beside her. "And what of your father? Where is he?"

Arud shrugged. Where was his father? "I don't know. He left for Vithalia Square to trade in the marketplace a few weeks ago and hadn't returned by the time Lykke and I left. He had never taken more than a few days on past trips."

"So your parents aren't following you?"

A tingling sensation swept up his neck and across his face. "No."

It was quiet between them as Scalvia set a second trap and stepped past him. "We'd better keep moving."

The rain had slowed to a drizzle, and a bit of sunlight cut through the thick clouds. Butterflies flitted and grasshoppers chirped, searching for bugs in the softened soil. Water dripped off the branches onto the leaves in soft patters.

"I'm sorry to hear about your father," Scalvia offered.

Arud said nothing. What was there to say?

"Come on. We're almost there." She skipped down a slight decline and over an embankment. The gurgling creek came into view. Arud lowered himself to the edge and scooped handfuls of water. Scalvia did the same, the water dripping off her red lips and down her dimpled chin. She sat up on her knees and wiped her face dry with her fingertips. Realizing he was staring again, Arud looked away and filled both waterskins in the creek.

He sat back satisfied. Out the corner of his eye, he noticed Scalvia now stared at him. He cleared his throat. "Are we going to wait here to check the traps or head back to camp?"

"We can rest for a bit," she replied coolly.

Arud ran his fingers through his hair, drank more water, refilled his skin, all the while feeling Scalvia's large round eyes boring into him. "We should be getting back to Lykke," he said, standing.

Scalvia took him by the hand with a light laugh. "Come on, Arud. I won't bite. Please, stay with me a little longer. Lykke will be fine. I promise." She did not release his hand.

Torn, Arud sat in silence for a short while. The fresh scent of the cleansed woodlands filled the air, and he breathed deeply.

"I've been roaming these woods since I was a little girl," she said. "It's like my home here." Her thumb playfully caressed the back of his hand and Arud felt both tense and relaxed at the same time. The creek gurgled and ebbed over stones and pebbles, lulling him into near sleep, until Scalvia jerked up with a twist to scan the woods behind them.

"What is it?" Arud asked. "Did you hear something?"

"Quiet."

Arud's heart raced as he waited, watching, wondering what was happening. Scalvia slowly stood. Her hand glided with practice to the sword on her hip. Arud stood, his eyes darting, his own hand reaching for his blade.

"Tell me," Arud whispered. "What is happening?"

"We are not alone."

Ψ FIFTEEN Ψ

Arud pulled his knife from its sheath and followed Scalvia to the top of the embankment. Her nostrils flared and she panted through parted lips. Tilting back her head, she pushed her nose into the air and closed her eyes. "There." She pointed to the thick wall of trees.

Arud stared into the woods. "There what? I don't see anything."

"Get behind me," she said, shoving him back. Together they crab-walked away from the creek, closer to the flat ground at the base of the embankment.

The growl of the ferine preceded it, a rumble that sent shivers through Arud's entire body. He saw yellow eyes weaving between the trees as the beast inched closer. The black ferine with the silver strands.

It had found him.

Scalvia stood as a buffer between Arud and the ferine. The blade of her raised sword reflected the sunlight the way the silver bodkin tip of Arud's bolt had in the early dawn. The ferine stepped out of the woods and padded across the embankment. Snarling lips rose. Saliva dripped off its menacing fangs. Long claws dug into the earth, flinging up dirt.

"Stay back!" Scalvia called to the ferine. "Or I'll slit your throat."

Arud's brow beaded with sweat. What was this girl thinking? She was crazy to taunt the creature. The ferine's lips pulled taut, as if smiling, enticed by

Scalvia's threat to be a formidable opponent. Growling, it paced the embankment, its glowing eyes trained on her. Arud realized he was taking small strides backward. What was he thinking? He couldn't abandon Scalvia the way his family had abandoned him. With shaking hands, he lifted his knife, waiting for the monster to make its move, cursing himself for leaving his bow behind.

"I'm not afraid of you," Scalvia told the ferine, tightly gripping her sword with both hands.

The ferine crouched, pouncing so quickly that Arud barely realized what was happening until the ferine landed heavy on Scalvia. The weight of the creature overpowered her as they tumbled to the earth; a blur of black fur and black hair. Panting, Arud jumped up, desperate for a way to help Scalvia who lay pinned beneath the ferine, the way she had beneath Arud the first time they met.

She screamed as the animal sank sharp teeth into her bare arm, her blood bright against her ivory skin. Uncontrolled rage funneled up Arud's chest, burning away his fear. He lurched forward, slashed his knife through the beast's broad shoulders and pushed the blade deep through its strong muscles.

With a pained growl, the ferine pressed off Scalvia and turned thirsty eyes upon Arud, menacing eyes, sending shivers through his bones. The ferine bayed, tensed its muscles. Foam clung to its exposed gums, ebbing over the edges of its gaping mouth. Spittle and blood flew as the beast shook wildly from head to tail. With paralyzed limbs, Arud watched it leap toward him. He covered his head instinctively. Why couldn't he move?

Scalvia screamed and pounced to her feet, with speed matching the creature's. She threw her sword at the ferine's chest in an attempt to distract it.

Her voice broke Arud from his stupor. Blood rushed back to his arms and legs with the tingle of pins and needles. He swung his knife through the air, missing the ferine completely as it barreled into him, throwing him into a tree several yards back, his breath knocked out of him. He scrambled to his feet, dizzy from the impact. His knife lay on the embankment out of reach. He rolled away, leaving the ferine biting at the space where Arud's chest had just been.

Scalvia yanked the creature by its hind legs. Arud's eyes bulged. It was impossible. The ferine was too heavy for a girl her size. The animal's jowls smacked the rocky terrain with a thud. A smear of black blood trailed behind it as Scalvia dragged the ferine away from him.

Arud lost no time scurrying to his knife. In the shuffle, the ferine had somehow gained the upper hand, back on top of Scalvia, who swung fiercely with her sword. The black beast covered her with its enormous body, its mouth wide open, ready to sink its serrated teeth into her neck for the kill. Arud spun his knife and flung it into the back of the ferine's neck. The creature shrieked and leapt off Scalvia.

Her sword's silver blade had begun taking its toll. The silver streaks through the ferine's fur had changed to a dark shimmer that seemed to smoke. With Arud's knife wedged deep in its neck, it turned, and stared at him with yellow eyes that seemed to have human qualities.

Eyes he somehow knew.

Eyes he swore looked right through him.

With a final rumble, the ferine turned and charged back into the woods. As it leapt up and out of sight, Arud's blade popped from its neck and landed on the embankment.

Arud ran to Scalvia, who lay heaving on the ground. He looked her over. Her face was scratched and bloodied. Her hair was matted down with black blood and dirt. A large wound exposed the pink flesh inside her forearm.

"Are you okay?" she asked through pained breaths.

Arud nodded. "Me? What about you?"

"I'm fine."

He helped her to her feet, then grabbed his knife, wiping the blade clean on his pant leg. She brushed herself off, then wiped her sword clean. Arud noticed the scratches on her face were healing. How could that be? He reached for her arm. The deep cut was now a red scratch.

He took a step back. "What are you?"

"Please, Arud. It's not what you're thinking."

"You're one of them, aren't you?" He gripped the hilt of his knife instinctively.

"There's no time. We have to go." She reached for his arm.

He yanked out of her reach. "Why should I listen to you? You've been lying to me from the moment I met you." He backed away, angling his knife.

Scalvia spoke softly, but earnestly. "We can fight about this later. Right now, we have to get back to Lykke."

Lykke.

All of Arud's anger lifted as he bolted out of the clearing and back through the woods. He wasn't sure which way to go, but he kept sprinting. He could hear Scalvia calling to him, her voice distant and muffled, like a voice underwater, and he moved away from her at each turn. He wove among the trees as if following a scent, cursing himself for breaking his promise and leaving Lykke's side. Branches snapped beneath him. Tree limbs swiped his skin. The forest lay still as death while his breath clamored in his head.

At the familiar sight of the leaning limbs he had turned into a burrow, he slowed his pace. He pulled back the outermost branch and gasped.

Lykke was gone.

Ψ SIXTEEN Ψ

"**L**ykke," Arud called. She was nowhere to be found. "Lykke!"

Scalvia's footfalls pounded to a stop behind him. She stared inside the empty burrow. Her hands covered her mouth. Her eyes teared.

In a quick jerk, Arud grabbed her and pinned her against a tree. His fingers clamped tight around her throat. All he saw was red. "Where's my sister? What have you done with her?"

"Arud...Stop..." Scalvia gasped for breath as he choked her.

"Where is she!" Arud shouted, tightening his grip. He wanted to break her delicate neck, or slice it, he didn't care which. But he couldn't do it. He knew he couldn't. He still needed her. Scalvia's white skin turned pink, then bluish, and her eyes rolled back. He let go in disgust, and she dropped to the ground like a piece of soiled cloth, coughing and gagging.

Arud seethed, the air around him suddenly stagnant and hot. He wanted to kill her. For the lies and deception, for letting a ferine—one that Scalvia probably led right to them—capture his sister. "Was this a set up? All of it?" He paced around her. "Did you make a deal with that ferine, lead me away to the creek to get Lykke alone so it could capture her?"

Scalvia's voice scratched as she cried, "No."

"What then?"

Scalvia looked up, tears streaming down her face. "I don't know what happened to Lykke."

"You're a liar." Arud reached around and grabbed a fistful of her disheveled braid. She clawed at his hands, while he dragged her back to the shelter, pushing her on the ground. "Sniff her out, dog," he said, shoving her face into the dirt.

"Arud, please," she cried, her voice muffled. "Please."

Her plea struck him, and he snapped back to reality. What was he doing? He had been overtaken by rage. Power surged through him. He had wanted Scalvia's blood. He listened to her cry as he took several steps back, and then collapsed.

"I'm sorry," he said softly. "I don't know what came over me."

Her whimpers quieted, but she did not reply. He watched, helpless, the way he had watched his mother when she cried for his father. He felt like such a coward.

"Scalvia?" he whispered.

She lifted her head, her face coated in a muddy mesh of dirt and tears. Shame filled him as he stared into her eyes, devoid of anger.

"What are you?" he asked.

She stared at him for a long while before answering. "I'm a Cur."

Arud's skin turned cold. "Why didn't you tell me from the beginning?"

She shook her head. "I was afraid you wouldn't have allowed me to come."

"And I'd probably have been right, seeing how you traded my sister to the monster."

"You have me all wrong. I would never let anything happen to Lykke. I swear it." She looked down. "This was a terrible mistake."

His anger bubbled up again. "Why should I believe anything you say?"

Her gray eyes pierced him, the yellow ring growing in depth. "Because I've been called to protect Lykke."

"What do you mean?"

"You need to promise me you'll listen."

He grinded his teeth, then opened his mouth to speak.

"And," Scalvia continued, "I need you to trust me."

Arud looked at Scalvia, the part girl, part ferine who had lied to him and tricked him and abandoned his sister. He shook his head. "I don't know, Scalvia. I'll listen, but I cannot trust you. Not yet."

Scalvia turned back. New tears moistened her eyes. "I would never hurt you or Lykke. Haven't I proven that?"

Arud re-sheathed his knife. "There's so much I don't understand, Scalvia. Everyone important to me is missing or lying, or both. No one's telling me the whole truth. I want to trust you, but I can't."

"I'll tell you everything I know."

"That's a start."

"Ahlgren is my stepmother. My real mother died giving birth to me. She was a ferine. For centuries, the ferine moved and lived among humans. Until one rose up against the others and created a legion of creatures whose intentions were death and destruction.

"With each kill and each passing new moon, these

vicious creatures gained power. Many of them rebelled, not wanting to join in the bloodbath. They were hunted down. Those that escaped found sanctuary in the world of men. They created new lives for themselves in human form by taking herbs to prevent transfiguration during the moon cycle. They built families and their offspring became the half-caste race know as *Cur*."

"And your birth mother, she is one of those who created a new life?"

"Yes," Scalvia said.

"What about your father?"

"Ferine are all female."

Arud scratched his slack-jawed mouth. "How can they keep the species alive without males?"

"They live for hundreds of years, Arud. They don't need to reproduce very often. And when they do, they find a way."

Arud shook his head. He didn't want to know. "Do you turn with the full moon?"

"Yes, but changing occurs differently for me. I don't need a full moon to turn, like a Pureblood. But my transformed size is much smaller and I am not as powerful."

Arud's mind clouded over. "So, tell me why you need to guard Lykke?"

"I can't explain it. I just know it's my calling."

"Then, how can you be sure?"

Her expression softened. "Haven't you ever just known something was true without any proof?"

He felt his face flush. "Of course." Arud looked away, trying to hide his reddened cheeks from her. He looked out across the woodlands, then back to Scalvia.

Her face was back to its creamy white shade. Her gray eyes focused on his.

A tingle pulsed through his body, and he pushed it aside. "I saw you—smelling the air earlier. Can you find Lykke's scent?"

"I can try." She placed her soft hand atop his. "I am sorry this is happening."

He nodded and stood. "So am I."

"I wish I could do something to make it stop."

"You can start by finding my sister."

Ψ   Ψ   Ψ

They backtracked through the woods for a full night and day, only stopping for brief rest and nourishment. The sun descended as night crept over the horizon, pushing daylight out of its way. Arud worried they would face the ferine again, something for which he did not feel prepared. He hoped they would find Lykke before it happened. He hoped they would find Lykke alive.

"This way," Scalvia said, her nose twitching. The limbs swooshed as she brushed them aside. Dry autumn leaves crackled beneath their boots. Stars popped out in the dusky sky and Arud was taken back home in his memories, to nights out with his father, learning the constellations and how to navigate by them.

Arud followed Scalvia over dead trees and ditches, crossing over clumped grass, between trees, and beneath spider webs large enough to span the trunks, glistening silver in the moonlight. Arud ran to keep up with her, knowing she wasn't moving at full speed after witnessing her fight with the ferine.

They ran and ran across the forest floor, Scalvia's nose twitching, her direction changing like a leaf in a breeze each time she lost the scent and found it again. They reached a rock quarry at the edge of the forest, dark and menacing, and Scalvia stopped.

"The scent ends here."

Arud stared down the flat wall dropping to the jagged rocks below.

The Dreadlands.

"You must be wrong," he said. "Try again."

Scalvia turned sharply. "There is nothing to try. She is down there."

He paced the edge, and peered at the sharp rocks. "How do we get in there?"

"We can't," Scalvia said. "It's too dangerous."

Arud squinted, catching sight of an object glittering on the peak of a rock formation in the quarry. He moved quickly to the edge, lying flat on his stomach to get a closer look. "What is that?" he asked, pointing. "Over there?"

Scalvia glanced over. "I can't tell."

Arud pushed to his feet and found a branch, which he hung over the edge of the chasm. "Brace me," he told her.

She grabbed him by the waist, anchoring them both to the cliff's edge. He carefully maneuvered the limb over the quarry, using it like a claw to grab the object dangling off one of the rocks. He touched it, trying to get the branch beneath it, holding his breath as it slipped dangerously close to the edge. He twisted the limb to a different angle and was able to snag the strange object by the limb's tip. Carefully, he swung the branch back around and set it on the ground. His heart wedged in his throat as he stared at what he had caught.

It was Vinter's beads, the ones she had given to Lykke before they left.

Ψ SEVENTEEN Ψ

Arud threw the beads around his neck and swung one leg over the ledge.

Scalvia grabbed him by the arm. "What are you doing?"

"I'm going to get her."

"Arud, this isn't the way. You'll die trying to reach the bottom."

"I have to try." He lowered his feet searching for a foothold.

"It will soon be dark. You won't be able to see—"

"I'm going," Arud said. "With or without you. Go home if you want. I'm not leaving without Lykke." He stared at Scalvia only briefly before finding a foothold.

"Okay. I'm coming with you."

The last shimmers of daylight cast elongated shadows through the quarry; menacing rock figures resembling monsters lying in wait across the trench. Stars popped out in the sky, and Arud noticed the cold air for the first time in several hours. He shivered.

Scalvia climbed over the edge much faster than Arud knew was humanly possible. Then again, she wasn't all human. He was still angry at her, but a part of him was actually glad to have her along now.

His crossbow hung off the side of his bag. Silver tipped bolts stuck up from his quiver. He wished he'd had it with him when he trekked to the creek. Then the ferine would be dead and Lykke would still be safe. With some difficulty, Arud managed to balance his gear and was on the move with Scalvia beside him.

"I'll lead," she said.

"No. I lead."

Scalvia's lips pinched together. "You still don't trust me."

"Can you blame me?"

She stared at him, wordless, teeth clenched.

"Find my sister and you will earn my trust." Arud grabbed the ledge and slowly dropped for the next foothold. He found an open spot and wedged his boot in the crevice. Hand over hand, he slowly descended the flat wall, carefully placing his feet, his hands, his center of gravity, hoping he wouldn't drop to the bottom.

The muscles in his back and arms ached, stretched to the point of ripping as he balanced his own weight, his and Lykke's bags, and his crossbow. Looking down, he could see the next ledge many feet below.

He could not reach it.

To his right, he noticed a shelf he could land on if he swung across the wall. He shimmied to the edge, placed his boots against the side and pushed, but the ledge tore off and he slipped, leaving him dangling by his fingertips. He kicked his feet, desperate for something solid to catch hold of.

"Arud!" Scalvia's scream echoed off the stones. She anchored beside him on the ledge he had been aiming for and extended her hand. "Can you reach me?"

"I can't. If I let go, I'll drop." His fingers grew tired. He tilted his head back. Not even a branch. He looked down, past his dangling legs to the bottom. Although the rocks were sharp, the bottom was close, and if he fell at just the right angle….

As if reading his mind, Scalvia said, "Don't do it. You won't survive."

She was right. He'd never make it past all those rocks. Sweat glinted off his brow. He let go with one hand and stretched out for her. He grimaced as his other shoulder bore all his weight. He was only a hands length short, but it might as well have been halfway around the world.

His fingers gave way.

Scalvia screamed.

He fell.

His arms flailed as he skimmed the sharp rocks. It was odd, but his momentum slowed, allowing him time to see each rock, every sharp point he passed. Somehow, he turned his body to avoid each one, pivoting midair, sidestepping rocks before finally landing with a hard thud on the quarry bottom.

But that's not what happened.

It was more like the ground met him, bouncing him gently on his feet by moving up then down to absorb his fall. Had *he* done that? He looked up at Scalvia, and heat rushed through him. Somehow, he had dodged the sharp rocks for over a hundred feet without a scratch. How was that even possible?

"Arud? Are you okay?" Scalvia hollered.

"I'm fine."

Scalvia sailed down next to him, a floating leaf tumbling in a gentle breeze. She stared at him incredulously.

"What?" Arud asked.

"How did you do that?"

"Do what?" he asked, walking away.

"You know what. How did you avoid all those rocks?"

He faced her. "How'd *you* do it?"

"We both know that."

He didn't reply.

Something shimmied between the rocks. They both turned. Several squeaking rats disappeared into the darkening quarry.

"This is so dangerous," Scalvia said. "The likelihood that—"

"It doesn't matter," Arud said, not hiding his frustration. "Without Lykke, none of this matters." Arud scanned the quarry, appearing darker and even more ominous than from the ledge. "Do you see well at night?"

She nodded.

"Well, I don't. So you lead."

Scalvia reached her hand out for Arud's. "Now you want me to lead?"

As much as he wanted to be mad at her, he couldn't. "Now I *need* you to lead."

Her smile faded.

"I'm sorry. I'm just worried about my sister."

"I know. Hold on."

She weaved between the rocks, avoiding the loose gravel traps, places that could suck them completely underground in a matter of minutes. Arud squeezed her hand to keep up, letting go only to climb large boulders intersecting their path. The chilled air blew across his sticky face, and he sweat under the fur cloak despite the cold weather. Their footsteps echoed across the rocks as they meandered through for at least forty minutes, before Scalvia stopped.

"What is it?" Arud whispered.

"It's Lykke. She's near."

"Is she alive?"

Scalvia turned, giving Arud a snide look. "I can't tell that from her scent."

She craned her neck, turning in circles until her eyes lit up. She pointed to a bulging rock wall where the stones overlapped unnaturally. "Over there." She reached for her bow and an arrow, the silver gleaming in the starlight. "Ready your weapon," she said.

Arud untied his crossbow and grabbed a bolt. They crept across the quarry. His heart hammered in his chest. He drew in ragged breaths. His cloak caught on the rocks. Scalvia waited while he unhooked the snagged fabric before inching forward, like a predator that had caught the scent of its prey.

She crossed effortlessly to the edge of the strange rock wall and motioned for Arud to join her. Small blue and white flowers the size of buttercups grew from the fissures, surrounding like a wreath. It was the only plant life Arud had seen in the dead quarry.

"A cave?" Scalvia mouthed.

Arud nodded. They pressed their ears to the cold stone. Arud heard muffled voices, one high and one low, bleeding through the rocks.

Scalvia held up two fingers with a questioning look on her face.

Now what? How were they going to get inside? They couldn't move the heavy boulder on their own. Well, maybe Scalvia could, but not without forewarning whomever or whatever was inside. The voices sounded human, but after learning about the creatures that shifted at will, Arud realized he could be facing a ferine in human's clothing. He shuddered.

"Arud." Scalvia's face indicated this wasn't the first time she had called him.

She motioned with her eyes to a flat spot above the boulder where the rocks leveled off. Then, she pointed to him, as if asking if he could make the climb.

He nodded, pointed to the boulder, and shrugged, feeling stupid for suggesting she move the boulder by herself.

Scalvia nodded.

Warmth flooded him. Somehow, he believed their plan could work, that she could actually move the huge rock alone while he waited from above to attack. He carefully sidestepped the gravel traps to the edge of the rock wall searching for a foothold, when the boulder began to shake, then shimmy to the side. Arud scampered next to Scalvia and readied his crossbow. She notched an arrow and pulled her bowstring to full draw. They took aim at the opening, at whatever had moved the boulder, waiting for a head to appear.

Even in the dull light, Arud could see the head peeking out the opening between the boulder and the quarry wall. He stretched his arm across Scalvia's bow.

"Don't shoot!" he shouted. "That's my father!"

Ψ EIGHTEEN Ψ

"**A**rud, is that really you?" Berg looked his son over, beaming.

"Father?"

"I knew you would come." He stepped out of the narrow space.

Scalvia did not lower her bow until Arud pushed it down to her waist. He stared at his father, unsure of what to think.

"I cannot believe you're standing before me. Come, come inside. The Dreadlands are not safe, especially at night."

"Father? How did you get here?"

"Well, that's a story now, isn't it? You and your friend come inside and I will tell you all about it."

Scalvia's hesitancy passed to Arud while they looked at one another.

"Lykke is here," Berg added.

"She is?" Arud grabbed Scalvia by the hand and led them both inside.

The cave was warm after Berg rolled the boulder back to block the entranceway. Arud crinkled his nose, the scent of wet animal layered faintly beneath the aroma of burning wood. Lykke sat on a rock eating. Her eyes lit up when Arud entered the room. She ran to him, and he pulled her into a tight bear hug. "I thought I'd lost you again."

She whispered in his ear. "You will always find me, Arud."

She giggled as he lifted her and spun in a circle. Berg and Scalvia watched from near the doorway, both smiling, although Scalvia's eyes remained cautious.

"And who is this young lady?" Berg asked, addressing Scalvia.

"I am Scalvia, from the Tess Woods. My father is Ek, a great warrior in the Liulfer tribe. I am a Cur."

Arud fixed his eyes on Berg. Why had she told him she was Cur? Would he be angry, confused, happy? Berg's eyes twitched with understanding as he took a step toward her.

She tightened her grip on her bow, her freehand slipping down her sheathe.

Berg reached out for her.

Her hand touched the hilt.

He placed his hands on her shoulders, staring deeply into her eyes. "Welcome, Scalvia of the Liulfer tribe. I am Berg of the Outlands, of the Sjurd clan, father of Arud and Lykke." His mouth widened into a square smile. White teeth like rows of soldiers guarded the laughter that shook his whole body.

Lykke giggled.

Scalvia smiled, maybe out of nerves, like Arud was, or maybe out of something more genuine.

"Son," Berg said. "Come over here."

Arud fell into his father's arms, his questions melting into a mist of blithe. His wall of doubt crumbled. Tears choked him, and he tried to restrain himself, but the musk of Berg's fur vest and skin prevented it. He looked up. "I thought I would never see you again."

Berg held him by the shoulders and looked into his eyes. "My son. It is so good to see you."

Arud smiled.

"Come, sit with me."

Berg led Scalvia and Arud to a hide stretched across the floor. They removed their boots and sat. Berg handed each of them bread and meat, which they ate hungrily, before he sat on the rug across from them. It was quiet. Tension hung in the air. Arud wasn't sure how he felt, torn between anger and relief. Questions resurfaced about his uncle, about the ferine. Where had his dad been? Where was his mother?

Finally, Berg sliced through the silence. "I am sorry to have left you and your mother without word. How is Vinter?"

"I don't know. We left while grandmother slept."

"I see," said Berg, seemingly lost in thought.

"What happened to you, Father? We were so worried."

Berg nodded. "Aye." He took in a deep breath. "I made my way to Vithalia Square, like I do each month for trading, and found nothing to be out of the ordinary." He took a bite of meat and chewed while he continued. "On my way home, a ferine attacked."

Lykke gasped, her eyes wide.

Berg gently touched her leg to comfort her. "Not to worry, *lovell*."

Lykke's face relaxed, her eyes still wide as she listened closely to the story, the way she always did when Berg spun tales. Arud said nothing about the ferine that stole his kill in daylight. Could it have been one in the same? Perhaps the black ferine with the silver strands which stalked them all?

"What happened next, Father?" Lykke asked.

"I was nearly halfway home when it attacked, too

far gone to retreat to the square, too long out to reach safely home." He paused, his face relaxing. "Prophecy speaks of a day when creatures emerge in daylight, hunters who become powerful without the full moon." He looked at Scalvia. Their eyes locked. "I believe that day has come."

Arud looked back and forth between them. "What of this prophecy? The same one you spoke of, Scalvia?"

"The Prophecy of Ulfhednar," she began, "speaks of a time when the ferine will rise in power to exterminate the half-caste breed and all who have joined with the Cur."

"Exterminate? Who, Father?" Arud asked.

"Where is Mother?" Lykke covered her ears and rocked, humming to herself.

"It is also written that during this time," Berg said, "an uprising will form, once again joining man and ferine in an alliance as it was hundreds of years ago. Before the separation. Before the evolution of the Cur."

"That is not how it occurred, sir," Scalvia rebutted. "Your history is fabricated."

Berg's disapproval shrouded his face. "Perhaps, you could enlighten me, young one."

"I want Mother," Lykke ranted, eyes closed as she rocked harder with her legs held tight against her chest.

"It is all right, Lykke," Berg said, lying her onto the blanket, ignoring his exchange with Scalvia.

Scalvia grabbed Arud by the hand while Berg tended to Lykke. Scalvia's whole arm was tensed.

"Why argue? This is a mere legend," Arud said.

"No," Scalvia answered. "It is a prophecy. One that will come to pass, perhaps before the next full moon."

Arud looked at Berg, trying to make sense of things. He looked to Lykke, her eyelids heavy as she fought off sleep. Something was out of place, like death without sorrow. Arud looked back to his father. "How did you find her?" he pointed at Lykke, who had given way to sleep.

"The ferine led me to her," Berg said. "I had made camp in the Dreadlands nearly a week ago. My assumption was that if I was to beat the beast, I should stay in its backyard. I heard a creature howling and readied my weapons. I followed its cries through the woods, but lost it. That is when I heard singing."

Berg looked at Lykke. "She was singing Vinter's lullaby. I followed the song and could not believe it was Lykke sitting alone in the woods. I heard the ferine moving closer, so I grabbed her. I knew you would be clever enough to find us both. And I was right."

Arud smiled. The uneasiness inside of him was subtle and dense, the voice of a conscience. Scalvia felt it too, he was certain, by the look in her gray eyes. The howl of a ferine interrupted them, and Lykke shot up from sleep.

"It is all right," Berg said. "She would not come here."

"Why not?" Scalvia asked. "She can smell us a mile a way."

Berg shook his head. "Those purple hooded flowers growing from the rocks are wolfsbane, the queen of poisons, and harmful to the ferine. She would not risk it."

"How can you know this?" Arud asked.

Berg turned, his lips pulled down, his dark eyes weary, and he absently rubbed his dirty blond beard. "Because I have been tracking her, and she has yet to come near my cave."

"Then why do you look worried?" Scalvia asked.

Berg looked to her, then to Arud. "Because she is tracking you."

The howl sounded again, a pitch different from the one Arud had heard in the Outlands, different from the ferine they had seen in the woods. He said nothing, only looked to Scalvia, whose eyes, like the deer he shot by the spring, showed her fear.

Berg stood. "Do not worry, children. Trust me. This is a safe haven." He turned and walked farther back into the cave, disappearing into darkness.

Scalvia wasted no time. "It isn't safe here." She began lacing her boots. "Not for any of us."

Arud whispered back. "What do you think we should do? My father's assured our safety here, and it's clear the ferine has no plans of letting up."

She shook her head. "Something is out of place. We must leave."

"And go where?"

Lykke sat bolt upright. Her unblinking clouded eyes stared at Arud though she was not focused on him. "Lykke?" Arud asked. "Can you hear me?"

She said nothing, then laid back to sleep. Arud stared as her chest rose and fell. "Lykke cannot leave. She isn't well enough."

Scalvia leaned closer to Arud. Her eyes had gained another ring of yellow, the cloudy gray like an overcast sky covering a full moon. "I don't trust your father's intentions."

Arud's skin grew hot. "And I don't trust yours, Cur."

Her mouth opened as she gasped softly. Immediately, he wished he could take his words back. Her face emotionless, she reached for her boots. "I won't stay here with him."

"Go, then," Arud said. "I'm not leaving my father."

Scalvia's lips and eyes turned downward. "I wish you would trust me."

Arud's brows lowered still. "I wish I had reason to. But you've done nothing to give me one."

Scalvia walked to the large boulder blocking the door. She moved it aside as if it were made of air. "I found your sister," she said, over her shoulder. Then she left, sliding the boulder back over the entranceway.

The cave became very quiet.

The nerve of that girl! Kidnapping him, leading him into a trap with the ferine, which she probably intended to do from the beginning, then losing his sister in the process. Sure, she found Lykke and even led him to his dad, but what did that prove? All she had said were a couple of lines from a prophecy Arud had never heard of before. All she had done was lie and trick him.

She was a Cur, after all.

He heard his father's footsteps shuffle from the back of the cave. Just before his head came into view, a stream of light danced across the shadows and reflected off his eyes. It happened so fast, Arud nearly brushed it off, the reality too incomprehensible.

Berg moved out of the shadows, pointing to the empty space on the hide. "What has happened to your friend?"

"She left," Arud said. "She didn't wish to stay here."

"Pity." Berg turned back to his preparations.

Arud stared at him; tall frame, muscular, handsome. His hair fell straight across his forehead and to his shoulders. It was his father. It was everything he wanted, to be reunited with him, to believe he had survived the elements and the night of the full moon. But the unease he'd felt the second he saw Berg peer out from behind the boulder still remained. And now Scalvia had left, her conviction strong enough to overcome her purpose in a prophecy she believed had come to pass. He was alone with Lykke. Expected to protect her; expected to take care of her, as fragile as she was.

He should have felt safe, being in his father's presence, without the Cur around. But he knew what he had just seen, even if it was for the briefest of seconds.

Berg's eyes had glowed.

Ψ NINETEEN Ψ

Berg sat beside Arud on the blanket, where Lykke slept peacefully. Arud felt his palms sweat. What seed of doubt had Scalvia planted so firmly in his mind that he was questioning his own father?

He remembered Ek's words, the night they sat outside his cave.

It is said that the oldest can shift into the images of other humans. But it is an uncommon occurrence, one that I am not sure I fully believe.

Could this be the case? Could this man looking like his father be a ferine in human form?

"So, Father. What are our plans? Will we return home to Mother?"

"I think not, Arud."

"Why?" he asked, shaken.

"There is some business that still must be attended to before we can see Mother again." He smiled. "But do not worry. Mother can take care of herself."

Arud forced a smile, suddenly wishing Scalvia were beside him.

"Father, how did you make it through the night during the full moon?"

He exhaled deeply. "I found this cave. It has served me well."

Arud fiddled with the blanket, listening. "But this is the realm of the ferine."

Berg rendered a cold gaze upon Arud, who shivered. "You know, Arud, not all of the creatures are evil. Their story is often misunderstood."

"But I've always been told that they—"

"The Cur, Arud. They corrupted the entire breed." His inflection rose as he spoke. "They are not Pureblood. They're a plague intent on poisoning humans and creatures alike. They must be exterminated."

Arud leaned back. "Father, you cannot be serious. Scalvia is Cur, and she—"

"Is a plague," Berg said, his pupils constricted. "Do not be confused by her outer appearance. Curs are cunning, and easily overtake men through their *physical* weaknesses."

Arud did not speak. This was not the mouth of his father.

"Well, then I suppose it's good that she left," Arud said.

Berg smiled. "That is right, child."

Arud's eyes widened. His dad never called him *child*. But he knew someone who did. Was it possible? It would change everything. Lykke, his mother, his whole existence. Her coldness seeped through Berg's features, and Arud knew without a doubt that he was talking to a shifter. And that the shifter was his grandmother.

Arud forced his eyes to hide his swelling emotions. He smiled at the shell imitating his father. He had to escape, but it would be near impossible while carrying Lykke.

Why hadn't he listened to Scalvia?

"Father," he forced his lips to speak. "I'm getting tired. Where shall I sleep?"

Berg motioned on the floor next to Lykke.

"And what of you?"

"I will sleep near the door. To protect my sweet children from the creatures lurking in the darkness." His smile was not carnal; it was forced, and inhuman. It made the skin on Arud's flesh crawl, his bones chill. What had Scalvia said about the Purebloods?

The Pureblood are cold. You can sense their presence and feel their thoughts.

Arud forced his lips to hide his emotions. There was no way he could sleep in this room with her, with this ferine in his father's skin. What would he do? How could he escape with Lykke and their gear? How could he even consider escape with the boulder to overcome? It was an impossibility.

Berg threw a second fur on the ground beside Lykke. Arud wondered if his grandmother had hunted and skinned these large animals herself, ripping them apart with her own teeth, on one of those mornings back home when she disappeared for hours at a time to unknown places.

"Do you think my grandmother is well?" Arud asked his eyes diverted to the ground.

Berg stopped midstride and stared at Arud.

Was the ferine inside trying to see through Arud's motives?

"Your grandmother? Why would you ask about her?" Berg said, his voice bitter.

Arud shrugged. "She is my grandmother, after all. And she's all my mother has at the time."

Berg nodded, his demeanor restored, apparently affirmed Arud had not seen through the mask his grandmother hid beneath. "Yes, she is. Your grandmother will take care of your mother. You can be sure of it."

His features were flawless, down to the tiny mole on his father's right cheek. Arud wanted to crumple in his arms, to feel safe in his musk and the strength of his words. But this was a mirage. His real father was probably dead somewhere. And Arud couldn't let the thought take hold that Berg had been murdered at Toov's hand. He shook his head clear of that evil. In a breath, like a breeze off the sea, a plan slowly grew in his mind. A plan he actually thought could work, if he executed it just right. "Father, I'm thirsty. Do you have a way to boil water for tea?"

"Of course, Arud. Did you bring herbs?"

Arud nodded.

"Then I will prepare the fire in the rear. It is dark, so please do not follow. I will return soon with the hot kettle."

Berg took a metal kettle from a small shelf in the rock wall and headed back down the dark hallway. Where Arud first saw his eyes glow.

He shuddered, pushing the memory quickly aside. If his plan was going to work, he had to convince the ferine inside his father that he suspected nothing. As Berg disappeared into the darkness, Arud called out, "Father?"

Berg turned. The light caught his eyes and reflected, exposing the animal hidden within. Arud concentrated to keep his impending fear at bay.

"Yes?"

"I'm glad I found you."

Berg grinned devilishly. Arud knew he had tricked her. She suspected nothing. Berg continued down the hall and out of sight.

Arud waited for her footfalls to turn to silence. He shot over to Lykke and shook her harshly by the shoulders. "Lykke! Wake up!"

Lykke did not move. Her skin looked gray. It was too early for her to be showing any symptoms. It had only been a few days since her last tonic. But Vinter had warned to keep an eye on her once she acted strangely. Arud felt her forehead. She was feverish.

He was on his own.

Arud moved to the boulder and tried to push it aside. He strained every muscle and the rock barely budged. He sighed, moving back to the center of the room. He looked to Lykke. To the dark hall. To the boulder. He stood frozen in the center, unable to stay, unable to escape.

He continued to scan the room for something, anything he missed that could help him. The herbs. Lykke's herbs. No, he couldn't use those on his grandmother. Even though they induced a deep sleep within the hour, Lykke was showing early signs of sickness and would surely need them soon.

What else could he use? The silver. Ek had given him powdered silver. If he could somehow get some into the hot water and get Berg to drink the tea...

It might work.

Arud tore into his bag, searching for the powder. He found a small pouch filled with a glittering substance resembling stars captured from a clear night sky. He rummaged further. There were other things Ek had packed, which Arud had not noticed before. A ring of metal, a wrapped portion of herbs and dried purple flowers with the roots and bulbs intact—Arud knew this to be wolfsbane—several marbled rocks that warmed in his hand when he touched them, and a book with frayed edges where the leather had worn down over many years.

Arud removed a mortar from the shelf where the kettle had sat and placed inside a small sprig of the violet flower. The scent was strong, like a dark, wet forest, and Arud feared it would give itself away. He pressed the pestle against the purple petals, crushing them into a fine violet mist. He sprinkled a handful of the powdered silver across the top and ground some more. The overpowering scent remained, and now it glittered, the wet forest with day's first light glistening through the trees. Surely, his plan would be too obvious. What else could he use to hide it?

His blood.

A trickle of blood would conceal everything. And perhaps her lust would overtake her common sense and the old bat would drink a whole cupful before coming up for air. Arud took out his knife and pierced his finger. He grimaced. Blood seeped out his fingertip and he squeezed it, over the mortar, onto the splintered wolfsbane and powdered silver. Instantly, smoke sizzled up, the glittering silver becoming dull, the forest scent masked.

Yes, it really might work.

"Are the herbs ready?" Berg stood in the opening. His eyes were dark and reproachful, glowering down at Arud the way his grandmother always did.

Arud jumped. "You scared me, Father." He climbed to his feet, holding out the mortar, willing his hands not to shake. "Mother's best recipe."

Berg took the bowl, breathed in the scent of the concoction with a smile. Arud was right. Her blood lust was taking over his grandmother's senses. She set the kettle down on the makeshift wood plank stacked on risers in the center of the room and emptied the mortar's contents into the kettle. Steeping the herbs for several minutes, she finally poured the tea into two mugs.

Arud smiled at Berg. "Let us toast, Father. To outsmarting the ferine and finding freedom."

The corners of Berg's mouth turned down slightly. His pupils dilated to near blackness. Arud held his breath tight in his chest until Berg lifted his mug. "To freedom."

Their cups clanked and they both brought them to their mouths. Arud turned his mug slowly, so the liquid pressed against his lips but did not enter, the way water does against a well-built dam. He stared from over the lip as Berg drank, his cup tilting higher and higher, the tea sloshing out the sides and down his beard.

Berg lowered his mug and Arud did the same, wondering how long the silver and wolfsbane would take to react with his grandmother's blood.

But he didn't need to wait long.

Berg's eyes widened. He started to shake violently. "What have you done, child?" He dropped his mug, the wood crashing to the stone floor with a hollow thud. He gripped his throat, his breath coming in staggers, and he began to wretch.

Arud quickly laced up his boots and strapped on his gear. Berg squealed and hollered, his voice rising and falling from Berg's tone to Toov's. Arud grabbed Lykke and lifted her into his arms. She did not stir. Beads of sweat had formed on her forehead and her hair clung to the nape of her neck. Arud hoped the fever had broken.

Berg grabbed his hair, pulling at the ends as he bent over and straightened, his body contorting into unnatural positions. His flesh shifted, the nude skin rippling as dark black waves pushed through, fur replacing flesh like rising icebergs in rapid motion.

Arud rushed to the boulder, threw Lykke across his shoulder, where she hung lifelessly moaning. He pushed on the boulder, but he did not have enough strength in one arm. He looked over his shoulder. Berg's face was melting like candle wax, lips drooping, eyes running, and he pulled at his skin with the claws of a ferine, pulling off long strips.

Arud turned away, petrified.

Berg's body continued to transform, and a low growl rumbled from the forming ferine's gut as Arud pushed frantically at the boulder, somehow moving it several inches. He sensed a strength unleashing inside of him, the way it had in the quarry. He turned around and his blood ran cold. Berg was gone, replaced by the massive body of a ferine. Its fur was black as charcoal with silver lines running through it that dulled to a dark gray and smoldered like smoke.

Arud's stomach knotted as he looked upon the ferine he had been running from since he left the Outlands; the whole time it had been his grandmother.

Her neck snapped in his direction, snout angled and snarled. White fangs dripped blood red. Glowering eyes reddened by broken capillaries. Arud desperately held his grip on Lykke and somehow found the strength to move the solid rock a few more inches.

Muscles rippled in Toov's hind legs and back. She

stumbled and fell, then rose back to her feet. Crouched. If she launched, she would kill him. Arud pushed and the boulder broke free of his hands. A silver arrow slipped through the opening and shot past him from outside the cave.

It landed in Toov's chest.

"Hurry." Scalvia reached out and yanked Arud through the gap. She moved the boulder back across the opening and pulled Lykke from his shoulder. "Run!" In the dark, she maneuvered across the rocks and gravel traps, with Arud chasing close behind. His widened eyes took in what dim light the stars provided.

Why was his grandmother trying to kill him? Why had no one ever told him what he was, what his family was? Deep in thought, his foot caught in a gravel trap. He tried stepping out, but he was sinking too fast. "Scalvia!" he screamed.

She stopped and jogged back to him.

"Help, I'm stuck."

"Don't move," she said, setting Lykke on the ground. "You couldn't just follow me?"

"Not now." Arud sunk deeper, to his mid-calves. He tried taking a step, but fell through to his waist.

"Stop moving! You're making it worse."

"What would you have me do then?" The gravel pulled him under to his stomach.

Lykke moaned.

Scalvia ran.

Where was she going?

Arud had trouble breathing, the gravel pushing on his chest and back.

Toov's sharp howl bounced through the quarry.

He had seen the strength in her eyes. She would not stay down for long.

Scalvia returned, a long branch in her hands. She flung the leaf covered limb toward Arud. "Grab hold."

Arud had one arm free, the other glued to his side by the gravel trap. "Ready."

Scalvia tugged. Arud moved a few inches. Scalvia tugged harder. He didn't budge. Toov bayed.

"She is coming."

"I know, Arud. I can't move you."

"Yes, you can, Scalvia. You have to!"

She tightened her grip, squinted in concentration, and yanked on the branch with a guttural scream. Her muscles stretched.

Arud closed his eyes. He imagined himself weightless. Imagined his body bending and weaving between each rock in the gravel trap. Slowly, he felt movement. His waist broke free.

"You're doing it," he yelled to Scalvia.

She pulled harder.

His other arm broke free, and he grabbed ahold of the limb as Scalvia dragged him completely out. She fell to the ground, heaving and panting. Arud reached out his hand and helped her up.

"Thank you," he said. "I owe you."

Scalvia smirked. "I know."

He stared into her eyes and for a moment, the whole world dissolved around them. Until the growl of the ferine less than two-hundred yards away rumbled through the quarry.

"Give Lykke to me," Scalvia said. "We'll move faster."

"No. I can carry her. You lead the way."

"Then you have to follow me."

"Go," Arud yelled. He scooped Lykke into his arms. "I've got you."

They hurried along the quarry bottom back to the rock wall they had scaled. Toov's howls drew closer. Lykke neared unconsciousness.

"Set her down and give me your hand," Scalvia said to Arud.

"Why?"

"Do it!"

He placed Lykke on the ground and reached out his hand. Before he could take a breath, Scalvia flung him up and over her head. He bounded like he was weightless. His arms flailed to break his fall on the hard ground above the quarry, and he dove into a roll, the wind knocked out of him. He winced. He had managed to crash into his bolt. The silver sliced through his shirt and nicked his shoulder blade, though it didn't break his skin.

"Arud!"

He dropped his bag from his shoulders and ran to the ledge overlooking the quarry. Even in the diminished light, he could see Toov closing in on Scalvia, who held Lykke's limp form above her head. "Ready?" Scalvia asked.

"Be careful."

"Just be sure to catch her."

Scalvia flung Lykke up, her lifeless body pummeling through the air. She slammed into him, knocking them both to the ground. Her eyes shot open from the impact, and she screamed at the top of her lungs.

In the distance, a ferine howled back, seemingly in

response. The ferine Arud had heard earlier, the howl he was certain did not belong to Toov. There were two creatures hunting them, thirsty for blood.

Scalvia jumped out of the quarry, like a cricket bouncing through the meadow back home, and landed on all fours beside him. "Give her to me," she said, taking Lykke from Arud's arms. "Let's move."

She ran through the woods. Arud chased her, grabbing his gear as he passed, and throwing it over his back. His shoulder stung where the strap crossed the wound, but his adrenaline surged stronger than the pain. Or was it something more? How was he keeping pace with Scalvia? Was she running slower than she was capable so he could keep up? He shadowed her across the downward sloping forest, through the trees, the leaves, the limbs, the logs, finally to the creek off the embankment. What had taken three days to cross, felt like only several hours to backtrack. What was happening to him? Shouldn't he be exhausted?

Scalvia set Lykke on the sand and dove into the creek. Bubbles popped above her, rain rising from the creek's bed to the surface. Several minutes passed. Several more. Arud began to pace. Was she okay? He needed her. He wanted her. But he could not leave Lykke alone on the bank. He would not leave her alone again until they reached the safety of the walls of Vithalia City.

Her fever had spiked, and Lykke breathed in short spurts. She needed the tonic. He had waited long enough. Arud removed the pouch from his pack and the iron cup Vinter had packed. He dipped the cup into the creek and set it down on the sand. He needed to make a fire.

He climbed the embankment searching for wood, keeping Lykke in sight, gathering weak branches and tinder before scuttling back to set up the fire lay. He looked to the water. Scalvia was still under. He layered the wood and scattered the moss and leaves. He struck his blade against a flint stone, scanning the still water for Scalvia, staring at his panting sister, watching sparks shimmer onto the bracken, searching the woods for Toov and the second hunter.

The sparks caught and the fire roared to life. Arud placed Lykke's cup in the center of the flame as he had watched Vinter do so many times before. He gazed into the tin. Soft bubbles formed along the bottom, slowly spread up the sides, and finally stirred into a rapid boil.

Scalvia popped through the surface of the water with a gasp, her braid unraveled.

Arud ran to the creek's edge. "What happened to you?"

She breathed heavily as she waded through the water toward him. Tendrils of black hair swam behind as water snakes. "I'm sorry. I needed to clear my mind."

"You scared me to death!"

"I'm sorry."

He glared at her. What could he say? She hadn't done anything wrong. "Next time you plan on nearly drowning yourself, let me know so I don't worry."

She collected her hair over one shoulder and wrung it out. "You were worried about me?"

He shrugged. "I guess. I mean, you are a girl."

"What's that supposed to mean?"

Lykke moaned loudly, clutching her stomach in a

tight ball. Arud moved closer. "I don't know what's wrong with her."

"She's changing," Scalvia said, crouching beside him.

"What do you mean she's changing?"

Scalvia lifted Lykke's eyelids. Dark empty irises peered out.

Arud didn't want to look; instead he removed the iron cup off the fire using his shirt to absorb the heat. He stirred in the herbs. "Lykke," he said, lifting her up. "Lykke, you have to drink this." She moaned again as he held the cup to her lips. White steam hung in the air. She pushed it away. Arud brought the tea to his own lips and flinched. It was too hot to drink. Lykke would scald her mouth if he forced her. He glanced at Scalvia. "What do you mean 'changing'?"

"She is Cur, Arud. And she is of age."

Arud nearly dropped the cup. Scalvia took it from his shaking hand. She said more, but her voice came to his ears distorted and distant. His vision blurred as blackness crept in along the edges. Lykke, a Cur? How could it be possible? But before he could ask, he heard a ferine growling loud and close, shaking him back to reality.

Toov was crouched on the embankment as the black and silver ferine.

Ψ TWENTY Ψ

They froze.

Scalvia whispered through clenched teeth, "Arud, do not move."

They were both without weapons. Arud's crossbow was attached to his gear while her bow and arrow lay sprawled out across the sand. Toov growled steadily, a rumble like distant thunder, as she padded toward them, taunting them, toying with them.

Lykke began panting; spit dripped off the tip of her tongue. Arud stood next to Scalvia whose hand rested on the handle of her knife. "Move away from me slowly," she whispered. "She can't attack us both if we're far enough apart."

Arud shuffled toward the bottom of the embankment while Scalvia slipped closer to the water. Toov crept forward, her head jerking, eyes darting from Arud to Scalvia while Lykke was left in the open between them. She screamed in a pitch that pierced as a siren. Arud jumped, forcing himself not to cover his ears. Toov bellowed a husky bark and charged.

Arud turned and ran, leaving Lykke alone. He felt like such a coward, but he hoped if he lured Toov away, Scalvia would think to grab his sister and hide her. He carried no weapons. He knew his fate.

Toov whined and Arud turned around. Scalvia's arrow stuck out of her side, the silver veins in her fur pulsating in dark grays around the wound. She growled, turning her sights on Scalvia who stood with legs braced and bow readied.

Toov charged and Scalvia shot off an arrow that skimmed across the ferine's back. She slammed into Scalvia, knocking them both into the water with a heavy splash. Arud ran back to Lykke, threw his pack on his back, and lifted her onto his shoulder. He carried her up the embankment and back through the woods, moving farther into the forest than he had ever been.

The sickening sounds of Toov's claws slashing into Scalvia's milky-white skin rebounded off the trees. He wished he could help her, wished he could save her, but how could he put his sister in danger? He continued to run, the air cold, the embankment drifting into the background like a forgotten memory. His sister moaned, her limp body heavy, and Arud pressed on not looking back.

Father, where are you? he wondered.

He ran for what felt like an eternity, before the hush of the river fell on his ears. He hoped he could make it. Maybe they could cross the Thiannes and their scent would be washed away. He sprinted, a hundred yards, two hundred, the river rising and ebbing like a beacon calling out to him, leading toward safe banks.

The trees opened and the river came into view, churning heavily in long sways before him. It was wide from bank to bank, wider than he had seen before, and he looked far into the distance at two mountain chains. He was on the path to Vithalia City. Those must be the mountains Vinter had spoken of. He neared the river, setting Lykke down on the bank. She was barely breathing, eyes cloudy, skin gray.

"Do not die," he whispered.

What was he supposed to do? He had no herbs for her tonic. He had left the hot tea by the creek. Then he remembered the various items Ek had packed, the cloth-wrapped herbs he had only observed briefly. Could he have intended those herbs for Lykke? Ek would have surely known she was a Cur, his own daughter being one.

Arud tore through his pack and took out the soft cloth opening it gingerly. The herbs were dried out and could not be boiled, but they would have to do. He had no other choice. Lykke was dying before his eyes. He forced her to sit upright and her head rolled, landing on his chest.

"Lykke, open your mouth." He forced her lips apart with one hand and placed the crushed herbs onto her tongue. He tilted his waterskin, spilling water out the sides of her mouth until she coughed, gasping. Her eyes opened wide.

"It's okay, Lykke. Drink."

She placed a hand around the base of the skin and drank, the herbs flushing down her throat. Instantly, her eyes cleared, the cloudiness pushed away by bright hazel orbs. "Arud?" her voice crackled.

He smiled, relief filling him. "I'm here, Lykke. You're going to be all right."

"What happened? Where's Scalvia?"

He could not bear to think of Scalvia's fate just yet. Toov's howl blasted at them and Arud feared the worst. "Lykke, can you move?"

She nodded. "I think so."

"Run behind those rocks near the river and hide. Don't come out, no matter what you hear."

"But Arud—"

"Promise me."

"Okay, I promise."

"Now, go."

Lykke ran downriver to a rock formation near the bank. Arud untied his crossbow and readied his bolt. Toov stepped out of the trees, her black fur bloodied, her silver strands weaving in deep grays. He took aim, waiting for her to move near enough for a shot in the heart, when a noise off to his left caught his attention. He turned, expecting—hoping—to see Scalvia.

His heart fell.

A second ferine stood in the glade, presumably the ferine whose howl Arud had heard twice now. It boasted a golden-yellow pelt and stood smaller-framed than his grandmother. He was alone. There was no way he could fend off these two creatures on his own.

He would need a miracle.

Ψ TWENTY-ONE Ψ

The golden-yellow ferine stalked toward Arud with the same methodical pace as Toov. He changed his aim from Toov, to the yellow, back to Toov. His brow beaded with sweat. Which was the greater threat? They rumbled low growls, both eyeing Arud. His heart raced in his chest. His hands shook with adrenaline.

Suddenly, Toov struck and Arud spun quickly around to take aim on her. He would be too late. He couldn't get the shot off in time. The yellow ferine blurred through the air, intercepting Toov's attack. The two creatures rolled in the dirt snarling and clawing, slicing deep grooves into each other's flesh.

The yellow ferine was Arud's miracle.

For some reason, this ferine had protected him. Perhaps it wanted Arud for itself. He would not wait to find out. While the creatures scrapped, Arud rushed past them to Lykke who crouched behind the rocks swaying back and forth, humming Vinter's lullaby. She looked up; her eyes filled with tears and she took his outstretched hand.

A loud whine caught his attention. He turned to see Toov limping away from the river and back into the woods. The yellow ferine panted on the bank. Blood pooled beneath where it lay on the ruddy sand. He crept closer to the injured ferine. His curiosity propelled him; his fear held him back. Lykke gripped his cloak, moving in his wake. He could feel her tiny body quiver. He reached the ferine.

A deep gouge exposed pink flesh while gaping lacerations oozing blood stained the pelt. He bent down and reached out his shaking hand to stroke its soft fur.

"Arud, don't," Lykke said.

The ferine lifted its head to look at him. They stared into each other's eyes. He believed the creature had come there to help.

"Thank you for giving your life so that we might sustain our own."

The ferine lowered its head back to the earth. Its breathing slowed. Arud shed a tear, stroking the smooth fur until it stopped moving, and escaped to death.

Lykke moved up alongside her brother. "Is it dead?"

Arud nodded.

"Poor beast," Lykke said, kneeling beside her brother.

As they sat near the river, the fur on the ferine started to shimmer. Arud and Lykke stood. The animal's pelt separated, like oil in water, as fresh skin pushed out the golden-yellow fur in clumps. The claws shortened to nails. The hind legs and front paws became human limbs. Long hair grew rapidly on the transforming head. The snout shrunk into a woman's nose and mouth.

Arud's eyes widened in disbelief. Ice coursed through his veins. He swept Lykke behind him so she could not see.

"Stop it," she screamed, trying to break free. "Let me go!"

Arud released his hold.

Her tiny frame convulsed as she crumpled to the ground. Her screams echoed as a gale passing through the trees and tears fell cold as winter's first snowfall to the bloodstained earth.

Arud covered the woman with his cloak, unwilling to believe it was her. His hand gently arraigned the amber-beaded necklace on the slender neck of the ferine who had saved them; the woman she'd transformed into—their mother. Vinter had said she would return for her necklace, and she had.

The necklace was hers, after all.

Ψ TWENTY-TWO Ψ

Arud toiled for several hours preparing wood for a raft. Lykke helped, her tears falling to the ground in streams. Rain fell cold, slicing through their clothes to their skin. He didn't mind the cold. It slipped between the fissures in the stones, where he knew it would freeze and expand, rupturing the once unbreakable stone. Rain could not break rock without being bitter. Rage toward his grandmother kept him hot. He would kill her for Vinter's death.

Neither Arud nor Lykke spoke as they worked, using the twine in their bags to latch together the fallen branches they found in the woods. Arud no longer feared the black ferine and actually found himself without fear for the first time since he'd left home. He lifted Vinter onto the raft lying on the river's edge. Her body was light in his arms, compared to his heart heavy. He didn't have a way to make fire, as was the custom in Vithalia to send the dead on to the afterlife. He only had the two stones from Ek that warmed in his hand, and he set them against her chest, along with a bouquet of wildflowers Lykke had picked. With his knife, he carved her name into the raft. If someone found her, they could perform the proper ceremony.

The sun was just coming up, its rays falling like a fine mist across their mother. Together, they stood over her. She could have been sleeping. Her face had softened in death, her skin smooth, her hair silken. Arud held her cold hand. He was not ready to let go.

Lykke hugged Vinter one last time. Arud kissed her cheek. With a heave, they pushed the raft into the wide river where the current caught. Arud ignored the tear rolling down his cheek. Lykke sang Vinter's lullaby. The rain turned into a downpour as they watched her drift downstream.

"Come on, Lykke. Grab your things."

Lykke did as she was told, her sobs coming unguarded. She took her brother's hand.

"We have to cross the river. It'll wash away our scent."

He did not have the strength to tell Lykke that the black ferine was Toov or how she had shifted into their father to trick them. He had lost everyone, except Lykke and an uncle whom he did not yet know. Even Scalvia was gone, and he had to assume the worst. She had not been upfront with him, but her actions had proven her loyalty. He owed her an apology, one he would not be able to deliver.

With their bags over their heads, they waded into the water. Instantly, Arud felt his muscles tighten from the cold, and he forced his legs to move. Lykke struggled beside him and he slowed to prod her along. The river was shallow as they trudged across the silty bottom. Rain poured over them and splashed up from the surface. Arud squinted. "Keep moving, Lykke. We're halfway there."

He glanced downstream. He could make out the faint outline of his mother. "Goodbye," he whispered, watching until the river curved, taking her out of sight.

They reached the opposite bank, exhausted. Lykke shivered, her lips pale blue. She would need a fire quickly or face hypothermia. He would need the same.

He scanned the area and spotted a rock formation where the sandy bank lay covered in leaves. They had no wood for a fire, and everything was soaked, but at least they could hide among the rocks in the makeshift shelter.

"This way," Arud said, running ahead.

The rocks formed a cove with an overhang. It was dry and protected from the wind and sideways-falling rain.

"Take off your clothes," Arud said. "Put on something dry."

Trembling with cold, Lykke stripped down to her underthings. She could barely function, her body shook so badly. Arud's wet garments lay on the ground beside him. He quickly dressed and grabbed his sister and held her in his arms, where she cried into his chest. He could no longer tell if she was shaking from the cold or from her broken heart. And it didn't matter. He held her until she succumbed to exhaustion, the freezing rain screaming all around them, the wind howling like the ferine.

He kept his sights upon the riverbank, anticipating Toov's appearance. She did not show herself that day. Perhaps she was wounded and recuperating back in her cave in the Dreadlands. He hoped she was wounded. He hoped she was in pain. She was an evil he could not comprehend. She had murdered her own daughter. But with everything he had learned in the past few days, maybe Vinter wasn't her natural-born daughter. At this point, anything was possible.

Arud remembered the book in his pack, with the frayed edges and the leather cover. When he could, he would read it. Hopefully it contained some answers.

$$\Psi \ \Psi \ \Psi$$

Arud woke up late in the night to the stillness of the Scynnthe Valley. Crickets chirped in the distance, singing to one another. The reeds bent in the breeze, playing hollow songs. The storm had cleared the air, cleansed the trees, and washed away the debris. The moon and stars twinkled light upon the frost-covered ground.

Lykke whimpered in her sleep, her dreams most certainly filled by Vinter, as Arud's had been. He shivered. The snow would soon arrive. They would need heavy coats again if they were to make it to Vithalia City.

Arud's gaze swept the valley, eyeing the two majestic mountain chains before him. The Torngats had many obstacles. The Sindri-Urd Range was dangerous to climb. Which should he take? Would it even matter? Without Scalvia to lead, without furs, and with Toov stalking them, they most likely would not make it either way.

He gathered some branches and tinder, finding pieces of wood that had managed to stay dry during the storm. He brought them back to their alcove and built a fire. The heat spread across his entire body. Lykke woke, smiled sweetly, then went back to sleep.

Arud stayed by the fire, wide awake. He took Ek's book from his bag and leafed through the pages, angling them to catch the firelight. *The Prophecy of Ulfhednar.* The musty scent reminded him of Scalvia's den. He missed her. He hoped she had survived. He turned to the first page and began reading.

Ψ TWENTY-THREE Ψ

In the days of the dark country, shifting creatures rose out of hiding. They became outcasts, legions of beasts that fit neither in the world of darkness nor of light. The she-wolf, who suckled the babies Romulus and Remus, received transforming powers from the demigods and became the mother of the shifters. She spawned hundreds of daughters who could shift into wolf form from the power of moonlight. A blood lust consumed them. They became known as the ferine.

A battle waged between these heinous creatures and man, resulting in the death of many and the near extinction of the ferine. The few that survived lived again in the shadows, lurking in the dark corners of the woods of Vithalia. They were waiting for the day when their numbers would grow and they could once again prowl freely without ties to the full moon.

A Cur child born of both human and ferine blood would rise up, during the four-hundredth and forty-fourth moon cycle. This Cur would hold remarkable powers lying dormant until the child's coming of age.

The mother of the creatures, whose identity had remained hidden for centuries, would reveal herself when her legion of beasts had grown into a formidable army. Both ferine and man would war to gain the allegiance of this child. Only with the blood sacrifice of the child could the ferine escape the darkness. Only in that death could the Great Mother ensure her children's survival. And likewise, only with the death of the Great Mother could there ever be true peace for the Cur and mankind.

Arud looked up. Could this really be true? Was Lykke the child of which this prophecy spoke? She couldn't be. He surely didn't want her to be. He closed the book, more confused than before he had opened it, still unable to sleep.

Lykke slept soundly as the sun rose, spreading its weak warmth like a shawl across the shoulders of the mountains. Arud slipped down to the river for a drink. He splashed water on his face, exhausted, wishing he'd been able to slumber. Dark clouds rolled in, covering the sun. They would need to move quickly.

He baited a pole with his cloak pin as a lure, and in no time, had caught a fat salmon, which he cleaned, filleted, and threw on a spit over the fire. Lykke stirred from the smell. She smiled, though the sadness of their mother's death crept through her eyes.

Arud smiled back. "Are you hungry?"

"A little." She sat up, looking to the river. "I had hoped it was just a dream. But I know it wasn't, for I had already dreamt of mother's death in Scalvia's den."

Arud stared at the fish cooking over the flame. He had no words to console his sister.

"Where is Scalvia?" Lykke asked. "Do you think she is all right?"

He didn't, but how could he tell that to Lykke? Arud swallowed the lump in his throat. "I hope so."

He took the fish from the fire and set it on a leaf. With two sticks, he separated the meat and he and Lykke ate the thick pink chunks.

"Are you feeling better?" Arud asked.

Lykke nodded, her mouth full of fish, and licked her fingers. She seemed like her old self again, like she always had after drinking the tea Vinter prepared. Arud hoped Ek's herbs would keep Lykke's sickness at bay long enough for them to reach the city.

They finished breakfast and dressed. Lykke shivered. "It's cold, Arud. I don't know how much longer I can stand this."

"Let's get moving. I'm sure there's an outpost nearby where we can get warm."

Lykke looked across the Scynnthe Valley. "I don't see anything between us and the mountains."

"Then we pray for help, and press on until it shows." He held out his hand to help her up. She was nearly ten, but looked much older after all they'd been through in the past week. "We have to keep going. We haven't any idea how long it will take to course across those mountains, or how far away the city is from their base."

With a trusting grin, Lykke said, "Okay, Arud."

He leaned over and kissed her cheek. "You're much stronger than you look, you know that?"

"I'm only strong because I have you around."

"And you always will."

"I know."

They put their packs on and began to cross the valley. Arud looked over his shoulder one last time before they left. He wanted to remember the place where his mother had given her life for them. He wanted to etch the scene into his memory. And secretly, he hoped to see Vinter standing on the bank, waving at them, her mouth in a wide smile, her hair falling over her shoulders.

But he saw no one.

They made good time to the base of the mountain chains, stopping to rest in the grassy valley only twice. Snow fell in light flits, catching in their hair and shoulders, but melting before reaching the ground.

Arud stared at the two ranges, still wondering which to take. The Torngats gently wound up in a steady incline with a flat pass paved by the feet of many travelers over the years. The Sindri-Urd Range grew like teeth, gnarled and jagged, and although Arud knew it would be the faster climb according to Vinter's words, he feared Lykke would be unable to make it.

"We head up the Torngats," he said, pointing north.

They took the pass up the side of the mountain, up the winding slope. Garlic mustard grew in tangles off the pass, and they picked stalks as they went, chewing on the leaves. The pass swept around, and Arud hesitated. Soon, the valley and river would be out of eyeshot as they trekked the mountain, truly alone for the first time since they left the Outlands.

Arud took Lykke by the hand and smiled. She looked up to him, her eyes trusting and loving. "I won't let anything happen to you."

She squeezed his hand. "I know."

They pressed ahead, around the smooth pass. The light breeze carried a bite. Thicker snow stuck in their hair and did not melt when it hit the ground. Arud worried they would not make it to an outpost in time.

The slopes on either side of the pass grew into two massive flanks of rock wall, closing in on both sides. The ground shifted into sandstone littered with snow.

143

Sandwiched, Arud took Lykke by the hand and whispered, "I do not trust this path."

Just before the arrow grazed his nose.

Ψ TWENTY-FOUR Ψ

Arud scanned the tops of the rock walls for movement. Shadows fell across the smooth stone, making it difficult to see the ledges in the crag. He hovered in front of Lykke as he circled, trying to find the location of the shooters.

"There!" Lykke pointed to the brink.

Arud spun. A figure disappeared in the shadows. Small rocks clattered down to the pass.

"Over there!" Lykke pointed to the opposite flank.

He checked the rock walls for an opening. Shadows deceived him, showing depth where it did not exist, a mirage boasting of a barren oasis. They needed to get out of the open and into those shadows. A curve in the mountain, hidden within the natural covering of the rocks, exposed a space beneath the narrow overhang. Harnessing his breath, Arud brought Lykke underneath the protective ledge. He continued to look around.

Come on. Something.

A shimmer of light bounced off the dark wall directly across from him. It flickered, pulsing in and out of sight. Was someone signaling him? "Scalvia," he whispered.

He could only hope.

Another arrow flew down from the ledge above them but missed; the angle too sharp for the shooter to reach them. It would only be a matter of time though, before the shooter changed positions and had a clear shot.

"We're going to have to run for it."

"Run where?" Lykke asked, as another arrow plunged to the ground, closer than the last.

"There." He pointed to the light, hoping she would see it.

Her eyes squinted. "What is that?"

"I think someone's trying to help us."

"How can you be certain it's not a trap?"

"I can't. But I know the intention of those above us. Eventually, they'll figure out a way to reach us." Arud paused. His pulse soared. His lungs heaved. "Are you ready?"

"Yes."

"RUN!"

Lykke sprinted across the dusty pass, leaving Arud behind, staring in wide-eyed bewilderment. She reached the far wall in mere seconds. An arrow caught in his sleeve. He looked up. Several shooters gathered at the brink of the wall. They appeared to be boys, not much older than Arud from the looks of them. What were they doing out here? And why were they trying to kill him and Lykke? He yanked out the arrow in his sleeve and bolted across the sand, screaming from adrenaline, fear, and rage. He slammed into the empty darkness of the hard, flat wall beside Lykke.

They were fully exposed.

"Now what?" Lykke asked.

"What happened to the light? Where'd it go?"

"There was no light. It was a mirage."

Arud looked at his sister and shook his head. "I don't believe it."

"Well, what other explanation—"Lykke screamed.

An arrow pierced through her arm. Arud pushed her behind him, resigned to the fact that they were alone; there was no one there to help them. They were going to have to shoot their way out.

He grabbed his crossbow and readied a bolt, searching, his eyes focused on the boys on the mountain. One of them, a boy with a shaved head, held his arm at the elbow and pretended to cry as he mimicked Lykke. He broke into laughter as Arud steadied his bolt, his sights on the boy, and released.

The tip sliced into his tattooed arm. The boy's face grimaced. He was no longer smiling. The other boys turned, aimed, and released an onslaught of arrows upon Arud and Lykke.

But Arud could see each one loosed, could project its flight, somehow, to avoid getting hit. Everything in the world quieted and slowed. He managed to dodge each strike, as if the arrows were falling leaves. He had no time to wonder how he was able to see so clearly or to give thought to the nagging suspicion that he was responsible for slowing the arrows velocity. He fired back in rapid succession, landing all but three bolts in each of the four shooters.

"Lykke, how are you?" he asked over his shoulder.

"It burns."

"It burns?" Arud checked the skin around the wound. It was smoldering.

"Why is it doing that?"

Arud didn't like this one bit. He reached for her arm. It was hot to the touch. She jerked away, her teeth barred. Was she growling at him? "Give me your arm."

"No. It hurts."

"Give me your arm!"

With tears falling, she stretched her arm. The base of the bodkin tip had not sliced through completely. He held just below her elbow and peered closely. The tip was silver.

Silver?

Why would they be using silver weapons? Then, his body flooded with the answer, like pins and needles.

They knew she was a Cur.

"We have to get out of here." Arud scooped Lykke into his arms and ran back into the open. The hunters no longer lingered on the mountain. Most likely they had headed back to their base camp to remove Arud's bolts and clean their wounds. They would be back though. He was sure of it. But for now, he had the upper hand: a head start.

He ran to the dead end of the dusty road where the rock wall sloped upward so steep and flat it was impossible to climb. Backtracking, he searched for a path near the mountain's base. Lykke's wound needed tending, not that he had any idea how. His mother was the healer. And she was gone. He would have given anything to hear his mother's words once more. He had always drowned them out, being of little importance to him: which herbs mix well for healing wounds and which herbs were in Lykke's tonics. He was a hunter, not a healer. He wished Scalvia was there. Was she gone too? And where was his father?

Lykke moaned.

"Hang on," he whispered.

At the edge of the narrow pass, where the walls leveled and absorbed back into the ground, Arud scrambled over the scree onto a second pass. He held tight to Lykke, who winced in pain, her skin clammy and cold. After a while, he saw a lee. It opened into the mountain itself forming an alcove, and he crept inside. The hollow enclosure spanned back several yards, and the ceiling was so low he couldn't stand upright. But the ground was flat, and it was warm. He lay Lykke down and gave her a drink of water.

"You're going to be all right," he said.

She nodded. "It hurts."

He pushed her hair out of her face. Pieces clung to her sweaty forehead and cheek. He studied her festering wound. The silver reaction was spreading. The arrowhead needed to come out. He hated what he was about to do. "I'm going to have to take the arrow out. And I won't lie, it'll hurt more coming out than going in."

"What?" She stared with panicked eyes. "No. I don't want you to."

"Lykke, I have to. I promise I'll be as gentle as possible."

Tears soaked into the hair on her cheeks. She stared up at the low ceiling.

He grabbed a handful of snow that had collected among the rocks outside their alcove and packed it around the wound. She cried out from his touch.

"This will help numb the pain," he said.

"Do it quickly."

He gripped the shaft. "Are you ready?"

She answered with fresh tears.

"Lykke, I'm about to take it out."

She cried harder, calling out for her mother.

He couldn't do it. How could he pull the arrow out

with her crying like this? What else could he do? "Hold on," he said, rummaging through his bag for answers he knew weren't there. He came across the wolfsbane. He knew it could be lethal to the ferine. He saw what it had done to his grandmother. But it hadn't killed her. Or Scalvia, who had stood near it at the cave in the Dreadlands. The pollen had had no effect on her. Maybe it worked differently with the anatomy of the Cur.

He opened a bulb and rubbed the gooey pulp into the exposed flesh of Lykke's wound. She turned her head to see her arm.

"What are you doing?"

"Does it hurt?" Arud asked.

"No. I don't feel anything."

"Nothing?"

She shook her head, her breath irregular as she sucked the air in hiccups between diminishing tears.

"Look away," Arud said.

Lykke faced the back wall of the alcove and sang softly, "Baru, Baru, sleep quietly."

He grabbed the shaft and twisted it.

"Let fear far from you lie."

The tip of the arrow made a suctioning sound, as the silver sliced back through Lykke's muscles.

"Baru, baru, fall fast asleep."

He rubbed more wolfsbane into the sides of the cut, watching it bubble as it mixed with Lykke's blood.

"For I will stay nearby."

He pulled again, his hand farther down the shaft, freeing the tip as her skin regenerated before his eyes. Her muscle rebuilt, pushing the shaft up like a sapling breaking through the ground. Her blood clotted. Her skin remolded.

"The darkness won't stay long, my love. Soon you'll walk in the light."

Arud finished and Lykke turned her head. He held the silver-tipped arrow in his hand coated with her blood.

"It's out? I didn't feel a thing." She looked at her wound and gasped. "Arud? What happened to my arm?"

"You have healed it, Lykke."

Smooth ribbons of fresh skin glimmered where the arrow had pierced. Not even a scar remained. She ran her fingers over the spot. "How is this possible?"

Arud looked into her eyes, holding his voice steady. "You are a Cur."

Ψ TWENTY-FIVE Ψ

Lykke's eyes filled with fresh tears. She shook her head, her skin blotched red, as if she had just finished running. Then, as if overtaken by something outside herself, her eyes widened and her pupils quickly constricted. "No," she screamed, punching Arud in the chest. "It isn't possible."

Arud grabbed her wrists, struggling to match her strength. "Calm down, Lykke."

She shook her head, her hair fanning back and forth in long streams as she tried to break free from his grip. He held tight, fighting for a stronghold over her while her screams echoed tenfold off the cramped walls of the enclosure. With a horrible gasp, she fell into his lap, wracked with sobs.

Arud's eyes widened as he stared down at his baby sister. Gingerly, he stroked her hair, trying to remember the day that felt so long ago, when he stroked her hair in the meadow behind their house. She had been cloud-gazing with their mother. That life was long gone. And Arud feared that little girl would never return.

Lykke cried out all her tears and had slipped into a lull, when she suddenly lifted her head. Arud's body went rigid, reading the sense of urgency in her posture. He followed her gaze to the world outside their enclosure, where the snow fell in steady drifts.

"What—"

She clapped her hand over his mouth and pressed a

single finger to her lips. He nodded his understanding, and she lowered her hand. Lykke crept to the entrance, crouching in the shadows. Voices of several boys trekking noisily down the pass headed their way. Without a doubt, Arud knew it was the same group that had ambushed them earlier.

He grabbed Lykke by the arm. "If they find us, we're dead."

She pressed her finger to her lips once again.

He shuffled to his bag and loaded his crossbow. He only had a few bolts left. Not that it mattered. He couldn't possibly land a shot crouched in the alcove. He looked around for a way out as the boys advanced.

"They couldn't have gone far," said the first boy with a scratchy voice.

"That's obvious," said another in an arrogant lilt.

"Not with the way I struck her," said the one Arud immediately decided would be his first target.

"There are no tracks anywhere. They must have found shelter before the snow picked up," said the one who sounded to be the brains of the group.

"They could be anywhere," said Scratchy.

"They're near here," said Target. "He couldn't have carried her far over these rocks."

Arud squatted near Lykke, listening, hoping the group would pass them by. They were only a few yards away. He heard the rocks shuffle as the boys marched across the pass. He hoped they wouldn't see the alcove.

"What happens if we don't return with them?" Target asked, his voice revealing a hint of fear.

"Then, you're in big trouble," Arrogant said, as they pounded up the rocks, almost within Arud's view.

"Me? Why would I be in trouble?" Target asked.

"Because you're the *skreyja* who let her get away," Brains responded.

He could see them now, four boys definitely his age, dressed in long, warm cloaks and carrying various hand weapons: axes, bows and arrows, and maces. Scratchy stood the tallest, with a mop of red curls on his head. Brains was the shortest, but the look in his dark eyes gave Arud the impression he would be the hardest to handle. Arrogant matched Arud's build, with a goatee that came to a sharp point, and Target was the kid with the shaved head who had wounded Lykke.

The four boys passed by the alcove bickering over who would be in the most trouble for losing the two in the valley. Their voices trailed the farther they moved out of sight.

Arud let out a sigh and faced Lykke. "We need to get out of here."

"Why are they after us?" she asked.

"I don't know. But we can't stick around to find out."

They gathered their gear and exited the enclosure. The boys were already far in the distance.

"Which way?" Lykke asked.

"Not that way," Arud said. "We may need to backtrack and take the Sindri-Urd Range instead." A sense of unease flooded him as he took a step onto the freshly fallen snow.

Lykke's hand wrapped tight around his wrist. "Something isn't right."

"You feel it too?"

"I smell someone nearby."

"It's probably just them," Arud said, pointing to the boys. "We're safe so long as we don't follow them." He moved farther out into the open, grabbing his sides tightly as a gust of wind bore into him. He scanned the area, but saw nothing to cause alarm, though the ominous sensation remained. "Come on, Lykke. Let's get out of here."

Carefully, she scooted out of the alcove, her flaring nostrils picking up what Arud's eyes had missed. "No," she said. "It's someone much closer."

The movement from the top of the alcove caught Arud's attention and he turned, just as the boy leapt, landing on top of him and knocking them both to the ground. An explosion of stars blinded him as the boy punched him square in the face. His vision faded in and out. Images flickered between spouts of blackness. Lykke running. A boy chasing her. The others returning. Grabbing her. Dragging her. Her screams straggling behind.

Their taunting was muffled, like a nightmare he couldn't wake up from, as the snow fell onto his face, numbing his busted nose; white mixed with gray sky, until he heard nothing and saw nothing but light fading to darkness.

Ψ TWENTY-SIX Ψ

Arud's head throbbed. While still in darkness, he heard voices and forced his eyes opened. He was lying on his back, looking up at the four, no five boys who had brought him here, wherever *here* was.

"He's waking up," said Scratchy.

The others turned. A broad smile crossed Arrogant's face as he pranced over to Arud. "About time. You been sleepin' for a full day."

"You knocked him good, Quinn," said Target, enjoying Arud's misfortune, another reason Arud couldn't wait to beat the kid to tears. Target nudged another kid in the side, one who Arud had not remembered seeing outside the alcove.

"Went down before he even knew I'd slugged him," said Quinn with a smirk. He pushed his dirty-blond hair out of his eyes and disappeared down the only hallway.

Quinn. So that was the kid who had knocked him out.

Arud pushed himself to his elbows. His pulse rocketed against his temples. The room spun slightly. He was indoors somewhere, maybe inside the mountain, maybe inside a home. There was a small opening in one wall, letting in streams of bright light that seemed to pierce Arud's skull. Along the opposite wall, a fire pit sank into the earth, billowing smoke up a chamber before exiting through the flue in the ceiling.

"What were you doing on my mountain?" Scratchy asked.

Arud studied the boy's blue eyes. "I didn't realize you were its owner." He forced himself to a seated position. "I thought it belonged to Skadi."

The other boys laughed softly. Scratchy shot a glance at Arrogant who clenched his fists and stepped forward. "Listen to me, you *bacraut*."

Arud pushed up to his feet in one second flat. He stood face to face with Arrogant, breathing hard, willing him to attempt to try anything. As Arud had guessed, they stood nearly the same height, though Arrogant looked heavier. "Well, I'm listening. *Bacraut*."

Arrogant cocked back his fist and swung, missing Arud who had ducked and weaved out of the way. He sent back an explosive punch into Arrogant's jaw. The boy teetered and fell to the ground. Arud stretched his fingers, his knuckles burning. The fast movement jarred his already splitting head.

The other boys jumped into motion. Scratchy came at him first. But his height was his disadvantage. Arud barreled toward him, lunged into his gut with a bear hug and plowed him into the wall. Scratchy curled up into a ball on the floor, cradling his stomach and retching.

"Why you little *tik*," said Target. He snatched Arud up by the back of his shirt and hurtled him across the room, where he landed with a crack against the heavy oak table and chairs.

Pain shot through every nerve in his body. He rolled over and crawled to his feet as quickly as manageable and readied himself for another blow from

Target. Scratchy had caught his breath, but still clung to the ground. Arrogant lay unconscious.

I may actually make it out of here alive.

Target stretched out his arms painted with symbols Arud recognized as Loki's and Odin's ships. Brains perched in the corner glowering, his skin a mocha shade, his eyes and hair as black as the ink on Target's skin. Arud wiped at the blood trickling down his forehead and positioned himself in the center of the room. He bobbed back and forth on the balls of his feet, waiting for whatever came next.

With a grunt, Target rocketed toward Arud. In that moment, that fraction of a second before the impact of Target's full weight, Arud snapped the cracked leg off the askew table dangling loosely within his reach, wound up his arms, and released a swing that connected with Target's cranium. The boy spun in a circle and crashed face down into the table, splintering what was left. He smacked the floor with a hollow thud.

Arud swung again, the solid wood connecting with Target's side in a sickening crunch and he swore he must have broken a few of the boy's ribs. It had happened so fast, Arud barely remembered doing it. He scanned the faces of the others. They looked scared. Target didn't move. Neither did Arud. Looking back down, Arud noted the distance between himself and the chair. It was far from his reach, yet he had somehow managed to snap off one of the broken legs and get into position to swing in less than a second or two. How had he done it? He forced his face to hide his emotions and threw down the stick for effect. Turning to Brains, he said, "Where's my sister?"

Brains looked at his friends lying battered across the floor. His hands shot up in surrender as he shuffled back toward the entrance. "Listen," he started, until Arud's fist shut him up. Brains covered his nose, most likely broken, as he dripped blood to the pinewood floor. His eyes teared. Arud grabbed him by the front of his shirt. "Listen to me, you *shortwit*. I will beat you for as long as it takes, but you're going to tell me where you took Lykke."

Brains shook his head, blood spraying across Arud's shirt. "I don't know. I swear it."

Arud punched him in the gut, and Brains let out an agonizing howl as he clutched his stomach and crouched to his knees.

"Why are you trying to kill us?" Arud kicked him. "Answer me! Why are you trying to kill us?"

"We were told to catch you…and to bring you here." His nasally voice quivered between pained grunts.

"Who told you?" Arud wrapped his hands around Brains's neck and pushed him flat to the ground. "Where's. My. Sister?"

Brains gasped, unable to speak, unable to breath. Arud squeezed harder. He had lost control again, the way he had with Scalvia when he had almost choked her to death. When he had learned Scalvia was a Cur. When he had lost Lykke. And here, he wondered if he could let go of Brains, even if he had wanted to. Something deep inside of him was awakening. And although he didn't understand, he enjoyed the rush of power.

Pain shot through the back of his head, and Arud released his grip. Brains rolled to his side gasping.

Arud was dragged backward across the splintered floor in a headlock. He tried to catch his footing as he went, but couldn't, his own weight pulling the arms around his neck tighter as he strangled himself.

So much for making it out alive.

As his hearing closed off, replaced by a high-pitched ringing, he vaguely heard a familiar voice in the distance call out, "Let him go!"

The arms holding Arud's neck released, and he slammed to the ground. He gagged and coughed. His breath rattled in raspy gulps. His throat felt like it might collapse. His lungs couldn't seem to suck in enough air. He rolled onto his stomach to see who had nearly killed him. Quinn massaged the muscles in his arm, apparently a side effect from trying to strangle someone his own size. Arud couldn't believe it. This was the second time Quinn had caught him off guard. And stepping out of the shadows, Arud saw the face of the familiar voice who had commanded Quinn to release him.

It was Vang.

Ψ TWENTY-SEVEN Ψ

Where's my sister?" Vang asked, staring down at Arud.

Arud squinted, still unsure what was going on as his ringing ears muffled Vang's voice. Arud's head pounded even worse, making it hard for him to pull to his feet. A wave of dizziness flooded him with every movement. Finally, he stood, his knees unsteady, and answered Vang, "Where's mine?"

Vang shoved Arud in the chest. "What have you done to Scalvia?"

"Nothing," Arud said, shoving back. Adrenaline and anger fueled his broken body.

Vang grabbed Arud's shirt and cocked his arm back. Arud matched him. Neither boy moved, waiting for the other to either strike first or back down.

"I'll ask you one more time," Vang said, spitting in Arud's face through clenched teeth.

"And I'll answer the same."

Quinn watched from the sidelines with narrowed brown eyes. The other boys began to stir. Except for Arrogant. He still lay on the floor, no longer unconscious, but not ready to move.

Vang slowly lowered his arm and lessened his grip. Arud shook free and took a step back, not wanting to give an advantage to any of his attackers. He locked-in on Vang, who from Arud's deduction, was the boy in charge.

"Just tell me…is Lykke all right?" Arud asked.

Vang nodded, then motioned with his head to Quinn, who disappeared down the dark corridor. Arud's knees shook as relief washed over him. He concentrated hard on stilling them.

Lykke stepped out of the darkness. "Arud," she squealed, rushing into his arms.

He grabbed her, looked her over, and said, "Are you all right? Did they hurt you?"

She shook her head. With a sigh, he hugged her briefly, then rotated her slightly behind him. "What do you want, Vang?"

"Scalvia."

"I've already told you, I don't know where—"

"I don't trust you. I haven't from the moment we met. My sister was foolish to believe you and even more foolish to lead you. She's only led herself to a sure death."

"And what do you think I've done with her, Vang? What abilities do I possess that a girl like Scalvia couldn't see through and overpower?"

Vang's muscles tensed. "I don't know. That's why I don't trust you."

"Please," Lykke said, her sweet voice carrying between them. "We have meant no harm to Scalvia. She fought off a ferine to protect us days ago, and we haven't seen her since."

Vang's shoulders hunched. "A ferine?"

"Yes," Arud said. "A powerful one."

"And you ran from it? Like a coward? Leaving my sister to defend it alone?"

Shame fell over him. He forced his stare to stay fixed on Vang's. "There was no other way. I had to protect Lykke."

"Why does your sister hold a higher value than mine?"

Arud couldn't answer him. There was no answer. He had been a coward for leaving Scalvia, and would never forgive himself. But if he had to face the same circumstances again, he wouldn't change his decision. He knew Scalvia understood, even if Vang didn't. Scalvia had given her life protecting Lykke's.

"It was her choice."

Vang moved off to the side, perhaps to regain his composure in front of his followers. Arrogant moaned and tried to get to his feet. Brains wiped blood from his face. Target braced against the wall as he tried to recover his footing. Scratchy seemed to be doing the same, shaking his head like a dog, his red curls flopping wildly.

Arud suppressed a smile. Despite the odds, he had managed to defend himself against all of them. He looked at Quinn. Well, *almost* all of them.

Vang turned back to Arud. "Can you take me to where you saw Scalvia last?"

Arud shook his head. "No."

"Why not?" Vang asked, his eyes filling with fire.

"Lykke and I must reach Vithalia City before the next full moon." He would not tell them of Lykke's need for a tonic each month or that she had already taken her dosage early. He would not tell them the ferine hunting them was a shifter who could take the form of even Scalvia and trick all of them.

"You won't pass over this mountain until you show me where my sister gave her life for yours."

"We don't know for certain she is dead," Lykke said.

Vang looked at her. "All the more reason why we must go back."

Arud knew he was right. He had to know for himself if Scalvia had lived or if she hadn't. His grandmother had already taken one person from him that he loved. He needed to know if she had taken Scalvia as well.

"Okay, Vang. I'll take you."

They stepped outside into the flitting snow. They had been inside a small cabin on the far edge of the Torngats. The mud-bricked dwelling was primitive at best, with a main room and a hallway connecting to what looked to be another small room. Beside the cabin, piled wood lay in corded stacks. The lip of a well missing its overhang clung to the dirt off to the side. Arud imagined it was an abandoned hunting cabin for those who wished to stay on the Torngats during wild boar or deer hunting season, since no city loomed nearby.

They crossed back through the valley, Arud cursing at his misfortune beneath his breath, back over the frost-covered ground, the cold no longer biting him as he wore Brain's leather coat, the boy stripped and left behind. Scratchy remained with him, too unsteady to make the journey after the beating.

Arud led the pack beside Lykke, who wore a warm jacket they had found in the cabin. No one spoke a word as they reached the river and Arud took a step in.

"What are you doing?" Vang asked.

Arud turned. "I'm taking you to where I last saw Scalvia."

"But that water is freezing," Vang said. "We'll be too cold to continue."

Arud approached Vang, his temper rising as his patience wore thin. "What would you have us do, then?"

"There's a bridge a half mile up," Quinn said, pointing east, the direction the river flowed.

"That'll put us too far downstream," Arud replied. "We cross here or we waste time."

"I won't cross here," Quinn said. "There isn't enough daylight to dry out in."

Arud shrugged. "Suit yourself. But this is the way we go."

Lykke tugged on Arud's jacket. "He is right, Arud. We wouldn't have any time to build a fire and dry out."

Arud threw up his hands, defeated. "Fine."

Vang led them along the soft bank. This time Lykke and Arud stayed behind the rest. He wondered if it was a trap, to lure them far away with the pretense of finding Scalvia. But why go through the trouble when they could have just killed him and Lykke in the cabin when they had the chance?

A late afternoon sun spread the warmest light of the day. Arud helped Lykke over the wooded ground and the toppled trees as the river again fell far beneath them.

"Will you stay with me, no matter what?" Lykke asked, her brown eyes looking up into his.

"Of course," he said. "Why would you ask such a thing?"

Lykke shrugged. "I don't know."

Arud stopped, turning her toward him. "Lykke, I would die for you. You have nothing to fear."

Lykke stared down, her eyes shielded by fallen

strands of hair.

"Come on, you two," Vang yelled from up ahead.

Arud took Lykke's hand. He felt like a prisoner being led to certain death. But he had no real choice. He needed to find the truth.

The trees opened up ahead to reveal the fallen trunk of a large oak connecting the two banks. Vang led them to the decayed log and stopped.

Arud looked down. The river surged far beneath. "This is your bridge?"

Quinn did not answer as he stepped up and crossed the creaking oak to the other side.

Arud shook his head. "I won't let Lykke cross this."

"Then she can stay here," Vang said. "But you're coming with us."

"No. Lykke stays with me."

"Coward." Vang thrust Arud closer to the fallen trunk.

Arud swatted him away and spun around. "Keep your hands off me."

"Or what?"

Arud's hot breath hit the cold air as a wall of smoke. A dull ache throbbed in his temples.

Vang stalked away in a huff. A cynical laugh followed. "Fennen you stay with her, and make sure nothing happens." He pointed at the kid with the shaved head, who Arud had labeled his first target. Fennen reached for Lykke.

So, his name was Fennen.

"Not good enough." Arud stood before his sister as a buffer. "I'm not leaving my sister."

"Like you left mine?" Vang seethed.

"I did not leave her, Vang. Nor am I leaving mine with him." He pointed at Fennen.

Fennen stepped closer. "What's wrong with me?"

"Nothing. Except you shot an arrow in my sister's arm."

Fennen smirked. "I was aiming at her head."

Arud shoved him in the chest and Fennen cocked his fist, released the blow, which Arud sidestepped, caught Fennen by the elbow, and twisted his arm behind him until the boy groaned. His face grimaced.

Arud pressed closer to Fennen's ear. "Hurt her again and I'll kill you." He bent Fennen's arm back a fraction more before Vang punched him in the small of his back. Arud and Fennen broke apart; Fennen rubbed his shoulder and Arud stretched his bruised back.

"We do not have time for this," Vang said. "We cross now."

"No!"

Lykke tugged on his coat. Arud turned. "It's all right. I can cross."

"It's not all right."

"Why not?"

"I can't explain why, but something about this is wrong."

She blinked, and the flakes of snow that had caught in her long lashes shimmered. "Then I won't cross."

She couldn't understand. He was supposed to protect her. He had promised his mother Lykke would reach the safety of Vithalia City. Tears wet his eyes. "I can't lose you." He shook his head. "Not again."

Taking his hand, Lykke said, "I can fend for myself. Fennen and I will walk back to the cabin and wait for you. We can find something for supper and share a warm meal when you return with Scalvia." Her smile was warm, redolent, like their mother's, and Arud wondered how she had grown so much in so few days. She even looked taller, more mature. A glimpse of the little girl in the meadow was all that remained.

He squeezed her hand, knowing she was right. Lykke was a Cur, and even if she did not have her skills keenly sharpened, she was fully capable of lashing out with the same strength and severity he had seen in Scalvia.

"Go find her. And bring her back."

Lykke placed something in Arud's palm. He looked at it. "The arrowhead," he said, surprised.

"To keep you safe," Lykke whispered.

Arud held her tight, kissed her forehead, and said, "I'll see you soon."

He crossed the large trunk, his arms outstretched for balance, and tried hard not to stare down or glimpse back. If he caught Lykke's eyes, he was afraid he would change his mind. His footing slipped, but his boot caught and he was able to stabilize. The ground loomed far beneath and did not appear welcoming, with large boulders and snapped branches waiting to break him, not just his fall. He quickly leapt to the other side while Vang and Arrogant crossed directly behind him.

"Which way?" Vang asked.

Arud glanced to where Lykke had stood. An empty space remained, as it had with his mother. His heart beat hollow. Pain and loss filled every ounce of his being. Would he see her again? He must. It was all that mattered, and as Arud led at a sprint, he had to believe it was true.

Ψ TWENTY-EIGHT Ψ

"**W**e rest here." Arud sat on a fallen log beneath a covering of trees, breathing in the aroma of pine. He tilted back his waterskin, draining half. The water soothed his throat and moistened his skin where the cold air had stripped it dry.

Quinn lay on a bed of autumn leaves and closed his eyes. Arrogant rested his head against the mangled trunk of a barren spruce knob, his waterskin clutched tight in his hands.

Vang sat on a boulder. Dark hair curled above his ears and near the nape of his neck from sweat. He wiped his forehead. "How much farther?"

"A couple miles."

"How can you tell?" Arrogant threw a rock against a mountain ash, shaking the ferns and white blooms. "It all looks the same to me."

"Well, not all of us are inbred dimwits like you, Gunter," Quinn said to Arrogant.

Gunter, not Arrogant. At least now he knew all their names.

"It only looks the same to you because you see yourself going through it," Arud said, "instead of being a part of it."

Gunter's eyes narrowed. His mouth opened at the edge. "What kind of poetic bull-scat is that?"

Arud shrugged. "You look at this forest as a means to an end, so of course each tree looks the same, each leaf something in your way, and each breeze another reason to shiver." Arud focused on Gunter's icy blue eyes. "But none of it is the same, no more than you and I are the same." Arud motioned to the trees surrounding them, firs and black spruce and aspen with white bark resembling broken limbs wrapped in shattered bindings. "Each tree hides its story within the rings of its trunk. Each leaf contains a unique crafted pattern. And if you listen carefully, you can hear the wind whisper its secrets."

Gunter, Quinn, and Vang sat silent.

A distant howl pierced through the air.

Toov.

Gunter pushed off the spruce knob. "That didn't sound like a secret."

"It was a ferine," Quinn said, looking around.

"Probably the one after you." Vang glowered at Arud.

"Time to move." Arud ignored Vang, and reassembled his pack, placing a silver-tipped bolt in his hand. "Arm yourselves."

Quinn carried a double-edged axe with an etched ivory handle. Gunter slid a curved dagger from his belt, the blade solid silver. Vang gripped a mace with barbed silver points. The weapon looked like it could smash through solid rock with little effort. Arud grinned. Maybe he could learn to like these bacrauts.

He maneuvered between the trees as sunlight trickled through the coniferous crowns. The forest floor faded into darkness as the sun dipped in the dusky sky. The ground angled upward as they neared the river's widest banks. Where his mother had died.

Another howl rang out. This one was different, far in the distance echoing through the woods.

Arud reached the bank of the Thiannes River. He did not glimpse downstream, did not let his emotions surface, as he led the pack of boys onward. They would soon reach the embankment where Scalvia had dove into the river, staying under for too long. He ran faster as he saw her, in his mind's eye, step out of the water, her hands pushing back her dark hair. As he rounded the hill, he spied the embankment. The creek.

Arud led the boys to the spot. He could still see Scalvia standing there, though she was only an apparition. The distant howl beckoned. Were these two ferine hunting together? It was unheard of for them to hunt in packs. But then again, nothing seemed to make sense regarding the ferine as of late.

They searched the embankment and found loosed bark, uprooted plants, and displaced soil. Remnants of the fight between Toov and Scalvia. Where was she? Why had she stayed and fought against Toov? A pair of prints led toward the embankment, heading south. Toov's prints, Arud was sure of it. But another pair led northeast, back toward the falls. Arud's heart lifted. "Vang!"

He ran over and looked down at the prints.

"Those prints are Scalvia's." Arud pointed to the pair trailing northwest.

"Are you certain?"

"Only one way to find out."

They trudged along at a jog, finding leaves spattered with blood and a dotted trail of crimson in the snow. The ferine prints evolved into Scalvia's bare footed impressions. Arud found his second wind, leading the group onward. The sky bloomed in burnt orange and rustic red as dusk settled atop the horizon.

Smoke plumed in the distance, cutting through the vibrant colors.

"Where's that smoke coming from?" Quinn asked.

Arud squinted. "Someone's lit a fire."

Vang ran ahead.

"Vang, no!" Arud feared what trap awaited them. Sure, it could appear as Scalvia, but Toov had fooled him once by shifting into Berg's form. Arud would not let it happen twice. He ran after Vang, with Quinn and Gunter fighting to keep pace. As he reached the clearing, he spied the fire outside a small burrow. Smoke billowed in a tall column. The air hung with the scent of burnt aspen.

Scalvia lay outside the burrow entrance. His heart sank. Her pallid skin was crusted with dried blood. Her black hair clung to her sweat-covered face and neck.

Vang reached for his sister. "Arud, help me."

"Wait!" Arud said grabbing Vang's wrist. "This could be a trap."

"What?" Vang screeched. "Why would you even think that?"

"Because the ferine has tricked me already by taking on my father's image. We have to make sure this is really Scalvia."

Scalvia groaned.

"And what if it isn't?" Vang asked. "What if it only shares her appearance?"

"Then you can't stop me when I kill her."

Ψ TWENTY-NINE Ψ

Vang yanked his arm free of Arud's grasp and touched Scalvia's forehead. "She's burning up. We need to get her back to the cabin."

Quinn knelt. "She won't make it that far."

"Didn't you hear anything I said?" Arud asked.

"What then?" Vang said, panic rising in his voice.

"Wolfsbane. It'll let us know who's in her skin."

Vang stood. "Are you insane? Wolfsbane will kill her. Have you seen what it does to the ferine?"

"Yes. But I've also seen what it does to the Cur. They react differently to it. And what better way to discover if she's a shifter or herself?"

"How do I know you aren't weakening Scalvia to protect yourself?"

Arud's arms fanned out. "Protect myself from what?"

"From Scalvia speaking the truth of what happened by the river, when you abandoned her. How you lured her there, then left her to fend off a ferine while you saved your own hide."

Before he could change his mind, Arud jabbed Vang in the side of the neck with a straight, flat hand. It was a move his father had taught him, in case he ever needed to stun someone. Vang fell limp to the ground, where he clutched his throat and gasped in rattled breaths.

"Enough, Vang! You don't know what you're talking about. Wolfsbane healed Lykke when Fennen shot her in the arm."

Vang stared in wide-eyed amazement. "She is Cur?" he rasped.

Arud slowly nodded as he offered Vang his hand. Reluctantly, he took hold and got to his feet. Scalvia moaned, louder this time, then began to pant.

"We're running out of time," Gunter said. "Do something."

Arud removed his pack and took out the cloth, which he carefully opened to expose the wolfsbane. He sliced through the bulb and caught the gooey plant matter oozing out in his cupped hand. As he stepped toward her, Vang thrust his hand in Arud's chest to stop him.

Arud caught his cautious eyes. "You must trust me."

Vang searched the faces of those around him, holding his gaze on his sister. "Everything inside me says I shouldn't."

"I know how you feel. I didn't trust Scalvia at first, but she showed me her allegiance by finding Lykke and saving her life. Offer me this same test. Then, decide if I'm worthy of trust. But not now. Scalvia needs this herb or she will die."

Vang lowered his hand.

Arud sat beside Scalvia and lifted her to a seated position. She screamed and tried shoving him away. Quinn and Gunter grabbed her limbs to hold her in place. Vang stared with rage-filled eyes, though he kept his distance.

"Sssshhhhh," Arud whispered. "I've got you."

Her clouded eyes scanned his face as foam brimmed over her lips.

Forcefully, Arud said, "Scalvia, I am opening your mouth and placing herbs on your tongue."

He pried her jaw open and smashed the wolfsbane inside. He tilted her head back and lifted his waterskin to her lips. Water poured out the sides of her mouth while it rushed down her throat. Within a second, her writhing stopped. Arud gently laid her head against his pack.

"What's happening?" Vang said. "What have you done?"

"Patience." Arud rubbed more of the plant residue into her cuts. Her skin smoked, shimmered, then molded into shape as if nothing had ever happened. Her breathing slowed to normal. Arud soaked a cloth with water and cleaned the dried blood from her face and arms.

Scalvia began to speak, though her voice was too weak to decipher.

"I'm here," Vang said, plodding closer. "It's Vang."

Her eyelids fluttered open and she found his face. "Hey." Her voice cracked. "What happened?"

"You were hurt badly, and Arud saved you."

Scalvia looked upon Arud and smiled. "Thank you."

He shrugged, knowing she was hurt because he had abandoned her. "How did you get away—"

She reached up and pulled him down for a kiss. Arud's heart pounded at the feel of her soft lips.

"All right," Vang said, pushing Arud away from his sister. "Enough of that."

Arud's face grew hot as he got to his feet and stepped away.

Scalvia scanned the faces of the boys surrounding her. A wide grin revealed she knew them well. Sitting upright, she said, "Well, the ferine had the upper hand and I thought for sure I would not make it out alive. Everything turned dark and I knew I was fading fast."

"What did you do?" Gunter asked.

"I thought to myself, *what would Gunter do in this situation?*"

Gunter puffed out his chest.

"Then, I did the opposite."

Everyone but Gunter shared a laugh on his account. "Very funny, but highly doubtful considering I've wrestled with you since you were a little girl and taught you all you know."

Scalvia smiled. "In your wildest dreams."

"So, how did you get away?" Vang prompted.

Scalvia stared off, as if the moment were too private to share directly. "It was mother."

"Mother?"

"Her voice. I heard her, but when I opened my eyes I was alone." She rubbed her arm absentmindedly. "Before too long, I realized I was sick and needed to find shelter before it was too late. And the next thing I knew, I heard your voice, Vang."

"Hail to The Red Thor," Vang said. "The Mighty Enemy of Hvitakrist!"

"Hail, Odin!" Arud said, and the group replied in a chorus, "Odin, Bless!"

With Vang's help, Scalvia stood and brushed herself off. She took the cloth Arud had used and disappeared into the burrow for privacy.

Arud rubbed the back of his neck, a smile permanently affixed to his mouth as he thought of her lips pressed against his own.

Vang approached. "I owe you an apology."

Arud shook his head. "Don't even think about it. I would have done the same in your place."

"No. Thank you. She would have died if you hadn't—" He looked away.

Arud thought of Lykke, wondering if she was all right.

Vang set his hands on Arud's shoulders. "I never should have doubted you. You're one of us now; in our brotherhood."

"The brotherhood," Arud repeated. "I like that."

Ψ Ψ Ψ

While Scalvia cleaned up, the boys rested. Arud stared up as the sky revealed the stars one by one. He thought of his mother. Was she sitting up there among the constellations staring upon him? He missed her.

Just after nightfall, Scalvia exited the burrow. The light from the fire illuminated her, a dark angel glowing from the embers. Arud couldn't understand how she managed to appear even more beautiful than he remembered. She came over to the group, putting her arms around Vang's neck.

"Where are the others?" she asked.

"Kron and Lager stayed back in the cabin," Quinn said.

"And Fennen took Lykke," Gunter said. "Probably back there as well by now."

Scalvia's smile faltered.

"What is it?" Arud asked. "What's the matter?"

"It's Lykke," Scalvia said. "She shouldn't have been left alone with him. We must go now."

Arud's heart fell to his feet, fully trusting Scalvia's sixth sense. She led back to the path Arud knew too well even in the darkness, through the woods, to the embankment. In the distance, the ferine howled in a dissonant harmony, masking their numbers. Arud didn't recognize their song, grateful it wasn't Toov's bay he heard among them.

Scalvia sprinted to the embankment near the river. She leapt in, and Arud followed. The others crossed without a word through the neck high water, and no one worried about their wet clothes keeping them cold. Scalvia led at a heated pace up the narrow path away from the river guided by the stars, her heightened scent, and her keen night vision.

The ferine howled continually as Arud and the others pressed through the valley toward the mountains. Starlight and the half moon's light bleached the grass as if all the color in the world had been stolen by the night. They neared the rocky mountain base, lined with balsam firs as guardians of the foothills, when they came to a sliding halt. Four pairs of yellow eyes stared out through the shadows.

"I think we found the ferine," Quinn said, as they all readied their weapons.

Ψ THIRTY Ψ

Time froze in the air. Arud loaded his crossbow. The silver tipped bolt promised a painful death to whichever feeble-minded ferine dared to move. Vang shouted commands and they filed into two flanking units. Gunter and Scalvia, armed with daggers and bows, formed a western defensive line with Vang spear-heading the center. Quinn sidled with Arud to the east, his axe as formidable as Arud's crossbow.

The creatures emerged from the treeline as stretched shadows in the evening sun. Each of their soft pads imprinted four circles in the dense layer of fallen snow as they marched; a wall of bristled hackles in varying shades: a caramel hue, a white and black mottled, a grey-back, and a deep goldenrod. But no black with silver strands. No Toov.

The mottled inched closer, joined by the one with the deep goldenrod pelt. Low, unnatural growls chilled something deep in Arud's bones. There was nothing to buffer him. Human and ferine faced off. Arud wondered which side would be first to strike.

A small-framed child appeared from out of nowhere, exiting a mist near the base of the mountain.

"Where'd she come from?" Gunter said.

It was Lykke. But it couldn't be. Arud screamed her name, but she did not respond. His knees grew weak. His heart pounded against his chest. She moved like one possessed by a ghost among the ferine who were ready to tear her flesh from her bones.

"What is she doing?" Quinn asked. "They will kill her."

Arud couldn't move. He had to be dreaming. Why wasn't he waking from this nightmare? How could this be real? How could *any* of this be real?

Because it was real.

Another of life's taunting reminders that he controlled nothing and that he understood even less.

Lykke raised a hand in the air, her fingers outstretched as if reaching to pet the beasts. The mist hovered around her, shrouding the valley in a crypt. The ferine turned their sights on the unprotected child.

"Lykke!" Arud leapt. Quinn yanked him by the coat, but Arud broke free.

Vang tackled him from behind, slamming them both to the ground. "Stop, Arud. Be still!" Vang gripped his arm.

Arud was too stunned to fight him.

Lykke treaded closer to the pack, her hands now raised above her head. Guttural clicks and inhuman garble uttered deep from within her throat.

The ferine focused on the girl, who plodded steadily closer.

Her full-throated voice intoned screeching pitches, and the creatures' growls morphed into pained whines. Their paws beat fervently against the snowdrifts. Several of them pawed at their bleeding ears.

Scalvia knelt beside Arud. "She's disarming them. Trust her. She's fulfilling her calling."

"What calling?" Arud could barely breathe as he watched his little sister walk into the presence of the enemy, commanding control. No one was doing anything to stop her. "We can't just let her walk in their midst. They'll tear her apart."

Scalvia grabbed ahold of Arud as he moved to stand. "Arud, please. Let her be."

"They will kill her."

"No," Scalvia said. "They would never hurt her."

He watched Lykke gather the attention of the beasts.

"They answer to her."

"Stand up and arm yourselves," Vang said, tightening the grip on his mace.

Lykke's erratic chant spread wildly among the pack. Goldenrod, copper, mottled, and grey paws smacked the snow as the maddened ferine howled their dissonant chords through the air. Lykke showed no fear, yet Arud feared enough for them both. Whatever was happening to his sister was beyond his control. He would have to take Scalvia's lead and trust that Lykke knew what she was doing. He had to believe the ferine had been rendered powerless by his sister's tongue, if only for a short time.

"On three," Vang said, and he counted down to one.

They charged upon the spellbound monsters lying in the snow. Arud's bolt propelled through the air, landing in the broad chest of Goldenrod. She fell to her side heaving as the silver reacted with her blood. Her body convulsed and entered a metamorphosis. Clumps of fur fell out. Claws dropped from pads. Arud smelled singed fur from where the bolt had struck.

Beside him, Scalvia shot arrow upon arrow into the sides of the ferine that had broken through Lykke's spell and were charging upon Vang and Quinn. Vang clubbed the copper ferine with his mace. The silver sliced through its abdomen as he flung the spiked ball through the air and back, over and over again. Quinn hacked Caramel's face. His double-edged solid silver blade split open the creature's black gums until its fangs fell to the snow.

Grey and Mottled charged. Grey sank its teeth into Vang's arm. Mottled leapt at his chest. Arud gripped the cylindrical handle of his full-tang knife as he jumped in front of Vang. The sweeping upward tip sliced through the mottled ferine's white chest, and Arud felt his arm shudder as he caught it in the hind legs as it passed. But the ferine used its narrow chest to push off the ground and whip around, raking its four inch claws through Arud's clothing and ripping his skin in strips. He fell face-first to the snow, quickly rolling over before the ferine could finish him off. He would feel the effects of the lacerations later. For now, he had to fight or die.

Vang was spared the full frontal attack, and able to use his unhindered hand to club Grey's head, smashing her skull in and knocking her to the ground. He grimaced and dropped the mace, grasping his wounded arm. Scalvia rushed to his side.

Mottled recovered too quickly. Her eyes trained upon Arud. He pushed off the ground, his bolt in one hand and crossbow in the other. She growled a menacing rumble as she angrily bared her teeth and dripped blood from her butchered chest, pacing around him as if human thoughts flooded her head. Arud took small strides back, not seeing a large root jutting from the ground. His boot caught, and he fell backward, just as Mottled loosed.

Arud notched his bolt, each movement perfect and

precise. Was it a stroke of pure luck, or an act of the gods? Any mistake would have cost him his life with each second counting, yet each second passed like several minutes. He felt a growing sense of power rush through him again as it had when he leapt into the Dreadlands. He released the bolt just as Mottled arched toward him, her eyes bloodshot and wild, her claws outstretched for his throat. The bolt struck her chest, though her trajectory still lined up with Arud breaking her fall. She would crush him to death.

He closed his eyes, waiting for the impact. He might live through this. It was a slim chance, but possible. Instead, he felt nothing.

Someone bellowed.

Arud opened his eyes. Lykke stood before him a full head taller than usual. Her arms stood out beside her, with long fingernails that had lengthened into six-inch sickles. Her chest heaved. Her face contorted in a rage he'd never seen cross her delicate features. Her eyes glowed greenish-gold in the darkness. Black blood covered her from head to toe. Beside her, dead in the snow, lay the corpse of the white and black mottled ferine she had sliced into two perfect halves, from snout to tail, using only her bare hands. Slowly, she faced Arud. Then collapsed.

Ψ THIRTY-ONE Ψ

"Lykke!" Arud rushed to her side.

Her shaking body convulsed in spastic waves.

Scalvia suddenly sat beneath Lykke, holding her head in her lap. She had moved so quickly, her image blurred across the snow.

"What's happening?" Arud asked.

"She's reacting to the change. It happened too fast." Scalvia looked up. "She has almost completed her transformation to full Cur."

"Will she be all right?"

Scalvia did not answer.

Arud paced, his hand covering his mouth. He felt helpless. He wanted to do something, anything to help his sister, but there was nothing to do but watch. Lykke's eyes focused briefly on Scalvia's face. She smiled down at her and whispered, "Hang on. You're almost there."

Lykke's face contorted again, and she clutched Scalvia's arm, sucking in air through her teeth, before suddenly falling limp and slipping into a deep sleep.

Arud stopped pacing, his blood cold in his veins. Was she dead? He didn't want to ask.

"She needs sleep," Scalvia said. "We make camp here."

Vang looked around. "In the clearing? We might as well walk into the ferine's warren and make camp."

"We'll be fine." Scalvia faced Gunter and Quinn. "Prepare a bed for her."

The two boys retreated into the woods.

"Arud," Scalvia said. "Make a fire."

He nodded, staring upon his sister. "I've already lost too much. I can't lose her."

"You won't," Scalvia said. "No go find wood for the fire."

He pulled his gaze away and entered the woods, gathering large branches in varying sizes, which he set in a pile. When he returned, he angled the branches beside Scalvia, who wiped blood off Lykke's face and neck, tenderly cleaning her skin, as if she were Lykke's mother.

Arud set tinder between the branches and struck the flint stone until a spark caught. Quinn and Gunter returned with large armfuls of leaves and moss, and set them on the ground near the fire. Arud used his coat as a sheet, then set Lykke gently atop the bedding. The orange glow of the fire reflected off her face. She looked peaceful. She looked like a little girl.

They clustered around the fire in silence. The crackle of burnt leaves and the wind rustling across the clearing were the backdrop for Arud's one thought: what in the world had just happened?

Breaking the silence, Quinn asked, "Where'd she come from?"

Ignoring him, Vang said, "We have to bury the bodies before we can rest."

Quinn shifted. "Killing them wasn't enough?"

"They aren't all dead."

"Are you serious?"

"To kill a ferine you must impale it through the heart with silver or sever its head," Vang said. "Only two of those creatures are truly dead."

"What do we do with the rest of them?" Arud asked.

"Bury them," Scalvia said, "and pour silver over the graves to mask their scent."

"You do realize we have to dig beneath the snow first," Gunter added.

Scalvia smirked. "Then I suggest you find a shovel."

The half moon shone bright in the clear sky as they worked their way back to the bodies. Quinn and Vang grabbed the hind and front legs of the grey ferine, dragging her into the woods and out of sight. Although Vang crushed her skull, she was still alive, since she had yet to shift into her human form. Arud wondered how they would do it, if they would cut off her head with Quinn's axe or force silver through her heart. He wondered if she would feel it, being alive, or if her nerves were shattered from Vang's wound.

Scalvia dragged the caramel ferine, while Gunter and Arud took the goldenrod, leaving tracks in the thickening snow like two runners of a sled. Mottled lay in two halves for whoever finished first.

"Wait," Arud said to Gunter as they entered the tree line. "Lykke can't be left alone."

"Are you serious? What do you think could possibly happen to her? We won't be more than ten minutes."

"No," Arud insisted. "I won't leave her."

"Fine," Gunter said, yanking on the legs of the goldenrod ferine. "I'll do it myself. You get rid of the last one."

Gunter disappeared into the woods along with the rest. Arud shuffled back toward Lykke. Was he overreacting? No way. Every time he had left Lykke alone something terrible happened.

"Who cares what that tik thinks of me, anyway," Arud said, kicking up snow. He passed the mottled ferine and shuddered. He would never forget how Lykke looked; heaving, covered in black blood, sickle-like claws replacing her fingernails. But something else caught his attention. The dark lumps lying on the ground were too small to be a ferine's body. Carefully, Arud approached the shapes. The shifted remains were human.

And even in two halves Arud could tell the body had once belonged to Fennen.

Ψ THIRTY-TWO Ψ

After more than ten minutes, the others staggered out of the woods, hunched over and drained of energy. Gunter collapsed next to the fire. Vang sat beside him. He pulled out a rolled leaf, like the one Ek had offered Arud outside his cave, and lit the edge with a smoldering piece of wood that had popped out of the fire. Quinn opened his sack and took out a hunk of cheese wrapped in layered basil leaves. He broke some off and handed the block to Arud, who passed it to Vang, then to Gunter after each took his share.

Scalvia came out of the woods. She showed no sign of fatigue. It must have been an advantage to having Cur blood. She looked to the two halves of the mottled ferine. "What about that one?" she asked, stepping closer. She stopped several yards away, and Arud swore her ivory skin went sallow. "Why didn't you bury that one?"

"I thought you'd like to see it first," he replied sharply. She turned downcast eyes upon the fire.

"What the blazes for?" Gunter asked.

"Because it wasn't a ferine."

"Of course it was," Vang said. "It already shifted when it was ripped in two."

"Why not ask Scalvia what she thinks?"

She looked to Arud. Tears sprung up in her half moon eyes.

"Enlighten us."

Vang looked to his sister. "What's he talking

about?"

"She said that Lykke wasn't safe alone with Fennen," Arud said, his volume rising. "I want to know how she knew he could shift."

Vang laughed. "A shifter? That's impossible. The ferine are all female."

"So I've been told. What was it you said, Scalvia? They find a way when they have need?"

The fire reflected in her eyes, the gray hue masked by the smoke. Only the yellow rings glowed. "I've had my suspicions about Fennen for a while."

"You wanna tell us about them?" Gunter asked. "And anything else that could be valuable in keeping us alive."

"It was just a feeling," she said sternly. "I thought it was absurd, so I kept it to myself. But something about the way he obsessed over my abilities as a Cur concerned me." She took a bite of her cheese and chewed slowly. "There's a lot about the ferine that has changed over the past few moon cycles." They were silent for several moments. "I'm sorry I never mentioned anything before."

Vang nodded. "It's hard to believe. What about the other two?"

"I was thinking the same thing," said Quinn.

"What do you mean?" Arud asked.

"Kron and Lager."

"What about them?"

Quinn shrugged. "Who knows? They live together with Fennen in the cabin. I can't imagine they didn't know about his secret. And if they kept it from us, maybe it's because they hold the same one."

"They'd decided to fight with the demon-dogs,"

Gunter said.

Scalvia shook her head. "It's more than that."

Arud paced through the slush of melted snow around the fire. Fennen had shifted. How? It wasn't possible. And what of Kron and Lager? If they also had this ability, they could not be trusted.

"Is it possible they have somehow become ferine?" Arud suggested.

The air chilled at the notion.

"That's some trick," Quinn said. "You don't just become a ferine."

"Then someone must be making them shift," Gunter said.

Vang shivered against the cold. "Who could be that powerful?"

Arud shook his head. "We'll have to go ask them."

"Are you crazy?" Vang said. "We have no idea what we're facing. They could be waiting to kill us."

"It could be a trap," Quinn added.

Arud thought of Lykke in the cabin alone with Fennen, Kron, and Lager. Thank God she had managed to escape. They probably would have killed her, like they had tried to in the valley. "Kinda like the trap you'd set for Lykke and me when you guys were shooting us in the valley?"

"*We* weren't shooting at you," Gunter said. "*They* were shooting at you, Fennen, Kron, and Lager."

"And they were only aiming at Lykke," added Quinn.

Arud stopped pacing. "What are you talking about? Why were they trying to kill Lykke?"

"No one said they wanted to kill her," Gunter added, "only wound and capture her. Something in the

Prophecy of Ulfhednar."

"You know the prophecy?" Arud said.

"We all know the prophecy," Vang added.

"So they think Lykke has something to do with the prophecy?"

"No," Quinn said. "They're convinced she is the Cur child of which the prophecy foretold."

Ψ THIRTY-THREE Ψ

Arud didn't know how much time passed before he was able to speak again. His tongue felt stuck to the roof of his mouth. If only his mother were around. She would know what to do. Or his father, wherever he was. Arud wondered if his uncle knew the truth about Lykke being a Cur, even the one in the prophecy. He hoped so, or else they would truly have nowhere to go. "How?" he finally said. "How can this be?"

Scalvia angled her body toward him. "She is a powerful Cur, Arud. Look at what she did with the black and white ferine...with Fennen."

"He must be buried," Vang said. "I'll take care of it. Quinn, a hand?"

"Gladly," Quinn said, following Vang into the growing darkness. "I'd kill the traitor myself if he weren't already dead."

Arud looked at Lykke, sweet Lykke. What was happening to her? Would she even be the same when she awoke, after she completed her transformation?

"I have never seen a Cur do what Lykke did to that ferine," said Scalvia, sliding closer to Arud.

Her body was warm. He wanted to collapse in her arms. He wanted to feel her lips pressed against his again. He wanted to feel safe. "What do we do now?"

"One thing is certain," Gunter said. "Kron and Lager will come looking for us if we don't return."

"And if we return without Fennen we'll know right away where they stand," Scalvia added.

Arud shook his head. "Lykke and I have to get to the city. I have to find my uncle."

"You won't make it alone," Gunter said.

"I still have to try."

Vang and Quinn returned and sat next to the fire without a word. Arud couldn't imagine what they were feeling, burying someone they thought had been their friend. Burying someone they thought had been human. The wood spat and crackled in the fire, lulling Arud, whose eyelids grew heavy.

"Is she the one?" Vang addressed Scalvia.

She tilted her head sideways. "There is something remarkable about her, leading me to believe it could be true." She gazed at Lykke with a soft smile.

"My grandmother tried to kill us," Arud blurted out.

The group stared at him.

"What are you talking about?" Scalvia asked.

"The black ferine with the silver strands," he said, "is my grandmother, Toov."

"How can you be sure?"

"She shifted into my father's likeness at the cave in the Dreadlands. Only Purebloods can do that."

"You were in the Dreadlands?" Vang asked, glaring at Scalvia.

"We were following Lykke's trail," she snapped. "Don't treat me like a child, Vang. I don't answer to you."

"That place is a death trap. It's a miracle you made it out alive."

"Well, we did," Scalvia said, glaring back. She faced Arud. "Why didn't you say something sooner?"

Arud tucked his arms in at his sides. "I don't

know. I guess I didn't want to say it aloud, like keeping it in would somehow make it untrue."

"I'm sorry, Arud." She leaned her head upon his shoulder. He breathed in her scent.

"Why would she be after you?" Quinn asked.

"Bloodline doesn't seem to matter to her." His heart dropped and the pain returned as he said, "She killed our mother."

Scalvia jerked her head up and gasped.

"My mother had shifted into a yellow ferine and appeared atop the embankment. At first, I thought she was there to kill us, until she attacked our grandmother." He stared into the fire, rubbing his palm. "My mother died by the river saving us—" His voice trailed off.

Tears caught in Scalvia's eyes and she took his hand.

"I don't understand why my parents kept this from me," Arud said, his teeth clenched.

"They were probably trying to protect you," Scalvia said.

"How? By releasing me into a world in which I can't possibly survive? By hiding who we are and who stalks us in the darkness? How is that protection?"

His body trembled as everyone stared at him. Why had he blurted out like that? "Forget it." He felt foolish as he stomped toward the treeline, his hands nestled deep in his pockets for warmth. His fingertips brushed the arrowhead and he took it out. He rubbed the smooth stone between his thumb and forefinger. His teeth suddenly clenched as rage overtook him. "There is no protection." He winged the arrowhead into the woods, uttering a grunt as he used all his strength. He collapsed to the snow, his face buried in his hands. He just wanted to go home.

But home no longer existed.

"Arud?" Scalvia stood before him, her breath a white shadow.

He stared at her with wet eyes as he slowly stood.

"Are you all right?"

Without thinking, he pulled her into his chest and buried his face in her hair, tears burning his eyes. After a few moments, she pulled back and Arud leaned in for a kiss.

It was longer than their first had been. And for a moment, Arud forgot everything: the ferine, Toov, the lies. Everything, except Scalvia. The way her lips felt. How their fingers entwined, and he couldn't tell them apart. Her taste. Her scent. It was all heightened, as if his senses were awakened. How long they held each other, he didn't know. All he knew was he couldn't be without her again.

Toov's howl rumbled far in the distance, pulling them apart.

"Was that your grandmother?" Scalvia asked.

"Yes," Arud said. "Sounds like she's recovered."

They sprinted back to the group, hand in hand.

"That was her," Arud said. "That was my grandmother. We have to leave now."

They jumped into action. Quinn kicked snow on the fire and ground it in with the soles of his boots until only a drift of smoke spat into the cold air. Vang packed the supplies they'd strewn across the ground while Gunter gathered what remained of their food.

"I'll carry your sister," Gunter said, lifting Lykke in his strong arms.

She barely stirred as she wrapped her arms around his thick neck.

"Where should we go?" Vang asked Arud.

"Back to the cabin."

They crossed familiar terrain up the Torngats. Arud wondered what they would meet in the cabin: creatures or boys?

Toov's howls resonated.

The wind gusted.

"Pick up your pace!" Arud yelled.

Late night settled, its veil of darkness covering the rocky mountain pass. A lamp burned in the window of the hunting cabin. They hid behind a rock wall, with Vang and Arud at the forefront. Arud scrutinized the cabin, searching for movement inside and around the stilted structure. Kron passed by the cut out window in the wall, his bright red hair unmistakable. Vang and Arud ducked. Arud slowly lifted his head after enough time had passed. It didn't seem Kron noticed them.

Vang turned, motioning for the group to break into two sections and move around either side of the cabin, appointing himself as head of one flank and Arud head of the other. Vang held three fingers in the air, bringing down one, then two, then…

Toov howled.

She was right on top of them. Lykke's eyes shot open. Kron peered out the window.

"Get down," Vang whispered forcefully, and they fell behind the rock barrier.

Arud stared at Lykke. She looked perfectly fine, except that the hue of her eyes remained deep brown. She grinned and he smiled back in relief. "How are you feeling?" he asked softly.

The wind suddenly shifted, and both Scalvia and Lykke twitched their noses in the air.

"She's coming," Scalvia said.

"I know that scent," Lykke added.

"What should we do?" Quinn asked.

"We wait," Scalvia said. "The black ferine approaches."

Arud scanned the rocks and tall black spruce lining the property for any sign of Toov. He saw nothing. The woodlands grew with underbrush and trees packed tight together. He wished he could sense with smell the way Lykke and Scalvia could. The way Toov could. He shuddered, facing Scalvia. "She can smell us." He tore open his pack, pulling out silver powder and wolfsbane. He passed pieces of the herb dipped in powder around the circle. Once everyone had a portion, he said, "I don't know if this'll work, but rub the wolfsbane into your clothing and skin. Hopefully it will mask our scent."

They matted themselves in the shimmering, sticky substance. No sooner had they finished, than a large black ferine edged out of the woods, creeping toward the cabin.

"They will be killed," Lykke said, tenderly, watching as the ferine reached the stairs leading to the cabin door.

With each step, the creature shifted. Paws slimmed to feet. Legs stretched, pushing the back into an upright position. Skin replaced fur. By the time the ferine reached the door, she was able to knock with a bony hand.

Lykke gasped, covering her mouth. She was staring at her grandmother. Arud squeezed her hand as

Lykke began to silently sob. The realization of who had killed their mother registered on Lykke's ghost-white face.

Toov rapped on the cabin door three times.

"What's she doing here?" Arud whispered.

Toov turned at the sound of his voice. Her animalistic eyes cut through the shadows. Arud and the others ducked further beneath the rock covering. Before too long, the cabin door opened. Toov said something too low to hear from across the way, and Lager welcomed her in.

"This is bad," Arud said to Scalvia. "She'll kill them."

"I know," she agreed.

"We have to get closer. I can't hear a bloody thing they're saying," said Gunter. He dashed to the wall beneath the cabin window.

Arud looked to Lykke.

"Go," Scalvia said. "I've got her."

He sprinted up beside Quinn and Vang, who had already joined Gunter. Clear voices drifted out the opening.

"Where is Fennen?" Toov asked.

"He left with them, but hasn't returned," said Kron.

"I see," Toov said in her icy voice. "And where are they?"

Lager's voice quavered as he answered, "I don't know. They should have been back hours ago."

The ground shook, and Arud imagined Toov stomping her feet against the boards. "You were supposed to stay with them."

"We couldn't," Kron said. "That idiot Vang

forced us to remain."

"Yeah," Lager added. "We had to keep up the whole 'you're our leader' thing or he'd start questioning."

Vang held his lowered head in his hands.

"He most certainly knows now," Toov said.

"How?" Kron asked. "We never said—"

"Fennen, you tiks," Toov said. "He fought with my soldiers against Vang and the others." There was a pause, silence, and Toov huffed in agitation. Apparently, Kron and Lager weren't the brightest stars in the sky. "He died."

"How do you know?" Lager asked.

"Because he hasn't returned."

After another pause, Kron said, "So, how does Vang know? I still don't understand."

Toov grunted. "His body, you *halftroll*. When he died, he must have shifted."

"Oh," Kron responded like a child.

"Which means they have *her*," Toov said. A chair scraped against the floor, followed by two others.

"Come on," Vang said, patting Arud in the chest. Vang, Quinn, and Gunter ran back to the others and propelled their bodies over the rocks to hide. Arud remained paralyzed. He needed to hear the words from his grandmother's mouth.

"Arud!" Scalvia whispered loudly.

He turned in her direction. She was frantically waving him back. He simply shook his head and focused his concentration back to the cabin. Footfalls shuffled across the creaking floorboards. Arud hugged the wall as he moved with them toward the front stairs. Their muffled voices siphoned through the logs, but he couldn't understand what they were saying. He slid beneath the stairs, waiting, until the front door opened.

"At all costs, you need to get her back," Toov said.

"Do you think they suspect anything?" Lager asked.

"Of course they do. They just may not suspect you and Kron, yet."

"What do we do, I mean, if they realize we are with the ferine?" Kron said.

Arud peered up through the spaces between the stairs above him. Toov took a step closer to Kron, whose body tensed. She pushed a bony finger into his chest. "You shift. I have given you that gift for a reason."

Kron nodded.

Toov paused long enough to watch Kron squirm with fear before she finally turned and crept down the stairs.

Say it. Say it out loud so I know it's true.

At the bottom step, Toov paused, then turned to face Kron and Lager. "She is the chosen one, the Cur child who will bring the ferine back to power. If she sides with the humans, the ferine will cease to exist."

"We know," Kron said. "We will get Lykke back, Mother."

A wicked smile that Arud knew all too well wormed across Toov's leathery face. The air around her chilled. "I know you will, child. Because if I don't have her blood to fulfill the prophecy, I will spill both of yours." She turned and pressed back into the shadows, shifting into the black ferine as she left. The door to the cabin closed, and the boy's feet scuttled away from the entrance.

Arud let out the breath he had been holding. It *was* Lykke, the child in the prophecy, and it was her innocent blood Toov required to sustain her species.

"I won't let it happen," Arud said under his breath. "I swear it."

He needed more than ever to get Lykke to the safety of Vithalia City. He must find his uncle. Maybe he would be able to help. Arud scooted out from beneath the stairs, listening for any voices drifting from the window. It was quiet. Scalvia, watching from the rocks, nodded that the coast was clear. Arud sprinted the distance, jumping behind the rock covering. Out of breath, he said, "She is the Great Mother, I'm sure of it."

"What did you hear?" Scalvia asked, her hand grasping his.

"Lager and Kron can shift," he said.

"That's not possible," Vang replied.

"Tell that to Fennen," Arud said, casting his eyes on Vang. "He shifted. We all saw it."

Vang silenced.

"What else," Scalvia said.

His heart was burdened as he spoke. "She's after Lykke."

"Me?" Lykke asked. "Why?"

"She believes you're the Cur child spoken of in the Prophecy of Ulfhednar."

"That can't be. I can barely eat a dead hare, let alone kill one."

Arud and Scalvia exchanged a glance. Vang and Quinn looked back over their shoulders.

"What?" Lykke asked, squirming.

"You don't remember what happened to Fennen,

do you?" Vang asked.

Lykke shook her head. "I remember walking with him toward the cabin and getting an uneasy feeling. The next thing I knew I was waking up in Gunter's arms." Her forehead creased in worry. "Why? What happened?" They were quiet as Lykke searched their faces. "Well?" she said irritated. "What happened?"

"He shifted into ferine form...and you tore him in half," Arud said. "With your bare hands."

She stared, then shook her head. "No, it can't be true."

"It *is* true." Scalvia spoke in a hush. "We all watched you do it."

Still shaking her head, Lykke said, "I couldn't have done that. Could I?"

Scalvia brushed Lykke's hair back with her fingers. "I know what you're feeling. At first, it was hard to believe I had ferine blood inside of me." She smiled, wiping streaming tears off Lykke's cheeks. "But I soon realized I didn't have to use my power for evil. I could use it to protect those I cared for." She glimpsed quickly at Arud before looking back at Lykke.

Chills swept down his spine while heat spread through his chest. Was she trying to say she cared for him?

Did *he* care for *her*?

"I remember, now. About Fennen," Lykke said, facing Arud. "I was only protecting you." Her lip trembled as a new wave of tears wracked her body.

Arud crouched beside her, holding her tight. "I know, Lykke."

She sobbed while Arud held her, letting her grieve

over the truth of who she was, over what she had done to Fennen, over a grandmother who had murdered her mother, and who was now hunting her. He wished there was something he could say, but comforting words had never come easily to him.

"What are we supposed to do now?" Quinn asked, after several silent minutes had passed.

"We go in there and tell those two traitors we know what they are," Vang said, motioning toward the cabin.

"Are you crazy?" Scalvia said. "They would shift and be right on top of us. More blood would be spilled. What point would there be in that?"

"To make them pay for what they've done," Gunter added. "I agree with Vang. They must be punished."

"No," Arud said. "We can't let them know we're here."

"Why not?" Vang said. "Are you truly that much of a coward?"

"Their sins will be discovered, Vang. What they do in darkness will be brought out in the light. It's Lykke who matters. She must reach the safety of Vithalia City."

"Why is that so important?" Quinn asked.

"Because if she really is the Cur child of the prophecy, then her blood will give the creatures the power they need," Arud said. "My grandmother doesn't just want to find Lykke. She wants to kill her."

Ψ THIRTY-FOUR Ψ

They crept along the rocks for hours, heading higher up the mountain. Lykke sobbed softly. Vang and Quinn led the group with Lykke and Scalvia next, then Arud, and finally Gunter at the rear.

"We can't go much farther," Gunter said. "It's too dark and our feet keep slipping."

Moonlight beamed on the crag as they trekked in a straight line along the inclined pass. Quinn called out, "Hang in there. We've almost reached a stopping point."

The mountainside plateau stretched over a valley. From this spot, Arud could see ahead where the mountain made its sharp northerly turn and snaked far in the distance back to an easterly direction. A large red pine grew out of the rocks, its boughs high and sturdy, overlooking the valley. Opposite the pine, a deep crevice in the rock wall pushed back several yards, forming a small burrow in the mountainside nearly six feet high by ten feet wide.

"This is camp," Quinn said. He pointed to the tree. "We'll be safe up there."

Scalvia peered into the high boughs. "Lykke and I will stay in there." She pointed to the dark burrow.

"No," Arud said. "It's safer higher up."

"And what would you know of that?" Scalvia said.

Arud's forehead scrunched as his neck pulled back. "What is it with you?"

"Me? I'm not the one trying to complicate things I

know nothing about." Her eyes squinted as she shuffled Lykke to the burrow.

Arud marched closely behind and grabbed hold of Lykke's hand. "When I hunt, I rarely see animals scan the treetops for predators. We will be safer higher up and able to see my grandmother or Lager and Kron, should they come looking for us."

Scalvia wrapped her arm around Lykke's shoulders. "And I feel it wouldn't be prudent to position ourselves where we have no escape. If something lies at the base of that tree in wait, you will be trapped. At least down here, we stand a fighting chance."

She was as obstinate as her father.

"There isn't much night left," Vang said. "Gunter and I will take watch in the tree. Arud's right. We have a better chance of seeing something coming from far away in the higher post. The rest of you get settled in the burrow and sleep."

And with that, it was decided.

$$\Psi \ \Psi \ \Psi$$

Arud helped Lykke into the burrow. "At least it's warm and dry in here. You should sleep soundly." He tucked her cloak around her as she stared at the uneven sediments lining the ceiling.

"Lykke, I wanted to—"

She turned sharp brown eyes his way. "I don't want to talk about it." She rolled onto her side, her back like a barricade keeping Arud out; a place he had never known before, outside Lykke's heart.

"Goodnight, then," he said, backing out. She did not reply. He hoped this would pass, that in time she would get a grasp on her new life, on the lies of her past, all the things Arud was dealing with himself. He would give her space, and when she was ready, he would be there for her.

Ψ THIRTY-FIVE Ψ

Arud opened his eyes to Scalvia's face. She was leaning over him, shaking him by the shoulder. He grinned, still half-asleep, enjoying what he thought to be a fantastic dream. Her voice sounded distant as he slowly came to, fighting the impulse to pull her down into his arms. He looked around an empty burrow. "Where is everyone?"

"It's past daybreak. Time to wake up."

Arud stifled a yawn. "Where's Lykke? Is she okay?"

"I'd say. She's already gone hunting and back with Gunter."

"Lykke—hunting?"

"Yes. And they've returned with two squirrels, a sack full of greens, and some tubers."

"She shouldn't have left without me. Why didn't you wake me?" Arud started to sit up and grimaced. His hands reached for his back.

"What is it?" Scalvia asked, lifting his shirt. "Your back is shredded. How did you not notice?"

Arud shrugged. "Busy day." He smirked.

Scalvia shot him a severe look. "It needs to be treated. Infection is already setting in." She ran her fingers across his bare back, and Arud shivered while grinding his teeth to block his scream. "I have a balm that will help. I'll go get it and be right back."

As Scalvia left, Arud lowered his shirt with a wince. Lykke poked her head into the burrow. "Good morrow. Did you sleep well?"

Arud smiled. "Yes. I see too well. I hear you've already been out hunting."

"Mm-hmm," she said squatting beside him. "I never knew how much fun it could be."

She looked the same,—sweet smile, blonde curls—but her eyes had aged. There was an edge that had never been there before. Arud felt a pang of sadness, knowing she no longer needed him to watch over her.

Scalvia returned carrying a satchel and a tin cup of water. "Lift your shirt."

"What's the matter? Are you hurt?" Lykke asked.

"See for yourself." He lifted his clothes to expose the strips Fennen had tore from his flesh. By the expression on Lykke's face, Arud knew it didn't look good. "It looks worse than it feels," he offered.

"I hope so," Lykke said frowning.

"Don't worry," Scalvia said. "I'll have Arud fixed up in no time."

"I'll leave you then." Lykke wrapped her arms around Arud's neck and kissed his cheek.

The same way she always had.

"And Arud...I'll always need you." She pushed to her feet and left the burrow, her voice trailing like the tail of a comet.

Why had she told him that? Had she read his thoughts?

Scalvia sat behind Arud and dipped a piece of torn cloth into the fresh water. Gingerly, she patted his wound. Arud clenched his fists, his nails leaving indents on the heel of his hand.

"I know this hurts, but I have to cleanse it. I'm

amazed you made it through the night. The wound is deep."

Arud wondered the same thing. "Must have been all the excitement distracting me from the pain," he suggested unconvincingly. Excess water, wrung from the cloth, ran cold down his back. His skin rippled with goose bumps. "Will she be okay?"

Scalvia stopped briefly, then went back to attending his wound. "She'll be fine."

"Why is she acting so differently?"

"The transformation to Cur is difficult. You have to understand she has not only undergone physical changes, but emotional ones as well. Her senses are heightened, her inhibitions lessened. She is much stronger than before and even stronger than she appears." Scalvia's voice softened. "She may be the most powerful Cur I have ever seen."

She tossed the bloodied cloth and removed the balm from her satchel. "Your wound heals quickly."

"I thought you said it was deep," Arud said wincing.

"It is deep. But already, I see lower layers of skin rebuilding." She gently rubbed the balm into Arud's wound, and he sighed. It cooled his skin, numbing the pain completely.

"What is that?" he asked.

"A blend of carrot and chamomile oils. My mother mixes them in beeswax."

"It's wonderful. I can't feel any pain."

"That's the point." She leaned forward, and he could see she was smiling. He smiled back. Scalvia took a piece of cheesecloth and pressed it into the balm, holding it in place. "There," she said, standing.

"That should take care of it. I'll redress your wound tonight."

Arud gently pulled his shirt back down, grimacing as the garment brushed the cheese cloth. Scalvia stared at him. He inhaled to say, "thank you," when she kissed him. He drew her in close, pressing tight. He didn't want to stop. He didn't want to let go. But the sounds of snickering pulled them apart.

Lykke, Gunter, and Quinn stood outside the burrow, their heads leaning in.

"You get everything taken care of?" Quinn asked with a snort. "Or is Scalvia attending to wounds we can't see?"

Scalvia turned and in one motion leapt into his face, pushing him back. Quinn guffawed loudly, until his back slammed into a tree.

"Not funny," she said. But her reddened face revealed that embarrassment overpowered her anger, and she released him.

Lykke puckered her lips, making kissing noises. Arud wanted to throw threw her over his shoulder and run circles around the camp to teach her a lesson. But his body was too weak, so he just gave her a reproving look instead.

"Time to eat," Vang said, leaning in; a look of dissatisfaction crossed his face.

As they sat around the fire, Vang took the charred squirrels and passed one in each direction so everyone could take their share. The greens remained piled in Lykke's handkerchief for everyone to grab themselves.

"So who knows the quickest route to Vithalia City?" Arud asked, hoping his and Scalvia's kiss had been forgotten.

"The only route is the mountain pass. There isn't much choice from here," Quinn said. "There's a village about halfway up where we can get fresh supplies, but besides that there's nothing except rocks and some trees."

"How long will it take?" Arud asked.

Quinn shrugged. "Depends. Two weeks, maybe less."

"Two weeks?" Arud said. "It's already halfway through the moon's cycle. We'll barely reach the city gates in time if we go straight through without stopping."

"I said maybe less," Quinn defended.

Scalvia took Arud's hand. "We'll make it. Don't worry."

"How can I not worry? It's already taken more time than it should've to come this far."

"Who lives in the village?" Lykke interrupted.

Quinn shrugged. "Vagrants, travelers like us, people running from the Vithalian guard."

"You mean criminals," Gunter corrected.

"Plus the occasional Cur who has chosen not to shift," Quinn added.

"A shady mix," Gunter said with a smirk. "We should fit right in."

Arud looked at Scalvia. "They can choose not to shift?"

"Yes," Scalvia answered. "And many have."

"Do we have to pass through this city?" Arud asked uncomfortably. "Isn't there any way to go around it?"

"Not unless you can fly," Quinn said.

No one spoke for a few minutes. The wind blew,

rustling the leaves on the lone tree. Arud looked down at the valley, a blend of greens from the vibrant shade of spring grass to the sickly hue of pond scum. The Great Expanse. It looked peaceful, completely undisturbed. It reminded him of the meadow in his backyard, when the apples were gathered for the harvest. It was the one place he felt completely safe, even with his grandmother lurking in the shadows...

"What about Lager and Kron?" Arud asked. "Do you think they'll be tailing us?"

"Oh, absolutely," Quinn replied.

"Wouldn't you?" Gunter asked. "You said it yourself: Lykke is the Cur in the prophecy. Do you have any idea what she is worth?"

"What in Niflheim oe Hel is the matter with you?" Scalvia snapped as she placed an arm around Lykke's shoulder.

"I'm not saying *I* think this way," Gunter said. "I'm just saying that for two lying traitors like Kron and Lager...you'd be a fool not to think they aren't looking for some way to grab her for profit. Probably boost their rankings in the ferine army. What better way to prove their indispensability?"

"That's not going to happen," Arud said to Gunter.

"No, it's not," Scalvia agreed. "She is able to fend for herself, aren't you, Lykke?"

Lykke nodded. For the first time since her change, Arud saw a glimpse of the fragile girl that was his sister. As capable as she was, she was still his responsibility, not anyone else's. And upon his life, he would get her safely to their uncle.

Ψ THIRTY-SIX Ψ

They left the plateau and moved along the well-trodden pass snaking with the lines of the mountain. Their waterskins were full, but Arud drank his in small sips, not knowing when they would find the next freshwater spring, and instructed Lykke do the same.

They stopped for lunch in a barren rock-littered crag and ate leftover greens and tubers. Arud still felt hungry when they finished. They packed up after the short rest and pressed on. The rocky pass inclined slowly. Snow began falling in light flits. The sun peeked in and out as the cloud formations passed, the warmth it provided insignificant, yet welcome.

By late afternoon the following day, they were exhausted. The terrain had not changed much: dusty rocks and upward slopes, tall pines and erratic undergrowth fanning up from the earth like stockings covering the long legs of the trees. The heavy snow piled in drifts. Arud collected some into his waterskin. The others did the same. It would probably not become warm enough for the snow to melt, but at least it would quench their thirst.

A snow leopard roared, and Arud jumped. The streamlined body of the cat paced on a rock shelf. It watched them as they crossed, but did not show any signs of attack. Perhaps it smelled the ferine blood in Lykke and Scalvia and thought otherwise.

Near sunset, they reached the curve in the mountain where it turned from a mostly eastern direction to a northerly one. The peak where the two chains converged and branched out into their horseshoe shape. Vithalia City came into view. It was the first time Arud had ever seen it.

From the Labrador seashore, a long single pass bridge, erected along a rock shelf, stretched to the city in the sea. White fortified walls ran long and sleek into the briny surf. The blood-red sky reflected off the ramparts as a glowing golden-red fire. The city looked like it had been carved out of a single enormous pearl, shimmering and glittering, polished and smooth, with many angular spires and watchtowers blooming skyward.

"It's even more amazing than I'd imagined," Lykke said, her wide-eyed expression almost reverent.

"I have never seen anything like it." Arud stepped closer to the mountain's edge.

The cliff stopped, and the face of the Torngats fell at a sharp angle, ending miles beneath. To the south, Arud saw the Sindri-Urd Range curving up into the dense clouds, snow blanketing what part of the mountaintop he could not see. The other side of the mountain sloped smoothly down into the valley that preceded Vithalia City. He scanned the Torngat Mountain pass heading north. Eventually, it would curve to meet the Labrador Sea where the capital had been erected.

A high, long road stretched through the breaking waves leading to the city's gates. The design, meant to protect the citizens from invaders who had to swim and climb the slick walls or cross the guarded bridge undetected, was also its greatest weakness. For it kept its citizens imprisoned if the stone parapet were ever infiltrated.

"Why can't we move between the two chains?" Arud asked.

"Look down," Gunter said. "Miles of flat rock slick as piss. Not even the most skilled climbers have been able to scale it."

"It's the main reason the city was built behind it," added Quinn. "Even though two mountains run near it, the rock wall between them is impassible. Intruders have to risk their lives scaling the steep rocks and sharp blades of the Sindri-Urd Range, or take the long, exposed route of the Torngats," Quinn said. "The city guards can clearly see from their posts in the watchtowers when travelers approach, even days in advance."

"How do you know all this?" Scalvia asked. "I thought you'd never been to the city."

"Books, Scalvia. Old scrolls. Tales spread through the realm for generations by those who have been here since the beginning. Unlike you, I don't sit around making myself look pretty all day."

"That's apparent," Gunter said, taking a swig of his slushy water.

Scalvia smiled her thanks.

"Let's keep moving," Vang urged. "We don't have much sun left, and we may have followers. There's a stream up ahead. A water source for us and other animals, meanins meat for dinner."

"What stream?" Scalvia asked. "How do you know there's a stream?"

"It's a mountain, Scalvia. Where do you think the Thiannes River gets its water from?"

She squinted her eyes. "But how do you know we

are close enough to reach it before nightfall?"

He shrugged. "Just a hunch." And Vang turned and began walking.

Gunter popped the last of the tubers into his mouth and followed with Lykke by his side.

Quinn adjusted his pack and filed in. "Your brother's like the North Star."

Scalvia grinned and took a step behind him. She looked back over her shoulder and saw Arud standing there. "Arud, are you coming?"

"I have never seen the city before."

She stepped beside him. "Nor have I."

Sunset dripped down the outer walls of Vithalia in ocean blues and rose pinks and the deepest last light of purple. Salt air clung to Arud's skin. The iridescent walls of Vithalia City gave way to the darkness as twilight faded. Nighttime lights ignited all along the city twinkling as falling stars.

"It's breathtaking," Scalvia said, as she beheld the city.

Arud focused on her profile. She looked over. He brushed her chin, softly angling it closer to his own. Their eyes closed; their lips touched. He pulled her closer, tighter; still she was too far from him as her fingers ran through his hair and down his neck.

"Come on, you two," Quinn hollered back.

Scalvia pulled away and smiled. "We'd better catch up with the rest of them."

Hand in hand they jogged across the mountain, the chain pulling away from the city. Arud felt elated, confident somehow, that they would arrive at the city in time with Scalvia beside him. This Cur who had shifted his heart. Who had gained more than his trust.

He stopped short. Had he heard something? He looked over his shoulder, but saw nothing in the shadows of dusk.

"What is it?" Scalvia asked, stopping with him.

"I'm not sure. I thought I heard something."

She scanned the flat terrain, her nose twitching. "There aren't many places to hide in these rocks. It was probably just an animal out hunting."

With an uneasy feeling, Arud turned. "That's what I'm afraid of."

Ψ THIRTY-SEVEN Ψ

They reached a second stream long after nightfall on the fourth day, exhausted and freezing. The clouds from that day's storm had cleared, and millions of stars blinked down upon them. The waxing moon edged toward three-quarters full, basking the mountaintop in yellow light. Arud worried they would not arrive at the city gates in the time remaining. He wondered if it even mattered anymore, with the Great Mother hunting them and giving ferine capabilities to whomever she pleased. Anyone could be the enemy. There was no way to tell by sight.

The mountaintop widened as it continued to curve. Withered grass pressed up between the rocks. Trees dotted the landscape, growing close to the shallow banks of the stream. They knelt using their cupped hands to drink, then cleaned and refilled their waterskins. It was too dark to hunt. This would be his first night going to bed hungry since Arud and Lykke had left home. Had it only been a few weeks ago? It felt like it had been months.

He longed for his soft mattress, for the cushioned chair and hearth where he propped his feet to warm by the fire. He missed sharing a pipe with his father, listening as Berg told stories of his journeys out to sea or to the market, or tales passed down to him by his own father and his father before him. Tales of Leif Erickson in Vineland and the battles between the Vikings and the ferine, of lavish banquets they held after each full moon had passed and the creatures had returned to the Dreadlands. Would his uncle know these same tales Arud had shared with his father?

Exhaustion hung in the air as they piled leaves and twigs to use as beds. It would still be cold, but at least the foliage would retain some of their body heat. While gathering, Arud stumbled into a hole, his ankle nearly twisting. It was most likely the entrance to some animal's den, and it gave him an idea.

"Get some wood," he said. "We can smoke out whatever lies inside."

With the prospect of a meal before them, Gunter and Vang gathered branches and laid them over the shallow burrow in the ground. Arud had no idea what type of animal would make its home here. It was a rather large hole, which meant a rather big meal should shuffle out. They stacked the wood, struck the flint, and smoked the tinder, waiting until whatever was inside could bear it no longer.

"I see it," shouted Lykke, standing several feet away from a second hole.

She yanked out a brown woodland mammal and held it upside down by a stubby hind leg. The animal, a wilderboar, wiggled and snorted, swinging ivory tusks and scratching thick claws that couldn't reach Lykke's arm. It had a long snout attached to a head much too big for its stout body protected by bristly fur with a cream-colored underbelly.

"What is it?" Scalvia asked.

"Dinner," Lykke said, and she snapped its neck.

Arud felt dizzy. He could barely breathe. It was like Fennen all over again. His whole world seemed to be turned upside down. Would he ever get used to this?

Vang took the wilderboar from Lykke and laid it on the ground to bleed it out and skin it. Lykke watched him open up the soft creamy underbelly, her eyes blank, as if she were entranced. Then, her face shifted; her brow and mouth turned down and her eyes welled with tears. Arud could see the recognition color her face as she understood it was her hands that had taken innocent life.

"Lykke, it's not your fault," Arud said.

But she'd already turned and fled.

Arud chased after her. What was she doing? He followed as she wound over the mountainous pass, battling branches hanging like bony arms and leaped over the leaf-littered forest floor. Even running full force, she outran him two strides to his one. Arud scrambled over stumps, his eyes somehow adjusted to the near darkness. He scanned the woods while trailing farther and farther behind his sister. Where was she going?

"Lykke!"

His breath came out staggered. His legs ached. He slowed, nearing collapse, unable to yell out her name any longer. Then, he saw her, scuffling near the downward slope of the mountain, the eastern side facing Vithalia City. And in that instant, he watched her disappear over the ledge.

"NO!" He burst to the mountain's edge and came to a grinding halt, flailing his arms to stop from toppling over after her. He stared down the flat wall to the valley miles beneath. "Lykke! Lykke!"

"I'm here," echoed a feeble reply.

Arud squinted through the darkness. "Where? I

can't see you."

"On the ledge beneath you."

"How did you get there?"

"I'm not sure. I slipped and somehow caught on this ledge."

"Are you safe?"

"I don't know. Arud, please don't leave me."

"I'm right here." He could hear her breathing, the panic rising in her throat. A breeze rattled the leaves on the limbs behind him. "Lykke, I need to know exactly where you are. Can you hold out your hand?"

"Okay."

Arud stood at the edge. Crumbles of snow and dirt slipped out from beneath his boots down the long drop. He scanned the mountainside, but saw nothing. "Are you doing it?"

"Yes," she called up.

"I can't see you. Wave your hand back and forth."

The movement caught his eye, and he could just make out the ledge she stood upon. It was below him, a crevasse in the mountain camouflaged by thick brambles. Arud wondered how many thousands of years it had taken to loosen the rock. How many storms had ripped through the soil? How many springs had melted the snow running off this cliff to carve out the tiny space that had saved his sister's life? "I see you," he said. "Now, push as far back as you can away from the ledge."

Her hand disappeared.

"I'll get you out of there. I promise."

"I'm scared."

Arud swallowed hard. "I'm right here."

"Hurry."

Arud lay flat on his stomach. Trees grew out from the side of the mountain, their thick trunks and solid boughs taunting him with help outside his reach. He had brought nothing with him to attach to the limbs; no twine or hooks of any kind. "Lykke?"

"Yes?"

"I'm moving away from the edge. I need to find something to pull you up with."

"Okay."

Arud swept back into the woods, searching for anything he might use. He lifted a hollow log. Too heavy. He tried a long branch. Too brittle. "Come on, Arud. Come on," he muttered. He pushed deeper into the woods, moving the curtain of hanging vines out of his way...

Hanging vines?

It could work. He sprinted back to the ledge. Vines hung like suspended rain on the trees several yards away. How had he missed them? "Hold on," he shouted. "I'm getting you out of there."

Arud yanked on a vine, stretching it out several yards. It held firm, and there was no way he could pull it from the tree. He launched off the ground, hanging by his full weight. The vine proved strong. Maybe he could swing on it? He didn't know exactly how far the vine would stretch, or if he even had enough slack to reach Lykke. He cringed. He knew what he had to do. "I'm coming, Lykke. Hang on and stand back."

Arud extended the vine to its full length and took a deep breath. "On three," he whispered. "One...two..." He launched, rushing to the edge where he swung out, far out, over the pit miles beneath him. Weightlessness consumed him. It was as if he could control the wind and air around him while he maneuvered his body at an angle to face the ledge. He could see Lykke several yards below. She stared. But even if he jumped, he would not be able to reach her. And if by some miracle he did reach her, how would they ever get back? They'd both be stuck in the fissure.

The momentum of his swing changed direction, taking him back to the safety of solid ground. He collapsed onto his knees panting from nerves and fear and exhaustion. There would be no way to reach her.

"Arud!"

He looked up. Scalvia and Vang were running to a stop beside him.

"Lykke went over," Arud said.

Scalvia covered her face as she gasped.

"She's all right," Arud quickly added. She's on a ledge a few yards below."

Scalvia let out her breath. "I thought you meant…"

Arud took her hand. "I'm sorry. I wasn't thinking when I spoke."

"What do we do?" Vang asked.

Arud showed them the vine, explaining how he had swung out and was able to see her, but not reach her.

"Let me try," Scalvia suggested.

Vang and Arud looked at her and in unison replied, "No."

Scalvia wrenched the vine from Arud's hand. "I wasn't asking for permission." She pushed her brother and Arud aside. With a running start, she launched herself out over the edge, flying with fervor and grace in a great sweeping arc, then back to the flat top of the mountain. "I think I can reach her, but I need more length."

Arud and Vang rummaged through the vines, but none were longer than the one they had used. "We can tie some together," Arud suggested. "It might work."

"Give me two, the longest you can find," Scalvia replied. "I'll work them into this one."

Arud chose two vines, as thick as his forearms, with a gray-green waxy coating. They were a different variety from the first, stronger in appearance and providing a better grip. Scalvia braided them in with the original one, producing a rope with the same precision she'd executed on the traps. Near the base, she double-knotted the vine around a small wood plank to form a seat, then tied several leaves around her hands to form a protective barrier from friction burn.

She wrapped her long legs, one at a time, around the knot and lifted. "This is perfect." She jumped down, smiled at Vang, and kissed Arud before backing as far as she could into the woods.

Arud looked over at Vang, expecting to catch his usual glare. Instead, the boy's features were tightened, concern for his sister stamped across his forehead. Arud turned to Scalvia. "Be careful."

"I do my best."

She ran with full force and lifted her body up over the knot hugging it tight with her thighs as she swung in the same graceful arc over the seemingly bottomless canyon. Her momentum slowed and she changed course, heading back to the mountain. This time, the additional length of the vine put her far enough below the ledge to disappear from sight.

Arud heard a hard thud followed by a grunt, and

he and Vang ran to the edge.

"Scalvia!" Vang shouted.

Lykke squealed.

"Lykke!" Arud called.

"We're okay," Scalvia shouted. "Pull us up."

Together, the boys heaved on the vine, straining against the weight of the girls. Vang slowly wound the vine around a notched stump, securing it with each loop, as Arud pulled the dangling girls up over the deadly valley. Sweat poured down Arud's face, stinging his eyes. He felt strangely dizzy, his vision swimming. Vang was also shaking his head. Exhaustion must have been setting in the both of them.

Arud's blistered hands bled. His foggy mind couldn't understand how. Shouldn't it take a long time for the blisters to form, then pop? Arud would have sworn his hands were red wax melting in summer's heat.

"What's going on?" Scalvia yelled up.

"Pulling—You—Up—" Arud huffed between labored breaths.

Vang fell face down on the forest floor, still as stone.

Arud leapt to catch hold of the slipping vine, bracing his feet against a log and a rock. He cried out, his shredded hands on fire. "Vang!" he shouted, his voice cloudy, even in his own ears.

The boy did not budge.

"What's happening?" Scalvia asked.

She spoke slowly, sounding as if her voice had been stretched or dropped to a deep pitch, mirroring the whale calls his father had imitated when Arud was a little boy. Ek would take month long sea voyages to meet with other Viking tribes to the north and south of Vithalia, searching for ways to destroy the ferine. Where was he now? Had he abandoned them? Had Toov attacked and killed him, too? She would kill Arud and Lykke, he was sure of it, before the next full moon. It was only a matter of time before she caught up to them and he watched her claws slice through Lykke's delicate skin. Was Toov watching them now? A cold shiver passed through him. It was all he could do not to scream…

"Arud! Pull!" Scalvia shouted.

Arud shook his head, his vision tunneling. His hands had somehow stretched yards away; his arms lengthened to twice their normal size. What was happening? He swept his hand across his face, rotating it to observe his palm covered in puss-filled sores, oozing the grey-green skin of the vine. White flower buds sprouted from the sores, growing rapidly into full blooms, then spreading vines of their own across his forearm, his shoulders, around his neck, choking the air from his lungs.

"Arud," Lykke cried, distant and slowed.

Arud grabbed for the vine around his neck, but it was gone. His hand, too, appeared normal again, the wax vision melted away, though his palm was still covered in blood where tiny spiked barbs protruded from it. Where had they come from? Arud glanced at the vine, forcing his eyes to focus. Barbed thorns covered most of the plant except where the shards had been plucked by Arud's palms. The vine moved in and out of focus; stretching, then shrinking; multiplying, then dividing.

"Arud!" Scalvia's faint voice registered in his ears.

And he remembered.

Lykke was over the edge with Scalvia. He had to pull them up.

Branches snapped in the woods around him. Leaves crunched. Someone else was there.

Arud reached for his knife, staggering off-balanced, as the vine slipped from his other hand. The girls had only dropped a foot or so, their screams sharp yet close by. He was grateful Vang had secured the vine loop by loop around the stump. Fumbling with his sheath, Arud finally secured the handle and dislodged his knife. He whipped the blade high above his head.

Ants crawled down his arm and across his shoulders.

He threw his knife to the ground, releasing the vine to swipe at the ants that were no longer there. The vine slipped another loop and Arud dove for it, grabbing ahold and sliding a few feet.

Gasping for breath, he scanned the ground for his knife. A short branch lay where he'd thrown it. He touched his sheathe. His blade was still there. Had he even taken it out? He looked at the vine wrapped around the stump. Each coil was locked in place.

He'd hallucinated the entire episode.

More footsteps crashed through the flora. Arud stumbled and swayed, searching for the intruder.

"Whose there?" he slurred through cracked lips.

His vision was closing in again. The ground fell out from under him, and he landed numb on the forest floor.

A pair of boots moved past. Two gloved hands reached for the vine slipping across the frictionless snow.

Arud tried to scream, tried to tell whoever was there that Lykke and Scalvia were on the end of that vine. Or maybe, he should be warning the girls of the stranger who was pulling them up, to what? Kill them? Help them? Arud wished he knew.

But his throat closed.

His vision had become slotted, like looking through the boards covering his bedroom window during the last full moon. And all he could see were the eyes of the ferine, but the face had morphed into Toov's.

She laughed, then howled, her teeth tearing through the slats. Claws ripped through the boards, splintering them to shreds. Arud turned around to grab Lykke and run, but she was gone.

A small ferine had taken her place.

It launched at him, and just before it sank serrated teeth into his neck, blackness overcame him and he fell into unconsciousness.

Ψ THIRTY-EIGHT Ψ

Arud's eyes popped open. A man's blurred face filled his vision before Arud fell back into blackness. He opened his eyes again. Had any time passed? He couldn't tell. The world still tumbled in waves around him, his head as heavy as the mountain he crossed.

The man was saying something, but Arud only heard pitches and tones. He recognized the man's dark eyes and brows, his sharp jaw line and cheekbones, but his identity remained muddled. It was as if the man was outside a lake looking through the water as Arud swam beneath.

A featureless palette of shades and motion.

His voice stretched like Scalvia's had been in his hallucination. What was going on? Arud's head pounded. Although he tried to fight it, his heavy eyelids closed and he swam once again in darkness.

After what felt like only seconds had passed, Arud opened his eyes. The sensation of movement had ceased. The hurried rush through the woods fell silent. Woodland and salty sea air had vanished.

He was lying in a room somehow, with a beamed ceiling and plank walls. The dark wood smelled damp. He reclined on a rough canvas mattress covered by a wool blanket that scratched his skin. Sweetfern-oil candles flickered, spreading their pungent fragrance. Darkness filled where the candlelight could not luster. Slowly, Arud touched his pounding head. At least it didn't feel like dead weight anymore. Where was he?

How did he get there? More importantly, where were Lykke and Scalvia?

He managed to sit up. His mouth was so dry he couldn't swallow. A wooden cup and pitcher filled with water sat on the nightside table. He lifted the pitcher, straining to keep his fingers wrapped around it, and poured himself a cup. He had to use both hands, his grip was so weakened.

After three cupfuls his thirst was quenched and he swung heavy laden legs over the edge of the bed. His barefeet touched cold wood. He put his weight on them and stood. Clean clothes lay folded on a crude wooden chair that had not been sanded. Arud slipped into the pants. His muscles cramped. How long had he been lying there? He grabbed the tunic with his bandaged hands, remembering how they'd bled in the forest. He slid the cloth over his back and winced when the fibers snagged on the scabs leftover from the ferine's slashes. He must not have been passed out for too long, if his wound was still this sensitive.

At least he was warm and dry.

He wondered how far he was from Vithalia City, for this rustic structure looked nothing like the glorious palace he had seen from the mountaintop. With each step, blood pushed through his tired muscles as he crossed to the door and opened it. The rough-hewn building seemed old and well-traveled with molded oak panels covering the walls of the cramped hallway. Voices drifted from somewhere. The scent of stewed meat wafted in the air.

Cautiously, Arud crept past the doors lining the hall framed with etched trim. Pitch lanterns illuminated the walkway. He reached a wide staircase where the voices grew louder and peered into the room, spying many candle-lined wheels hanging from the open rafters continuing out of his line of vision. As he descended, artistically carved support beams came into view, towering from floor to ceiling. Long hardwood tables surrounded by chairs ran in rows perpendicular to the stairwell.

Arud used the handrail to support his weight, the splintered wood catching in his bandages as they scuffed across. He heard Gunter's laughter, Quinn's snide remarks, Lykke's persistent questioning. Lykke was here, so Scalvia should be too.

The stairwell ended in a vast open room with a dozen more long tables running the length of it. At one end of the room, a storage area held grains, pots, pans, and utensils. Garlic hung in cloves from the rafters, patched with straw, along with herbs: basil, mint, and dill weed. Each spice layered in the air. Arud smelled the stewing meat, and his mouth watered. How long had it been since he'd last eaten?

At the opposite end of the room, a large hearth framed by white stones from floor to ceiling, burned a roaring fire. Encircling the fireplace sat Gunter, Quinn, and Scalvia. Arud did not see Vang. Lykke's laughter carried lightly through the air. She faced the fire with the others, their backs to Arud as they listened to a man telling stories in a voice Arud recognized. The blurry-faced man from the woods, perhaps. If he could only see him clearly. But Arud was too far away, and the man was looking down at his audience, entertaining them with stories of Loki and his wolf, Fenrir.

Arud shuffled closer, listening to the familiar tale.

"Then is fulfilled Hlin's second sorrow, when Odin goes to fight with the wolf, and Beli's slayer bright, against Surtr. Then shall Frigg's sweet friend fall."

Arud's pace quickened, the identity of the voice on the tip of his tongue, and fear swelled inside him. His friend's lives were in danger. He just knew it. Lykke's life was in danger. How could they not see through this man's façade?

The man continued. "Much I have traveled, much have I tried out, much have I tested the Powers; from where will a sun come into the smooth heaven when Fenrir has assailed this one?" He looked up. Arud saw his icy blue eyes. And he froze.

It was his father.

But Arud had already been fooled by this trick once before, when Toov had shifted into Berg's likeness. And here he was flaunting his trickery by telling stories of Loki, the great trickster himself. What could Arud do? He had no weapon. He had no strength to hold one, even if he carried his tang or crossbow and bolts.

But he had to do something.

"Arud," Berg said, exposing Arud's position.

Still frozen, Arud watched his friends turn and face him. Lykke ran over; wrapped her arms around his waist. He could not squeeze her back. "Run," he whispered in her ear.

She did not hear him.

"Arud, can you believe it? Father is here."

She did not know.

"Run," Arud repeated, as loud as his feeble voice allowed.

This time she must have heard him. Her furrowed brow showed her confusion. "Are you still feeling ill? You should go lie back down. I'll get Father."

"No," Arud said. Pain shot across his chest as his muscles contracted to reach for Lykke. "Don't let that creature touch me."

Lykke's face blanched, and she ran to her father.

And Scalvia.

What was Scalvia doing? Why was she playing along in this charade? She knew better. She should have been sliding a silver beam into the shifter's heart when she had the chance.

Berg, or the creature in his form, leaned down and gently stroked Lykke's golden curls, whispering something intimate.

Arud's stomach wrenched. "Get off her," he said, barely loud enough to call it a whisper. "Don't touch her." His knees quaked as his weight was unbearable.

Berg treaded toward him. Arud turned to flee, but fell, landing hard on the ground, unable to lift himself. What had they done to him? Had he been poisoned? Berg reached for him, and Arud recoiled. "Get away from me, Shifter." Arud kicked, trying to push away. "Don't touch me."

Scalvia ran over. "It's okay, Arud. It's your father."

"No! My father is dead. This creature is a shifter." He pointed at the ferine in his father's skin. "Stay away from me. You're not my father."

Scalvia turned to Berg. "He needs a bath immediately."

Berg scooped Arud into his arms and carried him out the front door to a shed in the back. Arud punched and writhed, but was too weak. Berg opened the shed door, and light pooled into the room. A long tub filled with water sat in the cluttered shed, the surface of the water scattered with dried herbs and coral tinted flower petals. Scalvia poured hot water into the tub, releasing the oils in the herbs. The room filled with a succulent, but bitter scent, reminding Arud of honeysuckles and root vegetables. Gently, Berg set Arud into the tub. He screamed, the hot patches in the icy cold water scalding his skin.

Lykke came up beside him. She streamed water through his hair and stroked his face. She unwrapped the bindings around his hands, and passed herbs across his blistered and calloused palms.

The vine.

He remembered the vine with its sharp thorns that had stuck into his skin. The barbs had been removed, leaving behind small scabs.

"You're safe," Lykke whispered, her soothing tone mimicking their mother's.

A mother's voice he'd never hear again.

It was too much; the pain, the confusion, the lies. His heart saturated; his soul worn. He let it all out in his tears as his loved ones surrounded him, waiting.

After some time, Arud settled. Water dripped from his hair and rolled down his face. "What happened to me?"

"You were poisoned by the barbs in the vine. They nearly killed you," Lykke explained.

Arud stared again at his palms. "Where's Vang? Is he okay?"

Scalvia glanced at the ground.

"He's fallen into a deep sleep," Lykke said. "We

don't know if he'll recover."

This was too much to take in. Scalvia and Lykke's teeter with death, his sister snapping the wilderboar's neck, Toov's attack, the boy's shifting, and Vang poisoned near death. Arud sat upright, his head clearing as the herbs absorbed the lingering poison. He focused on his father's face. "Who are you?"

Berg knelt beside the tub. "I am Berg Leidolf, son of Ylva and Grathco of the Skoll clan. You are my son, Arud, born of your mother, Vinter, daughter of the night, a ferine."

Water traced down Arud's cheeks, hiding his tears. "How can I believe you? How do I know you aren't a shifter?"

"Because I know you, Arud. You are flesh of my flesh. My son, of whom I am exceedingly proud, who has been given a great task in keeping his sister safe."

Arud stared into Berg's eyes. "Tell me one thing, Father."

"Anything, my son."

"How do you catch your prey?"

Berg smiled. "With patience. That is the first lesson I taught you, to wait until your prey thinks you have abandoned hope, then strike. They are caught before you even snare them."

And Arud knew.

"It's really you."

"Yes." He turned to Gunter and Quinn standing in the doorway. "Fetch some towels and clean garments."

"Yes, sir," they replied, turning on their heels.

Arud stared at Berg. It felt like centuries had passed since he last saw him. "How did you find us?"

"Your mother."

"Mother? But she's dead." Arud hung his head. "Grandmother killed her."

"Your grandmother?"

"As a ferine."

Berg hung his head. "There are so many things you should have known. So many ways I have failed you."

Arud's head spun with questions, though his anger began to soften.

Berg's face turned down. "I hadn't realized it was Toov's hand."

Fresh tears stung Arud's eyes. "I couldn't stop her. Mother died saving me and Lykke."

Berg took Arud by the shoulder. "As would I. Don't ever think her death was in vain. Life must be sacrificed to sustain the existence of another. It has always been this way. When you have children of your own, you will understand."

Arud stared into the water, listening. He couldn't bring himself to look upon Berg's face.

"Your raft carried Vinter to where I was staying. I recognized your carving. You have brought honor to your mother by sending her off properly. Her raft was ceremoniously lit, sending her into the afterlife."

Gunter and Quinn returned, carrying clothes and fresh towels.

Lykke kissed Arud on the cheek. "I love you," she said before leaving.

Scalvia smiled at Arud as she followed Lykke out of the shed, though sadness burdened her eyes.

"She will be all right," Berg said once they were alone. "She's a strong girl."

Arud didn't answer as he stepped out of the tub,

dripping water and herbs onto the floor. He stripped out of his wet clothes and Berg wrapped the towel around him. "So, how did finding Mother lead you to us?"

"I knew the only reason your mother would have left the Outlands would be if you and Lykke were in danger. Your carving confirmed my suspicion. I assumed she'd sent you to my brother, Bodolf's, house in Vithalia City, hadn't she?"

Arud dropped the towel and dressed. "We were headed there when..." His voice trailed. His eyes clenched as pain clutched his stomach.

"I know, Arud. The pain will dull, though I'm afraid it will never go away." Berg stared into his own thoughts as Arud turned upon him. His father hadn't had a chance to say goodbye. Berg breathed deeply and forced a smile. "I assumed you had passed the river and were traveling across the Torngats. Since you traveled with Lykke, I did not think you would attempt to pass the Sindri-Urd Range."

"No. I couldn't. She wouldn't have made it. Or at least, that's what I thought at the time. Now I wonder who's the stronger of us."

"Then you know."

"That she's a Cur?"

"Yes. And more."

"That she's the Cur in the Prophecy of Ulfhednar."

Berg nodded only once.

Arud slipped a tunic over his head, pulling it across his sore back and chest, then slid his feet into warm wool socks and hide boots. "So you came looking for us?"

"It is too dangerous for you to make this trek

alone. Lykke is in danger. Many follow this path, seeking to take her life. She is of great value to both sides."

"Why have you and Mother withheld this? What could Lykke or I have gained from not knowing?"

"We didn't want to put you in harm's way."

"But that is exactly what you've done." Arud's palms sweat, and his limbs tremored.

"I'm sorry," Berg said as they left the shed. "But we couldn't have known these things when Vinter and I made our decision. At the time it seemed the wisest choice."

They stared at one another for some time. The wind blew gently, the sun warmed their backs. Berg took Arud into his arms. "I have missed you so much. I thought I'd never see you again."

They remained that way for some time, and Arud drank in the musk of pine on his father's clothing. He never thought he would smell it again. And in that moment, his heart swelled, his anger shed, and he forgave Berg and Vinter for what they had done.

They pulled apart, and Berg began walking. "So why didn't you return from the market?"

"I never went to the market," Berg said, stopping to face him. "I went to Vithalia City."

"Why? I don't understand."

"A great battle is on the brink, for possession of the realm. I am helping Bodolf to organize the King's guard. Your sister holds the future of both species in the balance. But it is not her blood alone that makes the prophecy so powerful. The blood of two will combine to bring about the fulfillment of the Prophecy of Ulfhednar."

Arud's racing heart neared exploding. "What are you saying, father?"

"You, son, are the second child of the prophecy. Without your blood, the ferine will go extinct."

Ψ THIRTY-NINE Ψ

It took Arud awhile to work his way back to the inn. His blood? How was it possible? The evil had always come in female form. Only those granted shifting abilities by Toov were male. But Berg had not said Arud was Cur, only that his blood was as important as Lykke's. But how? The whole idea made him shiver and feel weak all over.

He eventually arrived in the large hall with the long tables and took a seat beside Lykke and Scalvia. An empty chair sat across from them. Vang's chair. He still hadn't awakened.

A burly woman wearing a dress with small flowers printed across the fabric carried a large cauldron to the center of the table. Her hair was pulled back beneath a handkerchief, her legs bare and hairy as a man's.

"Bring me yer bowl," she said to the group. "One at a time."

They took turns handing her clay bowls, which she filled with piping hot stew. Arud approached.

"Well," she said. "Aren't you lookin' better? Not that you were much to look at to begin with." She stirred the stew, releasing the scent of rosemary. "You took quite a bit of poison in yer blood. Fairin' better than that other one." She looked him over, and Arud noticed that her eyes were gray, eclipsed with yellow, like Scalvia's.

"Are you a Cur?" he asked.

"I am. And dontcha be forgettin' it." She threw a

ladle of stew into his bowl and shoved it into his hands.

Stew toppled over the edges, burning Arud's sore palms. He didn't say another word, simply wobbled back to his seat beside Scalvia. On the table, elderberry mead filled the glasses. Loaves of hot bread steamed on platters. Bowls of fall vegetables sat overflowing with eggplants, squash, and pumpkin in cream sauces seasoned with fresh herbs.

He couldn't remember the last time he had eaten. It felt like days ago. The woman was a good cook, but not as good as Vinter. His mother's bread was the perfect balance of crispy crust and soft center. Her stew was thick and rich, with just the right proportions of meat and vegetables. He missed her. He missed her smile, her touch, her laugh. He would never again eat a meal prepared by his mother's hands. Arud suddenly lost his appetite and pushed his food aside.

There were others, whom Arud had not met, seated at the table. There was a muscular man with olive skin and a beard whose name, Arud had overheard, was Bane. Another man, a sailor by the name of Deurff, was traveling with Bane, his face and arms covered in ink, his skin a deep shade of red.

There was also a girl, Falla, with dark hair and deep brown eyes, who was Bane's daughter. She was quiet and kept looking at Arud, then back at her plate. It made him feel like he had done something she disapproved of, or like she could see into his innermost thoughts. He tried not to look at her, but could feel her gaze peering at him throughout the entire meal.

The cook approached Arud. "Chew on this," she said, placing a sprig of wolfsbane on his plate.

"Why?" he asked.

"It will heal you completely. No more limpin' like a sailor who's done seen too many battles. Go on, now. Eat it."

Arud looked at Scalvia. "Listen to her, Arud. Ulga knows what she's saying."

Skeptically, Arud placed the herb in his mouth, chewing it like a goat. It didn't taste good, but he immediately felt his head clear and his lungs open up. He felt rejuvenated, alive, as if nothing had happened to him.

"This is amazing," he told Scalvia. "I feel fine."

She smiled. "Can we go somewhere and talk?"

"I'd like to go see Vang first."

"Okay."

They stood.

"Where are you going?" Lykke asked.

"To check on Vang," Arud said, rubbing his sister's cheek. "We won't be long. And you have Father to keep you company."

She smiled, a childish grin. "Don't be gone long."

Scalvia took Arud's hand and led him through the hall, back to the staircase that had taken him so long to climb down when the poison was still in his blood. Now, he seemed to glide up the steps without touching them. They reached the platform at the top and turned down the opposite hall. The laughter and chatter of those dining in the hall diminished the farther they went.

After passing several doors, Scalvia stopped before one. She rapped gently and pushed it open. Vang lay in a single bed beneath a fur blanket. His eyes were closed, and his skin had a grayish glint.

Scalvia sat beside her brother on the edge of his mattress and rubbed his forehead.

"Vang," she whispered. "Are you sleeping?" He did not stir. She turned to Arud. "He hasn't responded since we arrived. I fear he won't."

He took her hand. "Don't fear the worst. I thought my father was dead, and look at us now. Reunited. Your brother is strong, Scalvia. He'll pull through. Just pray and keep your faith."

Scalvia took Arud's hand and placed it against her cheek. Her ivory skin felt soft on his calloused hand. "I do pray, and I do have faith," Scalvia said, "but I also have fear."

Arud knelt in front of her. "You can't have both. No one can serve two masters, because they will always favor one over the other. You favor fear, but you shouldn't. Faith is the belief in what you can't see; not Vang healed, but the belief in Vang's full recovery."

She smiled sheepishly.

"What?" he asked.

"You always know exactly what to say to make me feel better."

He shrugged. "I only say what I feel in my heart."

Scalvia leaned closer, her gray eyes almost fully eclipsed by the bright yellow engulfing them.

Tingles ran through Arud's body as she stared into his eyes. What could he say? That he cared deeply for her? That he might even be in love with her?

But he didn't have a chance to say anything.

"Scalvia?" said Vang through a dried throat.

Scalvia whipped around to face him. "I'm right here, Vang."

"Why is my head pounding?"

"Drink," she said, lifting a cup of water to his cracked lips.

Vang polished off three cupfuls before he finally stopped asking for more. "Much better," he said, lying back down. He seemed exhausted after just drinking. "Where am I?"

"The Running Moose Inn. We have reached the village you spoke of. Skrivi Village."

"Er," he mumbled. "What happened to me?"

"You were poisoned," Arud answered. "Just like I was, by the barbs on the vines we used to reel Scalvia and Lykke up the side of the mountain."

He looked at his hands. "I remember now."

"How do you feel?" Scalvia asked.

"Famished."

"I'll bring you some stew and bread," Scalvia said, skirting out of the room. She turned at the doorway. "It's good having you back, Brother."

Arud took a seat beside Vang on the edge of the bed. "Thought we'd lost you."

Vang rubbed his eyes, shaking away the last of the poison's effects. "One minute I was in the woods, the next.... I was almost at the walls of Vithalia City."

Arud's forehead scrunched. "What do you mean?"

Vang looked up. "It was beautiful, the bright white lights and the glittering gate. I was mesmerized. Then, from out of nowhere I heard the growl of a ferine. I turned. Creatures were everywhere. I was completely surrounded. I unsheathed my sword and held a mace in my other hand. I knew I couldn't live through the assault, but I was taking as many of them into death with me as I could. I charged, slashing and cutting, their blood spraying into the air. Then, I saw you walking among them."

"Me?"

"You were glowing, and I couldn't take my eyes off you. That's when the ferine struck, slashed me through the chest. I felt myself dying. It was so real. Then it all stopped. I opened my eyes, and you and Scalvia were here." He smiled uneasily. "Do you think it meant anything?"

"I think it was the effects of the poison and nothing more." He stood. "After you eat, you'll feel like yourself again."

Vang nodded. "I suppose you're right."

Scalvia entered, carrying a tray with hot stew and bread for Vang. Arud moved out of the way so she could set it down. He watched them together, talking and laughing, as Vang devoured his meal.

Arud couldn't help but think about Vang's dream. He didn't understand why it bothered him. It was just a dream. But he thought of what his father had told him, about his blood being part of the prophecy's fulfillment. Suddenly, he feared the prophecy and the dream were somehow connected.

Ψ FORTY Ψ

It took three days for Vang to fully recover, leaving less than a week before the full moon would rise. Ulga had prepared steamed goat and vegetables over noodles for the late afternoon meal. They gathered at one of the long tables in the hall as a fire crackled in the background. Gunter and Quinn sat at the far end, across from Deurff, Bane, and Falla. Vang and Scalvia sat at the opposite end, across from Lykke and Arud. Berg sat at the head of the table.

"We have lost several days here," Berg said. "But now we are rested and ready."

Everyone nodded their agreement. Especially Ulga.

"We have a great deal of the mountain still to tread before we are close enough to the city gates. I hope there will be soldiers waiting, but it has been some time since I left Vithalia."

They quietly ate their meal as Berg continued. Bane and Deurff had agreed to accompany them to the city, with plans to reach the seaside harbor before the full moon.

"My greatest fear is that we won't reach the city in time. The ferine's powers are enhanced tremendously with the lunar pull, and we don't stand a chance facing them in the open."

"How many are there?" Bane asked.

"No one can be certain. There numbers have never been taken in census. Not to mention there has been a shift in their breeding patterns."

"What do you mean a shift?" Vang asked.

Berg scanned the faces of those around him. He seemed to contemplate sharing for some time. Ulga poured elderberry mead into goblets. The sailors drank distilled liquor.

"Father?" Lykke said. "What do you mean?"

Berg nodded. "The creatures have always been female. It is the matriarchal line which keeps the breed alive. There have been times throughout the centuries when the need of men has arisen, and ferine have done what was needed to create offspring."

"This is nothing new," Scalvia added.

"Yes," Berg said. "But the offspring of the half-caste are Pureblood. They shift the humans into animal form to keep their bloodline pure."

"While this is very interesting," Bane said, "could you make your point?"

Berg nodded. "Somehow the shifters have figured out a way to pass along their abilities to those who are neither Cur nor Pureblood."

"But it has never been that way before," said Quinn.

"That doesn't mean it's impossible," Berg said.

"He's right," Vang added. "We saw it ourselves at the cabin." He lowered his eyes.

"So what advantage does this give us?" Arud asked.

Berg shrugged. "I'm not sure, but there must be something we can glean from it."

"How are they able to do it?" Scalvia asked.

"No one knows."

They ate quietly for some time, until Arud turned

toward his father and said, "Could there be mention of this in the prophecy?"

Berg looked into his son's eyes. "The Prophecy of Ulfhednar?"

Arud nodded.

Berg raised his eyebrows while rubbing his chin. "I suppose there could be mention made of this anomaly. But the odds are…"

"Why not just check?" Vang said.

Berg laughed. "If it were only that simple. The prophecy was recorded so long ago, and most of those texts have been lost."

"I have the text," Arud said.

Berg shook his head. "I doubt that. You must have a different prophecy or a fabrication."

Slowly, Arud reached into his pocket and took out the book with the frayed edges. He looked back and forth from Scalvia to Vang and saw that neither of them recognized the cover. "It was a gift from a friend," Arud said.

"From what friend?" Berg asked. "Who would give away something of such value?"

Arud looked at Scalvia and said, "It was from your father."

"Our father?" Vang leaned forward on the table, pushing himself up. "Why would our father give that book to you?"

"I don't know," Arud said. "I found it in my pack after we left your home."

"May I see it?" Berg asked, reaching across the table. Arud handed him the book. Berg flipped through the pages tenderly, as if they were the petals of a rose. He read briefly, flipping to random pages in the tattered book. Arud spied Vang's face. After all they had been through, his eyes were filled with rage again. Or was it jealousy for having been slighted by his father?

What was there to be jealous of?

Berg stopped turning pages and leaned forward, focusing on the text. "This is very interesting," he said. "It says here that when the Cur child is of age, the ferine will open up dormant channels, allowing them to reconstruct their abilities and powers. But," he said, adding emphasis to the thought, "they will not be in form." He stopped reading.

"What does that mean?" Scalvia asked.

"It could mean a number of things," Quinn suggested. "Not be in form could refer to their shape, their shifting ability..."

"Their gender," Vang said bitterly.

Berg stared up at the rafters, lost in thought. The others quieted around the table, also considering the implication.

"This would mean an end to everything we know about the creatures," Scalvia said. "It would mean that anything is possible. Their strength and size could increase. Their abilities could enhance. Their numbers could grow."

"And they would be able to destroy everyone," Lykke said, in her soft voice. "Unless I am able to stop them."

Ψ FORTY-ONE Ψ

Arud sat near the open plateau overlooking the valley leading to the mountain chain ahead. The sky glimmered red and gold from the setting sun. Tomorrow morning they would continue their journey toward Vithalia City. At least this time Arud's father would be leading the way.

"Hey, you," Scalvia said.

Arud looked up. "Hey."

"You want to be alone?" she asked.

"Not at all."

She sat beside him on the rocky crag, stared at the rust-orange sky, and rested her hand on top of his. "I'm so ready to leave this place."

"Tell me about it. I wish we were safe within the walls of the city."

"I'll keep you safe," Scalvia said with a smile.

"I recall it was me who knocked you to the ground the first time we met."

She hit him lightly in the side. "You caught me off guard. That doesn't count."

"Like this?" Arud said, tickling her.

"Stop it!" Scalvia said between rifts of laughter.

"How can you keep me safe if you can't even get free of my grasp?"

She laced her fingers with his and unexpectedly twisted back his arm, broke free, and knocked him onto his back. They rolled on the grass, vying for position of one another. Scalvia finally pinned Arud, his arms above his head, his legs held down by her own. They were both breathing heavily, catching their breath.

"Who said I wanted to be free of your grasp?" Scalvia asked.

He rolled her onto her back, and then lay beside her; their fingers locked, as they shared a kiss, a laugh, a glance at the setting sun. He would die for this girl. He had never met anyone as amazing or beautiful in his entire life. And he knew he never would again.

So this is what love feels like.

As the stars materialized by the thousands, Arud pointed out the constellations he had been taught as a boy to Scalvia, who listened intently, although Arud was certain she already knew all of them.

"What else do you think is out there?" she asked.

"I'd like to believe a great and powerful Creator is up there watching over us. Guiding us. It would feel empty to believe I'm on my own in this world."

"You mean like Odin?"

Arud breathed deeply. "I'm not sure. Odin, while powerful and revered, is known to wander in self-reflection, leaving Asgard to ponder his own life. How can someone who is supposed to know everything seek answers?"

"I've never given much thought to it before."

"I think about it all the time, moreso now with everything changing." He turned on his side to look upon Scalvia's face. "There are other people who believe in only one God; an all-powerful Creator who has always been in existence and has no need to leave his kingdom in search of answers."

Scalvia faced Arud. "Why would a Creator who is

so great and powerful allow such death and destruction, such evil, to run freely through the world?"

Arud stared up at the stars, wondering the same thing. They sat in silence, listening to the wind. "I guess," he said after some time, "it all comes down to us. To our choices. I could no sooner stop a thorn from growing on a rose, even knowing someone could prick their finger and bleed. But would that make me evil? Or the rose for that matter?"

"No."

He looked at her. "Then how can you blame the Creator for the evil of the ferine?"

She smiled. "You place thoughts in my head I have never considered the answers to."

"Well, you have made my heart feel things I have never thought possible."

"Then, I suppose we are even."

Their lips touched, but only briefly, before footfalls approached, and they separated to sit up. Vang was running toward them.

"What is it?" Scalvia asked her brother.

"The ferine. They are here."

Ψ FORTY-TWO Ψ

Arud and Scalvia jumped up and sprinted back to the Running Moose Inn. The others were gathered out front, draped in weapons, including their new friends Bane, Deurff, and Falla. Ulga held an axe, her menacing frame standing nearly a foot taller than everyone else, and wider by far.

"Arud," Berg said, handing him his crossbow. "Ready your bolt."

"What direction are they coming from?"

"We don't know yet," Vang said. "They are throwing their voices, so their howls are coming in great numbers from many directions."

They grouped back-to-back, forming a large circle facing out, like the spokes on a wheel. Arud stared through the open spaces between the trees, down the sloping hills, for any sign of the creatures, or any familiar amber eyes.

Lykke stood nestled behind him in the center of the ring. She was panting, changing again, and Arud feared what she would become.

"There," Bane yelled.

Arud swept around in time to see a yellow ferine jump off a rock ledge and land on Deurff. Bane hacked between its shoulder blades with his silver mace. The creature rolled off and quickly jumped up, the wound bubbling and smoldering.

"I see another one," Scalvia yelled, charging toward the creature.

As she ran, Arud watched her skin change: fur pressed up between layers of epidermis, hair fell to the ground, clothes disappeared. It was the first time he had watched her turn. She ran full force into a tawny ferine, and the two wrestled on the ground, snarling and barking, frothing at the mouths.

Arud tore his eyes away.

Creatures appeared in droves. Arud faced a burgundy ferine with a white slice down its chest. It came at him, and he shot a silver bolt in its stomach. The ferine recoiled, then continued its charge. Arud reloaded his bolt and shot again and again, until the ferine slid dead at his feet. Five of Arud's bolts stuck out of its chest.

How had he fired so quickly?

"Arud!"

Arud turned quickly. Two creatures stalked Lykke, one the color of copper, the other of mocha. Somehow Arud knew who they were.

Lager and Kron.

Arud reloaded and launched an assault on the two traitors. His head turned slightly to the side. Berg stabbed the tawny ferine in the head a few yards away. Gunter lay pinned beneath a large brown beast, slicing his dagger through its narrow chest while the creature sank serrated teeth into his shoulder.

Arud released another bolt as he charged closer.

Ulga had shifted into a monstrosity with thick gray-blue fur. She slashed five inch claws into a speckled ferine. Blood splattered out, bathing the beast in black. Ulga showed no mercy as she tore it to shreds.

Arud released two more bolts.

Quinn had scrambled into the thick crown of an ash tree, launching arrows into the brown pelt of the ferine gnawing on Gunter.

Arud reached Lykke's side.

She stood taller than him, and her body had widened. Her nails stretched out into the razor sickles that had killed Fennen. The whites of her eyes showed. Snarling lips curled, exposing teeth sharper than her nails. Like an animal, she bounded forward on all fours, charging at Lager and Kron. Arud kept pace. One by one, they killed the ferine until they lay scattered across the snow, shifted into their human forms.

Catching his breath, Arud walked the grounds, taking damage control. Deurff was badly injured, his side sliced and gaping open. Vang had multiple lacerations and cuts along his exposed arms and the back of his neck, but would fair well with some ointment and a few bindings. Gunter's gouged shoulder would need stitching. Quinn climbed out of the tree, unscathed. Lykke slowly morphed to her sweet form, the beast inside hibernating until its next awakening. Her wounds were bad, but Arud could already see them healing.

Where was everyone else?

"Father?" Arud called. "Scalvia?"

Vang and Lykke ran up beside him.

"I don't see your sister or my father," Arud told Vang. "Ulga, the sailor, and his daughter are also unaccounted for."

They split up to search the plateau and clustered woodland, the battle having spread far from the inn. Arud checked between the trees, behind boulders and rotting logs, among burrows abandoned by animals that had migrated south before winter's harsh lashing. The still quietness seemed eerie after the din of battle. In the distance, he heard moaning.

"Hello?" He followed the voice coming from behind some low-lying shrubs, and pushed them aside.

Falla lay in the brambles, her hands clutching at the wet leaves covering her stomach. Arud's breath caught in the hollow of his throat as he slowly knelt beside her.

She looked up. "It's far worse than it appears."

Arud brushed aside the leaves. Blood pumped from the wound, soaking her clothes and the forest floor beneath her. He threw off his tunic and pressed it into her stomach. "You're going to be okay," he said. "I'll get you out of here."

"No," she said feebly. "There is no time. There is a stone inside my cloak pocket. Take it."

"I must get you back before it's too late."

"It's already too late. If you do not do as I ask, it will be too late for everyone in the realm."

Reluctantly, Arud pulled back her cloak. She grunted as the material tugged against her tattered skin. He slipped his hand across the soft fur of her cloak matted with Falla's sticky blood. He wanted to pull his hand free. He should have been going for help, not searching for a stone. But Falla's unwavering eyes beckoned for him to stay, and her voice whispered in his head.

Do not be afraid.

Arud's hand made its way to the inner pocket, where his palm clasped around the stone. He lifted it out. It was large, nearly filling his entire palm. The diamond cuts in the stone shimmered blood-red. "What is it?"

"It—will protect you and your sister—" she said between shallow breaths.

"I don't understand," Arud said.

"The prophecy—speaks—of the blood of two. You—Lykke."

She was going to die before she finished.

"This—will kill—the Great Mother—I—have— seen it—" She grimaced and coughed up blood, then clenched his hand. "I have kept it hidden—for such a time as this." Her eyes pleaded. His heart pounded. "You must save them."

"Who?" Arud asked, his voice quavering.

Her head dropped to the side. Life left her body. Arud sat, still holding his tunic against her stomach with one hand, her blood covering him, and the stone. The key to the Great Mother's death, to Toov's death?

But how?

Arud slipped the stone into his pocket and carried Falla's body back to the inn. Why had he not taken the time to get to know her? He hoped Scalvia and his father had returned as he approached the open doors and rushed inside. What was left of the others sat beside the fire, though Bane paced the floor. Ulga, Quinn, and Gunter were nowhere to be seen. Lykke let out a small gasp, and Scalvia and Vang turned. Relief, at seeing Scalvia alive, filled him. But where was Berg?

Bane stopped pacing, his eyes catching sight of his lifeless daughter. He cried out and took her from Arud's arms. With tears in his eyes, he kissed her forehead. Blood stained his lips. He laid her on the table, and the others silently gathered. Bane lay his head on her chest, sobbing. Lykke cried. Scalvia stood with her mouth covered.

"Come on." Vang said. "Let him mourn in peace."

"Where's my father?" Arud asked.

"He is in the shed, welding new weapons."

Outside, the stars were out, hundreds of lights so close to the mountain's peak that Arud could have grasped at them, as he would the lightening bugs in the fields back home when he was a small boy. "Where's everyone else?" he asked.

"Deurff suffered badly," Vang said. "He will remain here. Ulga is stitching Gunter, and Quinn is passed out."

"I think he passed out from fear," Scalvia said.

Arud turned to Scalvia. "Can you keep an eye on Lykke? I need to speak with my father."

"Of course."

Arud crossed the snow to the shed where he had bathed only a few days earlier. The tub was gone. In the back, Arud heard hammering. He rounded the corner and saw Berg leaning over a workbench. "Father?"

Berg dropped his hammer and reached for Arud. "Oh, thank God. I thought the worst."

"I'm fine."

"Where'd you go?"

"I heard someone calling for help. It was Falla." He looked at his feet. "She didn't make it."

Berg's mouth turned down. "I am sorry to hear of the loss of a girl so young." He continued hammering.

Arud pawed at the stone deep in his pocket. It was smooth and cold as ice. It electrified him as he stroked it. "She spoke to me before she died."

"Really?" Berg said. "I don't think I heard her speak a word this entire time. What did she say?"

Arud reluctantly held out the glimmering red stone. "She said this would kill grandmother."

Berg looked at the chalcedony stone in Arud's palm. He didn't blink. He didn't speak. He simply eyed it.

"What is it?" Arud asked.

"She did not say?"

"She said it would protect Lykke and me, and that it would destroy Toov. How could she know all this?"

"I don't know," Berg said, rubbing his bearded chin. "May I?"

Arud nodded, passing the stone to his father. "I have never seen anything like it. Did she say how to use it?"

Arud shook his head.

"I wonder if the prophecy mentions this stone." He passed it back to Arud.

"I don't remember reading about a crimson stone."

Berg smiled. "Probably not. But at the time, you were searching for answers of a completely different nature."

"What does that have to do with anything?"

"You may have missed mention of this stone because you were not looking for it." He reached into his tunic pocket and pulled out the Prophecy of Ulfhednar. "It's worth a look." He handed the book to Arud. "We have six days until the moon rises. Advise the others that our plans have changed. We leave in one hour."

"Yes, Father." Arud headed out of the shed, back

toward the inn.

The bleached ground and whitewashed trees loomed around him. His eyes had completely adjusted to the night as if it were day. Elated yet frustrated, he wished he could understand what was happening to him. He flipped through the leather-bound book. Near the back, in a section all to itself, was a chapter titled *The Bloodstone*.

Ψ FORTY-THREE Ψ

In the early days of the ferine, the world of men waned. Hundreds were slaughtered as the creatures began appearing throughout the moon cycles. Chaos ensued. Construction of a city began, a beacon in the Labrador Sea among the breaking waves, atop a coral foundation far from the grasp of the ferine.

King Ulfhednar ruled the throne, and his task was daunting. How could he protect his people from such a great evil? He sought sorcerers and seers, traveling the realm and beyond for answers as his kingdom fell into battle. There was only one answer he found: that of silver. Although it would raise his odds of winning a battle, it would not end the war.

King Ulfhednar's persistence caught the attention of Sorceress Edda, the Seer of Thrall. She took pity upon the king and offered a solution: The Bloodstone. A stone forged in the belly of the earth, beneath the Dreadlands, in the mouth of the Great Mother's lair. In return for this weapon, the seer demanded a child. King Ulfhednar complied.

The king led a quest to the Dreadlands where the ferine attacked his men. Hundreds died and hundreds more were wounded. The king himself battled the Great Mother, guardian of the lair. For hours they exchanged blows, his silver not powerful enough to take her life.

In the corner of the room, he saw a chalcedony streaked with crimson, the stone of which the seer had spoken. King Ulfhednar lunged at the creature, slicing through her forearm, rendering her useless while she licked her wound. With the beast preoccupied, the king leapt into the corner and grabbed the stone. Power surged inside him with its touch. The Mother towered over him, her limp forearm rapidly healing. She roared through her unhinged jaw. Bloody spittle flew from her tongue. She stepped toward the king, but his sword glowed hot. With a quick snap, she leapt, and he caught her in the chest, where his molten blade melted straight through. She dropped to the ground. King Ulfhednar wasted no time waiting to see if she would heal. He led what remained of his army back to Vithalia City.

Sorceress Edda examined the crimson-streaked gray stone, ensuring its authenticity; however, it needed the blood of a ferine and a half-caste Cur for its power to fully awaken. Sensing trickery, the king sentenced Sorceress Edda to the dungeon. For years, he summoned her to speak with his first in command, seeking the key to open the stone, for he knew nothing of this half-caste Cur of which the seer spoke. But she always answered the same.

After many more years of battle, the Bloodstone long forgotten in a chamber room, desperation drove the king to the dungeon, where he visited the seer face-to-face for the first time since he'd locked her away. But she was not alone. A beautiful young girl stood beside her, with hair as dripping honey and eyes as sea glass.

"She is your daughter, oh, King," the seer explained, "of human and ferine blood. The first of the half-caste Cur."

King Ulfhednar visited often, mesmerized by the beauty and charm of his daughter, even allowing her freedom to move about the city. He was intrigued by her strength and heightened abilities matching those of a ferine in shifted form without need of a full moon. This was the answer for which the king had been searching. Mankind could win by breeding with the ferine.

King Ulfhednar took blood from both the seer and his daughter to unlock the Bloodstone. The gray stone cracked, revealing a red diamond, though the king was still unsure of its powers. But on the next full moon, when the creatures attacked, running the long bridge to Vithalia City, King Ulfhednar stood waiting. The Bloodstone lay wedged in the highest tower at the center of the city. As the creatures approached, climbing the high walls from all sides, the king's guards lit their torches, casting a glow upon the stone. Radiant light shot out from the crimson veins, raining like blood upon the creatures. They screeched in pain, their claws retracting into their pads before they plummeted several hundred yards to the rock-strewn waters of the Labrador Sea.

King Ulfhednar stared at the broken bodies of beautiful women. Many had survived the fall. He sent his army on shore, where the turned ferine were captured and thrown into the dungeon. The guards were armed with silver weapons. The bars of the cells and the walls were exchanged with sheets of pure silver, forged from the mines of the mountain chains surrounding Vithalia.

For the next few years, the men of Vithalia forced the ferine to bear children, feeding their offspring *wolfsbane and keeping them out of the full moon's light. The kingdom was saved. Before each full moon, the Bloodstone was placed in the highest tower, and each month the creatures would retreat back through the woods to the Dreadlands. Until finally, out of fear and loss, the ferine ceased attacking.*

Upon the king's death, the Cur children revolted against the men who had spawned them. Many Vithalians lost their lives in the slaughter. Every Cur was killed. All except two. King Ulfhednar's daughter and the seer had gone missing. After a long search through the city, a trail of dead soldiers led to the chamber room, where the Bloodstone sat encased on a wooden stand beneath an ornate cover. Only the cover remained. The Bloodstone had been taken.

Ψ FORTY-FOUR Ψ

Arud entered the inn. "Where's Bane?"

The others looked up. Scalvia's face was etched in worry. "He's burying his daughter. What's the matter?"

Arud left without a reply.

He crossed the yard, passed the shed, back through the trees where the battle had taken place. There, he caught Bane bent over Falla, the ground already prepared to receive her.

Arud watched the man sobbing. The pain in the back of Arud's throat made it difficult to swallow.

Bane turned. "My boy. Thank you for bringing her to me." He embraced Arud tightly. "Were you...with her?"

Arud nodded. "Yes, sir."

Bane pressed his palms to his closed eyes, his head nodding incessantly. "She was lucky that you found her. No one should leave this world alone." He looked up at Arud. "Will you lend a hand?"

Arud gently took hold of Falla's feet while her father anchored beneath her shoulders. She was wrapped in a burlap burial shroud with only her face exposed. They lowered her into the ground and began filling in the hole, covering her with the same dirt she would soon become.

"I wish we could send her off properly, but it seems that's not an option here."

Arud shoveled dirt and listened.

"Her mother died in childbirth, but oh, did Falla have her laugh."

Arud's lip curled in a smile. "I don't remember hearing her laugh."

Bane's smile faded. "It has been awhile." He packed the dirt and stood back with Arud beside him. Freshly fallen snow clung to the dirt, masking its earthen hue beneath pure white.

Innocence must die to sustain life; the pure cleanse the earth.

Bane and Arud headed back to the inn. "I wish I could have heard her laugh one last time. And told her I loved her."

Arud nodded. "I know what you mean. My mother was recently taken from me." Arud's heart stung like ice cracking through stone.

"Death takes us all eventually."

Arud faced the old sailor. His olive skin stretched as supple leather across his bones, his eyes the color of storm clouds.

"Bane, there's something I have to ask you."

Bane smirked. "She spoke to you, didn't she?"

"Yes."

"Did she give you anything?"

Arud slowly nodded.

"Then I can assume you have figured out its meaning."

"I have."

"Then what troubles you?"

"Why are you here at the inn? Is it more than coincidence?"

He took several long strides before turning. "We are the Hallvar, guardians of the Bloodstone. We came to deliver the stone to Lykke, though Falla's premonition warned her otherwise. She believed Lykke was still unsure with which side to fight and that you had already chosen."

"It is meant for Lykke?"

"Yes, but she is not the only one changing. You are, also. Discovering strengths and abilities you never knew existed."

Arud stepped backward, placing distance between them. "How could you possibly know this?"

"My powers enable me to see things most cannot. It is the burden of the Hallvar."

"What is the Hallvar?"

"We are a select few who have carried the Bloodstone for many generations, keeping it safe, as we await the prophecy's fulfillment. The ferine grow restless. The four-hundredth and forty-fourth full moon has already come to pass. It is our role to find the ones that will restore Vithalia to its former glory. And Falla chose you."

"What do you see in me, Bane?"

"Your eyesight is keener. You have developed night vision. Your strength has doubled. You find nature bends to your whims. Yet with all this power, you are still unsure if it is you in control of any of it."

"This isn't possible."

"Your changes started when Lykke's began," Bane continued. "You are connected to her more deeply than you understand."

"I don't understand any of this."

Bane took Arud by his shoulders. "It is your love for her that strengthens you, that binds you to her. As her powers increase, so shall yours."

Arud pulled away. "I can't believe this. Any of it."

"Just because you don't believe in something doesn't make it untrue."

Arud shook his head. "How do you know this?"

"It's in the prophecy."

Arud looked at Bane, his eyebrows hunched down. "I haven't read about any of this in the Prophecy of Ulfhednar."

"There is another prophecy. The Prophecy of Myrkr beginning after the other is fulfilled. If you live through this one, perhaps you'll have the chance to read it one day."

"That is my intention."

"Ah, but it will prove a difficult task to take down an army of ferine from up here. We must reach the valley and the city."

"And what about the Bloodstone? Will we use it the way King Ulfhednar did?"

"If we reach the city walls in time we could be lucky enough to get it positioned in the tower." He faced Arud. "Times are different. The ferine are more powerful than they've ever been. They are fighting to save their species. To avoid extinction. You have read the prophecy. You understand what we face."

"Mostly. But I don't understand why they would be any stronger now than at any other time."

"Because, Arud, although your blood is important, your sister's is the key. If she sides with her fellow Cur and man, then the creatures stand no chance. King Ulfhednar's prophecy will come to pass. But if she does not..." Bane breathed heavily. "Then Heaven help us all."

They resumed walking, their pace quickened.

As they had reached the inn, Arud asked, "Do you believe the Cur were spawned to be used as weapons?"

"Of course, I do. That was the reason for their creation."

Lykke stood outside the doorway, her eyes filled with tears. Arud's ears burned. She had heard him. "Lykke."

She ran inside, and Arud began to chase her, when Bane grabbed him by the arm and stopped him.

"Explain the truth to her. If she begins to doubt the motives of man, she will side with the ferine."

"You can't be serious. My sister? She would never help those monsters."

Bane stepped closer to Arud. "Do not be so cocky and assume you know anything about her. The thought of her purpose or the purpose of the Cur as a weapon will not sit lightly in her heart. You must keep her focused on her duty to unite man and Cur against the ferine."

Arud yanked his arm away. "What if you're wrong? What is the motive of your heart?"

Bane spoke in a coarse whisper. "You know what I speak is true, because you have seen the powers unlocking inside of Lykke. Your doubt lies in your failure to admit that you have begun to see those same powers unlocking within you."

Ψ FORTY-FIVE Ψ

When Arud entered the Running Moose Inn, Lykke stood in Scalvia's protective arms, the looks on their faces a range from shock to disgust. "She heard you say the Cur are weapons," Scalvia said. "Please tell me this isn't true."

"It is according to the Prophecy of Ulfhednar, but that doesn't mean I believe it."

"Of course it does."

"Why are you mad at *me*? It isn't *my* prophecy."

"But you believe it. And it will only be a matter of time before you also see the Cur as weapons. Come on, Lykke."

"Where are you taking her?"

"To lie down."

Arud stared at Scalvia as if she were a stranger. "What's gotten into you?"

She glared at Arud. "Only the truth of who you really are." She led Lykke up the stairs.

He watched in stunned disbelief from the base of the steps. Something wasn't right about this. About any of this. Not what Bane had said. Not what Falla had said. Nothing.

"She'll be fine," Vang offered. "She gets this way sometimes."

"Scalvia is very passionate about things," Gunter said.

"And very stubborn," Quinn added.

Arud stormed off to his room and packed before

hauling his load down to the main hall, where everyone gathered around the hearth. He couldn't make sense of any of things and needed to speak with his father. But Berg was preoccupied with finishing new weapons before time ran out. The next full moon was just days away. They needed to get moving.

Looking around the group, Arud asked, "Where are Scalvia and Lykke?"

"They haven't come down yet," Quinn said.

"Has anyone checked on them?"

"I will," Vang said, headed upstairs.

The front door opened, and Berg entered carrying weapons, fresh bolts, and arrows. "Take what you need to replenish. The rest remain with Ulga in return for her generous hospitality."

"And delicious food," Gunter hollered.

Ulga almost cracked a smile.

Berg brought Arud several bolts tipped with silver. "Where is your sister?"

"Upstairs with Scalvia."

Berg's eyes narrowed, apparently reading the uncertainty upon Arud's face. "What's wrong?"

"Lykke heard me say the Cur were created to be weapons."

"What? Why would you say that?"

"Because that is what the Prophecy of Ulfhednar says. You told me to read about the Bloodstone."

Berg rubbed his chin. "I'll go talk to her and smooth this over. The last thing we need is for Lykke to choose the wrong side."

Arud crossed his arms. "What did you say?"

"Arud, her choice will decide which species survives. It isn't fair, but it is her fate nonetheless."

What was going on? Did Arud know anyone? He had never felt more alone in his life. He had no home, no family, nothing at all. Could anyone be trusted? "You see her as a weapon, too?"

"That's enough. Get ready to move out." Berg pressed past him and up the stairs.

He was met at the top by Vang. "They're gone," Vang said, winded. "This is all that was left behind." Vang held up a pair of knitting needles.

Arud felt the air harden in his lungs.

Those needles unmistakably belonged to Toov.

Ψ FORTY-SIX Ψ

Berg sprinted down the stairs. "How extensive of a headstart do they have?"

"A half hour to forty-five minutes," Arud guessed. "I saw them go upstairs just after I left you in the shed."

Berg packed ammunition along with his tri-action crossbow, capable of launching three bolts at a time. Arud packed the bread Ulga had given him.

"What's happening?" Quinn asked.

Arud couldn't speak.

"A shifter has taken Lykke," Berg said.

"What shifter?"

"We have lost two," Arud said, looking at Vang. "Scalvia never returned. The girl we thought was her, was a ferine in her skin."

Vang's eyes glimmered with understanding. "She could be wandering the woods. She could be wounded…"

"No," Arud interrupted. "Don't even think it."

Vang deliberately stepped into Arud's space, embracing him by the elbows as he had by the river. "Then we have both lost our sisters. Which will you go after?"

Arud trembled. The two girls he loved, missing. "I go with my father and Bane to find Lykke. You, Quinn, and Gunter find Scalvia. We have less than a week to reach the city. You know Scalvia better than anyone. There's no doubt in my mind you'll find her."

"And if I don't?"

"You will." Arud pulled away and strapped on his pack. "Now go, find her."

Vang, Quinn, and Gunter rushed toward the front doors to leave, when Arud called out to them. "Wait!"

They paused and Arud ran up to Vang. "Take this with you." He held out the cloth wrapped Bloodstone.

"What is it?" Vang asked.

"Something the king will need to protect the city. If he's wise, he'll know what to do with it."

Vang took the object and pushed it deep into his bag.

"And this," Arud said, handing Vang the Prophecy of Ulfhednar. "It belongs to your family. Share it with no one but the king."

Vang placed the book beside the stone.

"Vang, please find her."

"I will, or die trying."

And with that, the trio left.

"Arud, are you ready?" Berg stood in the front entrance of the inn. He wore a fur vest, and silver plated gear covered his arms and legs. His face glowed bronze against the red fox pelt.

"Yes, father."

Bane smiled, gripping a long spear tipped with silver. "Let's go kill those monsters."

Arud led his father and Bane outside.

"Which way?" Berg asked him.

Arud scanned the mountaintop. One direction would lead them down the mountain to Vithalia, the path he wanted to take, the one Vang was wandering. The other pass meant backtracking. But he knew which way. He could almost smell it. "We go back the way we came." With purposed steps, he headed back down the mountain pass.

"Are you crazy?" Bane said. "If we move that way, we will be out in the open when the creatures come."

"It doesn't matter what happens to us. We have to save Lykke. She still thinks she's with Scalvia."

"It's suicide. If we go after her with a small guard of Vithalian soldiers, then at least we stand a fighting chance."

Berg was silent. Arud assumed he was weighing both sides of their argument and wondered when his father was going to stick up for him.

"He is right," Berg said, pointing to Bane.

"What?" Arud protested. "You can't be serious."

"We won't survive out in the open," Berg said. "We can't save Lykke if we're dead."

"I don't believe this."

Berg turned to Arud, his hands on his shoulders. "Son, I know how much you love your sister, but that love is blinding your judgment. You have to trust me when I say this decision is in our best interests. All of ours."

Arud felt a tear stream down his cheek, then drip off his chin. He would not meet his father's eyes.

"The faster we get to the city, the quicker we can gather reinforcements and go looking for her."

"And you could be wrong, boy," Bane said. "She could be down that way, not back toward the river."

"If the moon rises and she isn't with us, we lose our chance of saving her." Arud looked at Berg. "I'm not wrong. I'll go find her alone if I have to, but I would rather die than let her stand one more second in the presence of that evil." His lip was trembling as his tears fell unguarded.

Berg and Bane stared at him. No one spoke.

Finally, Arud wiped his face dry and took in a quick breath. "Don't try and stop me." He turned, pacing back toward the curve in the Torngats chain.

"Wait," Berg said.

"Father, no," Arud said. "I won't just stand around when—"

"I'm coming with you." Arud looked upon his father's face. "I won't let you risk your life alone for your sister. We turn it over to Odin's hands and trust he will protect us."

"Count me in," said Bane, moving up from behind.

Arud nodded. "Let's get her back."

They ran across the mountain, along the curve, down the slope for two straight days, following footprints in the snow left by Toov and Lykke. Bane was a skilled tracker, able to notice disruptions in the branches, blades of grass, and unearthed leaves, until a snowfall on the third day left them without a trail.

Was Toov deliberately leading them so far away? She must have been. They would never make it back in time. They slept in two hour shifts, then covered more ground. They hunted, ate, and slept another two hours, until exhaustion fell heavy across the men, and the little food they'd packed ran out.

Finally, they passed the cabin at the bottom of the Torngats. It looked abandoned, and Arud knew it was. They had killed its last two occupants on the mountaintop: Lager and Kron. As daylight slowly filtered across the horizon like a distant memory, they crossed the Scynnthe Valley and reached the river.

Pressing back across Vithalia, Arud thought of his mother, lying dead on the riverbank, of Scalvia shifting into ferine form, and of Lykke's face when she overheard him speaking with Bane about the purpose of the Cur. Three of his greatest loves, all gone, all just outside his reach. He prayed Vang would find Scalvia and bring her safely to the city. Even if he never saw her again, he hoped she lived.

But Lykke, sweet Lykke, with her golden curls and contagious laughter, she was his to protect. For the benefit of the entire existence of men and Cur alike. What would happen if he could not succeed? What would happen to Vithalia if Lykke were lost to the wrong side? He couldn't let those thoughts consume him. He had to keep his focus on her rescue. She had been taken by Toov before. The only difference was this time Arud knew there would be more than one ferine to face. And more importantly, he realized that this time, Lykke may not want to leave.

Ψ FORTY-SEVEN Ψ

They were not far from the river when Toov's howl flooded the air.

"What was that?" Bane asked, tensed.

"That was my grandmother," Arud said, his moss-toned eyes scanning the woods. "She's shifted again."

"How can you be sure it was her?"

"I know her howl. She's been stalking us since we left the Outlands."

"What do we do?" Bane asked, his baldhead reflecting the faint winter sun.

Several howls answered Toov's in the distance. Dense trees patched in tight clumps hindered Arud's view. "We get ready. She is gathering her pack. She is intent on bringing about the Prophecy of Ulfhednar."

"How many do you think?" Berg asked, rubbing his thick beard.

"I don't know, Father. But if Lykke is as important as the prophecy says, then we could be facing a ferine army."

"That's not good, boy," Bane said.

Arud didn't respond.

"Well, let's stop standing around like prey and gear up," Berg said. He loaded his crossbow, then wedged a knife into his belt. His long spear leaned against a birch tree off to the side.

At least thirty bolts forged of pure silver filled Bane's quiver. Arud unlatched his crossbow and notched a silver bolt of his own. His hands trembled as another round of howls resounded in the distance.

"I hear at least three," Bane said.

"Then prepare for ten," Berg told him. "Circle up. Back to back."

They huddled together, collectively able to watch every angle of the surrounding woods. The howling echoed eerily through the trees, ferine calling and answering in a shrill song. Sweat formed across Arud's brow. How could they ever survive this? The stillness of the forest seemed to grow louder.

"They are coming," Berg said.

"No," Arud said. "They're already here."

A pair of familiar amber eyes glowed in the dark shadows between the trees facing Arud.

"I see three," Bane said.

"I see two more," Berg added.

"And I see my grandmother," Arud seethed.

"Take aim, but wait until they are within range," Bane said.

"Tell me, Arud," Berg said over his shoulder, "how do we defeat our enemy?"

"By letting them think they've won, then striking when they least expect it."

"Good. Remember, your blood also holds value to the ferine. Bane and I will take out as many as we can, but it's unlikely they will let us live."

"That's encouraging," Arud said.

"You *should* feel encouraged. Toov will not let her pack harm you. Lure her in. Make her think you have given up. Then kill her."

Arud swallowed gravel, his pulse pounding in his ears.

Two identical snow-white ferine appeared first,

followed by a smaller one with a yellow coat and another, red as flames. Toov stepped out of the shadows, her massive bulk sending chills across Arud's flesh. Sharp teeth called out for blood. Her black fur glistened, the silver strands running through like veins, pulsating, alive. The rest of the pack prowled behind her, their pointed ears alert, their long legs pacing. A sandy ferine smaller than the rest strayed out of the shadows and crouched beside Toov.

"What are they doing?" Bane asked.

"I don't know," Arud said. "Maybe they sense our silver."

"Then now is the time to strike," Berg said, pulling his bowstring to full draw.

He released three bolts in one snap. Two landed in the red ferine's side; the other missed its mark. The ferine yelped, its body smoking from the silver. In a vicious fury, the creatures attacked, fangs bared; froth dripped from pointed muzzles. Arud struck the white one and Bane's bolt caught its twin. The howling creatures did not die immediately, but the silver disabled them, giving Arud, Berg, and Bane time to gather stray bolts and reload.

The red ferine recovered quickly and launched through the air, pushing Bane to the ground. He swung his blade, the silver bubbling through muscles and tissues, splattering the creature's blood across the snow. It bit Bane's hand and he cut into its pink mouth till the ragged jaw hung only by stretched skin at the hinge. It jerked back. Bane slipped underneath and sliced its belly. Intestines piled into a steaming heap on the snowy forest floor. The ferine collapsed, then shifted back into its human form; the outline of a long-haired woman all that remained.

Berg tramped upon the yellow ferine pinned to the ground by his bolts. The ferine slashed sharp retractable claws at Berg, who used his spear to stab its narrow chest over and over again, cracking bones, piercing muscle, and puncturing organs. One last wheeze rattled from the beast's throat before it ceased moving and began its shift. As Berg withdrew his weapons from the carcass, the other white twin pounced on his back, barreling him into the ground. Its teeth tore into Berg's flesh and he screamed in agony, unable to roll away.

"Father!"

Arud notched his crossbow, launching bolt after bolt upon the white ferine, its body writhing and smoking, gradually shifting back to human form. It was not dead yet, the halfling sprawled naked on the ground, barely able to breathe.

Arud stood over her. "Where is Lykke?" he demanded. Where is my sister?"

The wide-eyed shifter stared up at him, and hissed through grinding teeth. "She is one of us now."

"No!" Arud shouted, unsheathing his long knife.

He hacked off her head, watching as it spun down the steep slope. He glanced over at Berg. He was not moving. In a blur, the second white ferine charged. Arud ducked, and the ferine flew overhead, slamming into a tree. The dazed creature wandered away before returning, shaking its head.

"Bane! White!"

Bane stopped hacking at the corpse of the yellow ferine and turned his eyes on the white one. Together, Arud and Bane took aim on either side of the white ferine, shooting three bolts each into its muscular body. The disoriented animal attempted to charge, staggering back and forth from Bane to Arud, until finally, overcome by the silver, she collapsed at Bane's feet.

"Get the others." Bane sliced off the ferine's head just as its metamorphosis began.

Arud turned. Corpses of human women, the transformed versions of all the ferine, lay scattered across the ground. But two teenage boys about Arud's age lay alongside them.

Just like the Prophecy of Ulfhednar predicted would happen in the end.

Toov stood sentinel beside the sandy ferine, who growled threateningly, exposing bloody gums and fangs, pawing frantically at the snow. Toov appeared to be hampering her attack. Arud glanced at his father. He still hadn't moved.

"Bane, check Berg!"

Bane lurched over, covered in black blood mixed with his own, and felt for a pulse. "He's alive!"

Arud closed his eyes, nodding compulsively. "Stay with him, Bane. The black one is mine." Arud advanced upon Toov. "Where is Lykke? What have you done with her?"

A sick smile crept across Toov's canine lips.

Arud notched a bolt, aiming it at his grandmother. "Where is she?"

Toov nudged the sandy ferine she guarded.

Arud shook his head. "No. No! That's not my sister." But then, Arud peered into the ferine's bloodshot, hazel eyes and glimpsed Lykke, beneath the fur, beneath the evil possessing her. His shoulders slumped forward. "What have you done to her?"

Lykke snapped sharp teeth at the air, staring upon Arud like he was nothing more than a meal.

Arud faced Toov. "I'm not afraid of you anymore."

As if to prove her dominance, Toov swatted Lykke, sending her hurdling through the air. She slammed into a tree with a painful squeal before her body fell limp to the snow. What was Toov doing? She needed Lykke, didn't she? A sick thought hit Arud as he realized Toov needed only her blood, not her life.

He screamed; released his bolt. Toov turned, growling from deep within as she attacked, battering Arud, leveling him to the ground. Together, they tumbled across the forest floor, Toov's teeth tearing at Arud's flesh, his knife shredding through her thick pelt. Her weighty body crushed him with every roll. How was he going to get the upper hand?

Let her think she's won.

Their momentum slowed and Toov wasted no time pinning Arud down, her nails like a grapnel digging deep into his shoulders, drawing blood. He howled in agony. She barked, spraying bloodstained spittle across his face. Bane's footfalls grew nearer. "Stay back!" Arud shouted, but Bane wouldn't listen.

Bane released two bolts, both landing in Toov's side, where they smoldered, bringing out the silvery veins like shooting stars across a midnight sky. Toov howled, a piercing howl, turned rabid eyes upon Bane, before she leaped off Arud to charge upon her new target. Bane notched a fresh bolt, but not before Toov plunged into his chest, her claws swatting and slicing in erratic sweeps. Bane fell to the ground, his chest streaked red where Toov's nails had carved him.

"Hey!" Arud shouted. "Leave him alone. It's me you want."

Toov jerked her bloody muzzle in Arud's direction. He drew back the string on his notched crossbow. "I know you need my blood to fulfill the prophecy. But you can't have it. You and your kind will not live to see another full moon." Arud's bolt bulleted through the air, and Toov leapt out of the way, catching the silver tip in her muscular back leg. As she pivoted, he reloaded and took aim, ready for the final assault that would take her life, when a blur off to the side caught his attention.

Arud's heart fell. He could never defeat two. But he wouldn't be easily beaten. He braced for the new foe, a jet black ferine, who edged from the shadows of the trees, slunk directly to Lykke, and nudged her awake. With a rush of warmth he realized who protected his little sister.

It was Scalvia.

Toov growled, her eyes fixated on Scalvia, who rumbled back, placing herself as a shield before Lykke. Toov charged, and Arud felt time slow to a crawl. Toov's muscles tensed. She sprung in long strides at Scalvia, who snarled and barked, still somehow the beautiful girl with long black hair in Arud's eyes. Lykke lay helpless, shifted back to her sweet self, her fur in clumps beside her, her pale curls veiling her face. Something inside him raged, filling him with a strength that melted his despair.

He released his draw.

The bolt caught in Toov's side.

Then another.

The impact threw her off-balance.

Scalvia leapt.

Arud raced closer, hammering another bolt into his grandmother.

Toov and Scalvia collided midair, hurtling to the ground. Toov sunk serrated teeth into Scalvia's flesh, and raked sickle-like claws across her skin. Scalvia slashed back, but she was outrivaled.

Toov was going to kill her.

Arud scanned the battlefield and noticed Berg's long spear. That was it, his only hope to save Scalvia. He grasped it, sprinting close enough to launch the silver shaft. Scalvia's whines were almost too much to bear. In the midst of it all, Lykke stood, completely healed, staring as Toov ripped Scalvia to shreds.

Lykke slipped closer as Toov continued her barrage of claw and teeth.

Lykke glided nearer.

Arud took aim.

What would she do? Would Lykke help Scalvia? Or was she under Toov's command? Had his grandmother succeeded in convincing his sister to fight with the creatures? Arud raced closer as Lykke neared. Toov clamped her teeth around Scalvia's neck.

Arud couldn't bear to lose Scalvia and Lykke. But he was too late. Scalvia went limp. Lykke reached for her, but then Toov extended an arm, grazing Lykke's chest and neck with lethal claws.

Arud hoisted back the spear as Lykke spun around and fell onto her stomach, wounded. Arud roared, slicing the spearhead through Toov's spine and chest. His brute force surpassed human capabilities. Animal instinct had overtaken him. Growing muscles pressed against his taut skin, ready to burst.

Toov writhed on her hind legs, flailing at the spear with her front claws, abandoning Scalvia, who began to shift. Toov collapsed on the snow as her blood pooled beneath her.

Arud angled over her. Every coldblooded way he could hurt Toov passed through his brain. And she deserved it, for murdering his mother, for afflicting Scalvia, for capturing Lykke. Vengeance rushed from his heart as he pulled out his knife. "This is for my mother." He plunged the blade into her neck and sliced her from ear to ear. Toov's head thwacked the ground, and what was left of the black ferine shifted into the form of Arud's grandmother.

Bane hobbled over to Scalvia clutching his chest. He carefully removed his cloak, drew in air through clenched teeth, and covered Scalvia's body. "She's dying," Bane said, searching for a pulse "They're all dying."

Arud sat next to Lykke. He knew if she didn't heal, she would die like the other women lying on the battlefield. And Toov would have fulfilled the prophecy by spilling her blood and taking her life. Tears fell onto his sister's canine body. Her neck bent acutely to the side.

Bane gawked at Toov with a smirk. "I think it's safe to say this one's dead."

"We're taking her head with us to Vithalia City," Arud said, "as a warning to the others."

Lykke moaned. Arud cradled her against his chest. "Please, Odin. Don't let her die."

But it wasn't just her. It was his father. And Scalvia. He couldn't lose them all. What point would there be in living? No family. No amazing girl whose gray eyes he'd get lost in. He watched Scalvia's chest expand as she panted in steady breaths, but she still hadn't transformed. "Don't let her die, either." He continued rocking Lykke in his arms, running his fingers through her curls.

Leaves crunched, the sound growing louder. Arud looked up sharply, scanning the woods, knife out, dripping with Toov's fresh blood. Bane pushed himself to his feet and readied his bow, his hands shaking, his breath labored.

Arud was exhausted. He couldn't fight anymore. He had nothing left. He closed his eyes, prepared to give his body to whatever approached. To let them just take him. Scalvia's parents exited the forest.

"Ek? Ahlgren?" He couldn't believe what he was seeing.

"Scalvia told us you might be in trouble and need help," Ek said.

"We figured there would be wounded," Ahlgren said. She let out a gasp as she saw Lykke lying on the ground. She bent over her. "She is healing, but not very quickly."

"Scalvia, too," Arud said. "And my father. I fear the worst for him."

Ahlgren handed Arud a cream dotted with green and pink herbs. "Rub this into Lykke's wounds. This will speed up her metabolism."

"Ek, take care of Scalvia. I will attend to Arud's father."

Bane led Ahlgren to Berg. She first looked Bane over, giving him some medicine from her pouch and a long strip of cloth to wrap around his gash. She quietly bent beside Berg, touching his body, listening to him breathe.

Arud watched Ahlgren for a moment.

Turning, she met his eyes with a cold stare.

Something wrong in her eyes. Was she blaming Arud for what had happened? No. He was seeing things from hunger and sleep deprivation and stress. He continued rubbing ointment into Lykke's lesions. He looked down as his fingers pressed into her carved flesh. His tears spilled out. "Please don't leave me."

She coughed and her eyes fluttered open. She tried speaking, but couldn't.

"Shhhh," Arud whispered, kissing her forehead. "Don't talk. Everything is going to be okay."

Arud stared over at her, relief flooding him. Lykke shut her eyes again and Arud sighed. She was going to be all right.

Scalvia gasped and sat upright. "Father?"

Ek grinned. "Yes, daughter. Now rest and heal."

Bane stared at her human form. "Her arm is mending. How can that be?"

"She is Cur, Bane," Arud said. "Like Lykke. Of ferine and human blood."

They sat in the woods, bloodied from battle, as both girls rapidly healed. His father lay stone still, and Arud's chest ached as he prayed Berg would hold out a little longer. Arud closed his eyes, trusting Ahlgren would heal him too. Tears seeped out the edges as he looked heavenward. "Hail, Odin," he said. "Odin, Bless."

Ψ FORTY-EIGHT Ψ

It was a hard trek back to the river with Berg and Bane wounded. Lykke had revived although Scalvia was taking longer. Toov had wounded her badly. Arud carried his grandmother's head in a tied off bag, the great ferine mother.

According to the Prophecy of Ulfhednar, the creatures would be unable to rise without their Great Mother. And although tomorrow night the full moon would shine, Arud felt relieved in knowing there would be no attack.

Arud and Lykke helped Berg hobble to the riverbank. Ek and Ahlgren had Bane balanced between them, absorbing his weight. His blood had soaked through his bindings, and he was growing weak.

"They must cleanse in the river," Ahlgren said. "It will sting, but the water will be healing."

Together, they helped the men strip down to their underthings. Scalvia hung their clothes on rocks to dry.

"I'm going in too," she said, moving further downstream.

"I brought you clothes," Ahlgren said. "And Arud, I brought some of Vang's things. I am sure they will fit you."

Arud looked up at Vang's mother, who was clutching her son's clothes before her like a shield. He took the clothes with a curt nod, then helped his father sit on a rock in the water. Berg pinched his lips tightly to keep from shaking, a grimace on his face that lingered long after he slid into the icy water to wash his wounds. After a few minutes, he was submerged and appeared relaxed. Arud left him alone and returned to Ahlgren. She didn't acknowledge him at first, staring at her chapped hands cupped in her lap.

Arud cleared his throat. "I don't know where Vang is," Arud started, "but I'd like to think he's reached Vithalia City by now, although I'm sure he's thinking the worst not knowing Scalvia is safe."

"He doesn't know Scalvia is with you?"

"We split paths to find our sisters after they went missing. It seems Scalvia found you first."

Ahlgren nodded. "They are both lucky to have you."

Arud leaned forward and kissed her on the cheek. He wasn't sure why, except if it had been his own mother, he would have done the same. Arud moved down the bank to jump into the river. He saw Lykke splashing downstream with Scalvia. It was odd to him, seeing her shift back and forth between personalities, one moment a playful child, the next a hideous killing machine.

While everyone bathed, Ek set traps and Ahlgren gathered wood for the fire. The men left the river with much help from the others. Ahlgren rubbed heavy creams and solvents into Berg's and Bane's wounds. She fed them medicinal herbs that numbed their pain and tenderly covered them with strips of cloth fastened tightly in place.

The girls had returned, clean and refreshed. Scalvia wore a simple dress that hugged her curves. She smiled at him and he felt his cheeks redden.

Lykke held her hand. Giggling, she said, "Scalvia

and I are going to gather greens for tonight's meal." She stretched on tiptoes and kissed Arud's cheek. "Don't worry. I know it's her this time."

Arud smirked. He knew it was, too. The head in his bag confirmed it.

After several hours, sunset neared and Ek returned carrying three rabbits. Lykke and Scalvia followed closely behind with two armfuls of edible tubers and weeds.

"Well, now," Ahlgren said. "We will be feasting tonight." A pot of boiled water and mint leaves sat to the side, cooling. "I am afraid I only have two cups. We will have to share."

She filled the two cups, passing them around and refilling them as needed. Ek roasted the rabbits over the fire spit. Lykke and Scalvia plated the greens on flat pieces of bark. Arud smiled. He hadn't remembered feeling this safe and happy since he was back home in the Outlands.

The meal was served, and Ek led them in a prayer. "Thank you, great Odin for your protection and care. For guiding us to where we were needed and keeping us safe."

"All of us," Ahlgren added, most likely thinking of Vang.

"Yes, all of us. Your mercy is undeserved."

They ate hungrily, laughing and carrying on in high spirits. The air was cold, but the fire warmed them. Bane and Berg's bodies relaxed as Ahlgren's creams numbed the pain and healed their wounds.

After the meal, Ek lit one of his leaf-rolled herbs. This time, Arud accepted his offer. He inhaled the thick smoke. Instantly, he felt every muscle in his body relax. All the tension he'd been holding since the ferine came to his bedroom window slowly melted away.

He needed to be alone. He left the adults' company to sit on a dry rock by the river. He smiled as he watched Ek use exaggerated arm motions to relay some story while the others laughed, then shared tales of their own. Arud stared up at the stars, wondering what his future would hold. The memory of his mother stung fresh. He missed her tremendously.

"Hey, you." Scalvia sat behind him, her face beaming.

"What are you so happy about?"

She shrugged. "Knowing my parents are here. That we are safe. Hoping Vang has found a haven."

Arud grinned. "I know the feeling."

They held hands, lying back on the rock, gazing at the glittering stars, reminding Arud of the beauty of Vithalia City at sunset. He stared at Scalvia. No star compared to her beauty.

"I think you were right," Scalvia said.

"About what?"

"About their being a Creator in charge of things," Scalvia continued. "I just feel like all of this happened outside of our control. You know? Like the way I felt something guiding me at every turn. Like I feel something guiding me toward you."

She squeezed his hand, kissed his cheek. Arud snuck a glance at the adults. Ek was telling another of his elaborate tales, with Bane and Berg holding on to every word. But Ahlgren was staring in his direction, while Lykke slept in her lap.

"There is something else, though," Scalvia said.

"What?"

"I feel like we've missed something."

"What do you mean?" Arud asked as random images of what could be flashed through his mind.

Scalvia sat up. "What if Toov wasn't the mother?"

Arud's face twisted as he sat up. "Why do you think that?"

Scalvia shrugged. "I can't put my finger on it, but something is still out of place."

Fear gripped his chest with icy claws, and Arud fought to keep his face neutral. He lifted Scalvia's dimpled chin so their eyes met. Covering, he said, "I think it's all those herbs your mother has fed you." He smiled, waiting for her to return one of her own.

But she didn't.

"Scalvia, we're safe now. We've taken down the Great Mother. Lykke is safe. Once we secure Vang's safety, everything will be as it should."

She nodded, then slowly relaxed on the rock beside him. He could barely breathe. His illusion of safety had been shaken. Scalvia's words resonated deep inside of him. And they scared him to death. What if she was right? What if Toov wasn't the Great Mother?

Ψ FORTY-NINE Ψ

Arud opened his eyes to bright morning sunlight and the smell of cooking fish. He sat up and stretched. Cool air swept over his face, carrying the crispness of fall. Smiling, he watched Lykke and his father together. Berg looked much better than he had the day before. Whatever herbs were in Ahlgren's concoctions, they seemed to be working.

Arud strolled over to join his family.

"He awakens," Berg said with a smile.

"We thought you would sleep clear through breakfast," Lykke said, hugging him.

"Not when breakfast smells so good," he answered, kissing her forehead. It seemed strange how much taller Lykke had grown since the trip began. He assumed it was simply one of the changes. He scanned the campsite, looking for Scalvia. Ahlgren and Ek sat near the river. He walked over, his boots crunching the snow.

Ahlgren and Ek turned to face him.

"I can't thank you enough for what you've done for my father," Arud told Ahlgren.

She smiled. "Think nothing of it."

"Please, sit with us," Ek added.

Arud took a seat beside them, watching the current lazily carry a leaf downstream.

"I am told that you saved my daughter's life," Ek said.

"No more than she saved mine."

Ek smiled, then turned his attention back to the river.

"Scalvia is lucky to have met you," Ahlgren said with a grin that conveyed secret knowledge.

Arud couldn't help but notice. What was it with her? Was he reading into things? Coldness passed ever so gently across his neck, like the current barely moving the leaf in the river. He cleared his throat. "I am the lucky one."

Ahlgren nodded with a tight expression.

"Scalvia is checking the traps for squirrels," Ek said. "She has always been a hunter, since she was a little girl."

"It is in her blood," Ahlgren added. "Even before we realized she was a Cur."

Arud faced her. "You mean you didn't know right away?"

Ahlgren shook her head. "No. Scalvia's strength remained hidden long into her childhood. It wasn't until she was past the age of recognition that her Cur abilities blossomed."

Arud nodded. "I didn't know it worked that way."

Ahlgren placed her arm around Arud's shoulder. "The Cur are the people that you care for and love. Like Lykke. And Scalvia."

"Talking about me, Mother?"

Arud turned. Scalvia stood behind them, holding two rabbits by their hind legs.

"Yes, we were," Ahlgren said, quickly taking her arm off Arud.

A chill passed and Arud's head felt groggy. What had happened?

"Wanna help?" Scalvia asked, lifting her kill.

Arud stood. He forced a smile at Ahlgren and Ek before walking off with Scalvia.

She looked over at him. "What was that all about?"

"Nothing," he lied, taking the rabbits from her. "Just hungry."

Arud reached the campsite and began skinning the rabbits fervently. Scalvia followed him, watching him bludgeon the meat.

"They're already dead, you know," she said with a smirk.

Arud didn't respond, focused on his task.

"What's wrong with you?" she asked, grabbing his arm.

He yanked free a bit too hard and threw her off balance. She nearly tumbled back on the bramble before regaining her footing.

"Okay, Arud. You don't want to talk to me, just say so."

Arud covered his eyes with his hand.

Scalvia knelt beside him, her voice tender, her hand soft on the nape of his neck. "What is it?"

"I don't know. Everything. Nothing. I can't tell up from down anymore."

"We're safe, remember? It's time to relax and enjoy ourselves. That's what you said."

Arud let his gaze linger on her face for a moment before returning back to the rabbits.

"Arud, tell me what's the matter."

"I haven't been able to shake what you said last night about Toov, you know, not being the mother."

"Arud…it was a feeling, that's all." Her smile went unmet. "Come on. It's absurd." Her eyes were wide as she stared at him. "Isn't it?"

He wanted to tell her yes, that Toov was the mother, and she was dead. No more creatures. No more living in fear of the darkness. Nothing but a happy future for them both. But he couldn't. He took her hand and whispered, "No, Scalvia. I think your premonition may be right."

"Based on what?"

He let out a long breath. "On nothing. But just because you can't show the proof of something doesn't mean it isn't true. And my gut is telling me to trust you. It has since we met, and you haven't let me down once." His words lingered in the air so thick, Arud felt he could grab them and take them back. But in his heart he knew he spoke truth. And that night, when the moon rose, they would be facing the army alone.

Scalvia looked down. "What are we supposed to do?"

"There's nothing we can do. We have to keep moving toward the city and pray that we are wrong."

"Have you even heard or seen any ferine since the Great Mother's death?"

"No."

"Isn't that proof enough we are safe?"

"Why are you trying to convince me that everything is okay?" His anger flushed his face red.

"I was confiding in you. I didn't realize it would make you angry." She stomped to the fire, carrying the skinned rabbits with her. After spearing them and setting them over the flame, she joined her parents by the river.

"Don't worry about her," Bane said. He sat by the fire, warming his feet, his eyes closed. "Women get like that sometimes, especially around the full moon."

"I'm fine," Arud lied.

"Just remember, whatever it is you two are fighting about is a good thing."

"How could our fighting be a good thing?"

Bane opened his eyes. "Cause if she didn't like you, she wouldn't fight with you."

Arud glanced over at Scalvia, who glimpsed over her shoulder and caught his stare. She scrunched her eyes, and whipped her head around, her hair trailing like the tail of a comet.

"See," Bane said. "That girl is crazy about you."

Arud shook his head. "Thanks for the advice, Bane."

"Any time."

Arud moved away from camp to be alone. So Scalvia was crazy about him, and fighting was her way of showing it. It didn't make any sense to him, but he'd never been in love before. He'd leave her alone for now and hopefully, when she cooled off, he could apologize. Maybe she was right. Maybe she *was* just bouncing thoughts off him; not actually inferring Toov wasn't the ferine's Great Mother. He had taken things too far. Why had he yelled at her? Toov was dead. She was the one who'd been hunting him from the start. Why was he even considering that there was someone else? He turned back around and paced directly to Scalvia.

"Can I talk to you?" he asked.

She gave him a non-committal look. "I guess."

They walked off through the woods in silence, until they were far enough from camp to be alone. She stared down with her arms crossed.

She wasn't making this easy for him. "I'm sorry."

Scalvia looked up. "For what?"

Arud paused. "For upsetting you. For fighting with you. I'm sorry I took what you told me too far. Did I forget anything?"

She fought back her smile, but lost. "I'm sorry, too," she said, reaching up for a kiss. Their lips were just about to touch, when a shrieking howl filled the air and they froze.

"That sounded close," Scalvia said.

"Like it came from camp."

They sprinted through the trees, back to camp, where everyone was gathered around the fire.

"Is everyone all right?" Arud shouted. "What's going on?"

No one answered, their eyes trained on Lykke crouching on the ground panting, pawing, snarling at them. Scalvia took Arud's hand as Berg swung his arm across Arud's chest, blocking him from stepping any closer to Lykke.

"What's wrong with her?" Arud asked no one.

In a jerky motion, Lykke tilted her head back and let out a howl. The same one he had just heard in the woods. And as horror slipped down his spine, he listened.

Far in the distance, something howled back.

Ψ FIFTY Ψ

Berg touched Lykke's shoulder and she jumped, sinking her claws deep into his hand. He recoiled instinctively, cradling his injured limb.

Arud crouched beside her. A white film glazed her eyes, the pupils long gone. "Lykke," he whispered, as he did to the deer dying in the woods. "Lykke, you're safe."

She growled a low inhuman rumble that coursed up from her belly to her snarled lips. Her yellowed teeth had grown into sharp points as the ferine transformed inside her.

"Lykke." He shook her hard by the shoulders.

She launched up and out of his grasp, crouching several yards away. Her face shifted, the skin pulling taut across the brim of her nose, her cheeks bunched and wrinkled. Bloodshot eyes filled with animal rage locked on Arud. His hands shook as he looked at the others. Their faces were shrouded in the same shock he felt covering his own.

Scalvia touched his hand. "Let me try." She crept toward Lykke on all fours, head lowered and eyes downcast, as Arud had seen people do when they approach an aggressive animal. She was able to move within a foot of Lykke. "You can trust me."

Scalvia slinked closer, her hand next to Lykke's on the dirt, their outer fingers touching. "I love you, Lykke."

Lykke stopped panting for just a second while

Scalvia's voice registered somewhere in her brain.

Scalvia seized the moment and grabbed Lykke by the shoulders, pulling her close so they stood face to face.

The cloudiness retreated from Lykke's eyes as they returned to hazel. Her lips softened, her face smoothed, and her teeth shortened into a row of white. "Scalvia?" Lykke murmured.

Scalvia smiled and brushed Lykke's hair back behind her ear. Lykke fell into Scalvia's chest, sobbing. The ferine howled again in the distance. Lykke shot up, her skin flushed.

Arud's hand gripped the handle of his full tang knife. "We have to get out of here. Now."

Quickly, they gathered their belongings. Berg and Bane needed help, so Ek wedged beneath Bane while Ahlgren helped Berg to his feet.

Lykke's upturned nose sniffed the air.

"I sense it too." Scalvia said, mimicking Lykke. "Something is very, very wrong."

Arud moved toward her. They stared into each other's eyes. Scalvia's were nearly pure white orbs, like two full moons, her irises hidden beneath. They shared no words, but they both knew.

Toov was not the Great Mother.

They had to get out of the open. They had to reach the safety of the city's border by nightfall, yet they hadn't even crossed the valley. It would take weeks to reach Vithalia City. They would never make it, especially not with two wounded.

"We leave now," Arud said.

"For where?" Scalvia asked. "There is nowhere safe from here to the city except the village, and we would never make it there in time."

"Don't tell me what I already know. Either help me make a way or get out of mine."

Arud swept past Scalvia and plunged into the cold river, crossing alone to the other shore. He turned. "Let's go." He marched across the valley, hearing the water sloshing as the others crossed behind him.

Lykke ran alongside him. "What is your plan?"

He shrugged. He didn't trust her. He hated himself for feeling that way, but he couldn't help it. She was more ferine than human, just like Scalvia.

"Arud," Lykke said. "Stop. Look at me."

Arud reluctantly stopped and looked down at his sister. Blond curls, bright eyes, beautiful. He hugged her tight. "I'm sorry. I'm just so scared."

"I am too. But we can win this together. Like we always have."

They pulled apart, and Arud nodded. The others had caught up. Scalvia stayed to the back of the group. He shouldn't have yelled at her. What had he been thinking? This wasn't the time to fix it, though. If they didn't get out of the valley, none of this would matter.

"Let's head to the canyon between the mountains. There may be a way to climb through." He turned and paced forward without waiting for discussion. He knew it was a stupid idea, but it was the only one he had. Hopefully, something would come to him before they reached the flat wall, marking their final dead end.

Ψ FIFTY-ONE Ψ

The canyon stretched eerily ahead as Arud led the group through the high rocky walls, glistening as the minerals buried within reflected late afternoon sunlight. It had taken them hours to cross both the river and the valley, with Berg and Bane still unsteady and requiring help.

Lykke was distant. Her eyes had glazed again to milky-white. Her breathing had become labored, her mumbled words now mere whispers in a windstorm. They trekked to the canyon entrance. Arud craned his neck to study the depth of it. He remembered the last time he had been there, when Vang's crew had attacked from the upper levels. They had been completely defenseless on the low ground. Finding courage, he stepped forward.

Scalvia grabbed his arm. "Arud, what are you doing? There is nothing ahead."

He turned sullen eyes her way. "I know. But what choice do we have? We can't cross either mountain by nightfall."

"But there is only flat wall ahead. We can't break through it."

"I know!"

Lykke touched Arud's hand, speaking as if in a trance. "It is the only way." She moved ahead in smooth, long strides.

Arud took in a deep breath. He plodded ahead of Lykke, pushing through the long canyon toward what he knew would be a dead end.

What's the point? Why are we even trying? The pack will be here soon, and we won't survive.

But he needed to keep going.

"Arud," Scalvia said, her voice shaky.

He turned. With her eyes, Scalvia motioned up at the top of the surrounding cliffs, where the dark silhouettes of creatures scampered to and fro. Slowly, Arud removed his bolt. "Ready your weapons," he said. Calling up, he shouted, "Show yourselves."

One by one, ferine lined the edge of the cliffs, until thirty or forty stood in two rows towering above them. Arud gulped hard. His heart hammered in his chest. He faced Scalvia. "You must guard Lykke."

"She no longer needs guarding." Scalvia stepped closer. "I fight beside you." She wrapped her arms around his neck and kissed him more passionately than she ever had. Arud held her close, and for that brief moment, they were the only two souls in existence.

"Arud, they're coming!" Ek yelled.

Creatures slipped down the mountain's edge, catching sharpened claws in crevices for support. Scalvia backed away, protecting her family. Her lips in a snarl, she bared lengthening teeth as she slowly transformed from the most beautiful girl Arud had ever laid eyes upon into her Cur form.

Arud plunged ahead to stand beside Lykke. She was panting and heaving as her eyes rolled back into her head. Sharp claws began growing in place of her fingernails as her teeth spiked and her gums glowered.

"I love you, Lykke," Arud said. "And I'll give my life protecting you."

She faced him, a remnant of the little girl fighting

to show through her barren eyes.

Creatures leapt toward them in droves. Arud landed bolt upon bolt, the silver tips sizzling in their flesh. Ek slammed forward with his axe readied and brought it down into the skull of a gray ferine. Its head cracked and its body fell limp to the ground. Bane shot bolts with perfect aim into the chest and sides of the ferine that leaped from the mountain.

Arud sliced his knife into those wounded creatures lying beside him. He slit through the throat of a mahogany-hued beast, its own blood pouring down its lungs until it suffocated. He wedged his knife's tip through the back of a golden ferine's throat and out its spine. A ruddy marbled creature pounced, and Arud flung his knife at it, the blade catching midair deep in the ferine's chest. It dropped heavily, and its blood pooled beneath its fallen corpse.

The creatures fought hard with sickle-like claws and serrated teeth, biting with an evil rage. A paw caught Ek in his chest, knocking him back several yards, destroying his armor as he smacked into the rock wall.

Two creatures bounded at Scalvia, who stood before her family, the way she had protected Lykke from Toov. Growling. Snarling. Barking. Showing blood red gums. The creatures attacked, and she met them midair, a bombardment of slashing claw and raised fur, before they tumbled to the ground as the three fought to the death.

Scalvia knocked one in the side, pushing it to the ground, and sank her teeth into the other, ripping out its throat. The recovered ferine launched onto her back and chomped between her shoulder blades. Scalvia whined as she struggled to break free, but the ferine clung on.

"Scalvia!" Ek screamed, his voice hoarse from knocking into the wall. He reached his shaking arms for a bolt.

"No!" Arud shouted, charging toward Scalvia. He slammed several bolts into the white ferine's back, its fur pink with Scalvia's blood. It slumped over dead, and immediately its claws retracted back into padded paws then became a woman's bloodied hands.

Creatures continued to slide down the mountain. Arud realized they were grossly outnumbered. They wouldn't be able to fight them off much longer. He looked ahead to where Lykke stood, untouched. Not a single ferine had gone near her. Had they been told to leave her unharmed? But by whom? And as the thought reached his mind, the ground trembled and rumbled, and Arud braced himself by stretching out his arms to either side for balance.

"What's happening?" Bane asked.

The ground shifted, sending Arud to his knees. The creatures instantly disappeared up the mountain side, moving out of the valley and out of sight, as if called away from their prey by their alpha.

The Great Mother.

Berg and Ek stepped away from the mountain as rocks rained down around them. Scalvia transformed back into her human form, slipping quickly into her torn black bodice and furs. Her blood-caked skin began healing as she tromped up to Arud.

"Why is the ground quaking?" she asked.

Arud didn't answer.

Lykke howled, a deep, dark animal sound from

some part of her that Arud wished hadn't existed. The group huddled in the center of the valley as the ground continued to shake. Ahlgren stayed up against the far wall of the mountain. Dust rose thick around her, nearly camouflaging her from Arud's view.

"Mother," Scalvia said, reaching out her hand. "Step away from the wall."

But Ahlgren did not move.

"Ahlgren," Ek said. "What are you doing?"

With a sharp crack, the rumbling sound grew louder, and the flat wall behind her fractured. Long fissures cut through from the ground, spindling upward and separating the two chains. A hideous screech filled the air as a cloud of black rushed out the split in a single fluid motion.

"What is it?" Scalvia asked, covering her head.

The black cloud whirled as a wave and spun back around to assault them. It skimmed just above their ducked heads before popping back up into the sky.

"Bats," Arud said.

Thousands of bats flew through the air. Inside the mountain, a wail pierced the air, bone-chilling and unnatural. Camazotz? Arud swallowed hard, afraid to ask, as the final bats exited the mountain, following the swarm into the distance. A sickening feeling of dread flooded him from head to toe. Those bats had been locked inside that mountain for a reason.

He just knew it.

Ahlgren motioned to Lykke. "Come, child."

Obediently, Lykke walked over to her. Arud screamed out her name, but Lykke didn't respond. Ahlgren placed her arm around Lykke and whispered in her ear. Lykke nodded, slipping her hand into

Ahlgren's, whose smile told Arud everything he needed to know.

"It's you," he said.

Scalvia turned. "What are you talking about, Arud?"

He stepped closer to Ahlgren, his bolt held tightly in his fist. "You're the Great Mother, aren't you?"

Scalvia's eyes trailed toward her step-mother, her entire body shaking like the mountain.

Ek steadied his daughter, his arms wrapped protectively around her. "Is this true, Ahlgren, what Arud speaks?"

Ahlgren's twisted smile widened.

Scalvia covered her mouth, her head shaking violently. "No. No! It can't be true."

"It is true, child."

"Who are you?" Ek asked. "Really."

"I am the seer, the Sorceress Edda."

Ahlgren stepped backward, heading toward the severed mountain, taking Lykke with her. "King Ulfhednar lied to me. He lied to us all, defiling the beauty of our species with his men, who violated us to breed his weapon." They stepped over the crumbled rocks.

Arud matched her step for step, not allowing any more distance between them. "Where are you going with my sister?"

"To take back what is rightfully mine. Vithalia City. It is where we are supposed to live. It is our home. Not the Dreadlands, where the food is scarce and the conditions are treacherous. My place is the king's palace, where I gave him an heir before he locked us away in the dungeon as detestable monsters." Her face changed, her mouth curving down at the edges. Her eyes almost softened. "His own daughter. His flesh and blood." And as quickly, her face warped in rage. "*I* am the heir to the throne. It was stolen from me. *I* am the queen of the realm!"

Arud couldn't breathe as Ahlgren held Lykke, taking small backward strides, nearing the mountain's edge. What was she planning to do? There was nowhere they could go.

"The king gave me a child, his heir, the rightful ruler to the throne of Vithalia. And tonight, I will take it back."

"Where are you going with Lykke?"

Ahlgren laughed. "You foolish boy. You ask questions for which you already know the answers."

He did not respond as he moved closer, Scalvia marching alongside him.

"I need blood from the royal line to fulfill the prophecy," Ahlgren continued. "To take the kingdom back. The ferine will no longer be imprisoned to the light of the full moon. I will give them the power to shift freely, to roam the realm whenever they please. Man will be left to live in fear and destitution. Your kind will have to huddle in the Dreadlands starving, fighting with one another for diminishing resources. Humans will pay with royal blood for King Ulfhednar's decisions."

"So why do you need Lykke?"

"Her blood is blue, Arud. She is my great-granddaughter."

Arud's head grew light as darkness ebbed along the edges. "That isn't possible. King Ulfhednar lived and died centuries ago."

"Our kind is very old and we live much longer than men. King Ulfhednar gave me a child. The first Cur."

Arud shook his head, his knees weakening.

"She was beautiful, strong like the ferine, yet with the freedom to roam the realm like the humans."

"Stop." Arud stretched out his hands, as if trying to prevent her words from taking shape.

"She had a daughter, a powerful herbalist whose gift lay dormant most of her life."

"Shut up," Arud begged, tears stinging his eyes.

"She was your mother, Arud. She was my granddaughter."

Arud fell to his knees.

"Toov was the daughter that King Ulfhednar gave to me. The first and most powerful Cur created. Until Lykke."

Arud wept. His entire life had been a lie. Everything he had ever known had been a lie. Nothing was as it seemed. No one. He was alone, amidst family and friends.

"Toov's powers were greater than those of the ferine. With time they diminished, then fell dormant when Vinter was born. Your mother showed no signs, not until she gave birth to Lykke. When she was born, Toov regained her powers and Vinter's awakened. That is when I knew Lykke was the savior we had been waiting for."

"You're lying," Scalvia roared. "None of this is true."

"It is true, child, whether you believe it or not."

Berg raised his blade. With a flit of Ahlgren's hand, he shot through the air, landed hard in the rubble, and slumped forward.

"Father!" Arud screamed, rushing to his side. Berg lay unconscious. Arud turned rage-filled eyes upon the seer. "What have you done?"

Ahlgren cackled. "That is your biggest weakness, Arud. Your blind love for others." With a hiss, she turned on her heels, holding tightly to Lykke's hand, and stepped through the broken rocks.

Arud sprinted after her. He could see Vithalia City behind them, far in the distance. "Ahlgren, stop!"

The woman turned around, teetering on the ledge, holding Lykke, the valley spanning miles beneath them. "My name is Edda."

"Take me. I know the prophecy requires blood and mine is the same as hers. Take my blood instead."

She cackled. "How very honorable of you, Arud. But I'm afraid not. Your gift is a side-effect, if nothing more. Lykke's powers are greater than any Cur I have ever seen, greater even than the ferine. Her skills emerged even before her birth, an anomaly prophesized by King Ulfhednar himself regarding the end times. If she had been allowed to shift before her coming of age, her powers would have disappeared. Who knows how many more centuries would have passed before a child such as Lykke was born?" Ahlgren bent over Lykke. "Do you want to come with me, *lovell*?"

Lykke tightened her grip on Ahlgren's hand and slowly nodded.

"What have you done to her? You have put her under some sort of spell."

Ahlgren simply smiled a demented grin before she turned and jumped.

"Lykke!" Arud stared down as Ahlgren coasted through the air to the bottom. He heard Lykke scream until she was too far away and her voice dissipated. He turned. They were all staring at him for direction, with eyes full of heartbreak and loss: a parent mourning a dead daughter, two husbands grieving lost wives, and children without mothers, all searching Arud's face for answers. How could he help any of them? He was just a boy from the Outlands, an apple farmer, an adequate hunter, a child. Wasn't he?

Not anymore.

He had powers awakening in him, too, abilities to manipulate the space around him and strength to overcome this present darkness. He could almost hear his mother's laughter, overjoyed that he finally understood his place and purpose. He had promised her he would bring Lykke safely to Vithalia City.

He knew what he had to do.

"Father, head with Bane and Ek to the abandoned hunting cabin at the base of the Torngats. Secure it, arm yourselves, and don't leave till dawn. I'm going after Lykke."

"No," Berg said. "We must go with you."

"There's no time to argue. This is the only way."

"Listen to the lad," Bane said. "We must go now if we are to prepare in time for the creatures."

"What of you? What will you do?" Berg asked.

"I'll go down the same as Ahlgren. I'll meet her in the valley. And I will kill her."

"We will kill her," Scalvia said, taking Arud's hand. "She has stolen from me too and I won't allow her to take Lykke from us."

Arud nodded. "I need you to protect her so I can

deal with the Great Mother."

Berg grabbed Arud around the neck and squeezed him tightly. "Be careful. Both of you. And bring Lykke home safely."

"We will, Father."

Berg pulled away with a wry smile. Touching them both, he said, "Odin, far-wanderer, grant wisdom, courage, and victory. Friend Thor, grant your strength. And both be with You."

Ek stepped forward, his eyes hardened and misted. "Take care of each other. And understand that that creature is no longer my wife. She has been taken over by evil. My wife is long dead." Tears filled his eyes, and Scalvia held him tight. "I'm sorry, Scalvia."

She said nothing, only kissed his cheek and wiped hers dry, before she sidled beside Arud.

He studied her, taking in her smooth skin and dark hair, her lips and eyes, the essence of her beauty. He did love her; he knew it now.

Scalvia took his hand. "Do you trust me?"

"With my life."

And with a running start, they leapt off the mountain.

Ψ FIFTY-TWO Ψ

They soared in freefall for what seemed hours to Arud, who marveled at the beauty of the setting sun casting off the smooth walls of Vithalia City. He glanced at Scalvia, her black hair tossing in the currents like an angry wave around her face. He didn't know what would happen when they neared the bottom. He only knew they would somehow be safe. The flat plateau moved closer and closer. Scalvia's grip clenched tighter.

Arud closed his eyes. He was in the meadow behind his house again. Vinter walked toward him, wearing a long white gown. The air blew warm and smelled like spring. Backlit, she looked like an angel. He met her among the tall grasses, and they hugged.

"Mother," he cried. "I have missed you so much."

"And I, you," Vinter replied.

He let go and looked into her eyes. She smiled tenderly, brushing his hair back like she did when he was a small boy.

"You have grown into the man I always knew you would become."

Arud shook his head, his eyes downcast. "I have failed, Mother. I have lost Lykke to the Seer."

"You have not lost her."

He looked up.

"It will take the blood of you and your sister to give power to the enemy. You will decide your fate, not her."

"But I can't win. I don't even know how I'm going to reach the valley alive or how I'll keep Scalvia safe."

"Oh, but you, do. You have known for a long time. You have just been too afraid to speak it aloud."

Vinter kissed his forehead and backed slowly away. "Open your eyes, Arud. You're nearly there."

Arud's eyes shot opened. The ground was frighteningly close. But he wasn't afraid. He spoke to the ground, calling for it to soften his fall.

He felt it respond.

He called out to gravity, demanding that it release its grip upon him and Scalvia.

It obeyed.

Vinter was right. He had known for a long time. He was the descendant of a great king and a powerful seer. The first male in the lineage of the ferine.

He had the seer's powers all along.

They hit the ground gently and rolled to a stop. Scalvia's blanched face turned his way. "How did you do that?"

Arud smiled. "It's in my blood." He helped Scalvia to her feet. "Come on. We have to catch up to Lykke."

Ahead, Ahlgren and Lykke scurried along the plateau toward the city gates. The descending sun stretched long orange rays across the valley. Shadows appeared in crags that warped into the bodies of ferine, demented and frothing, pawing at the earth. Their eyes seared like hot coal burning crimson. The smell of death hung in the air.

He ran with Scalvia toward the city as the sun filtered its last light. The moon rose like a menacing foe, showering stinging white light upon them. They weren't going to make it. "Lykke!" Arud screamed.

She did not turn.

In a dissonant chorus, howls filled the air. A chill swept through the land, crawling up Arud's spine. They were surrounded. Stepping out of the shadows, countless creatures slipped into the valley. Where was everyone?

The trumpet sounded.

The city gates opened. The king's army appeared on horses, clomping across the long road leading across the ocean. Waves crashed up foamy surges on either side of the bridge, coating the men with balmy spray. They marched in the thousands and Arud felt power pulse through his body. The creatures grew restless as the army drew closer, biting the air with froth covered muzzles. They released their oily, earthen scent that Arud could smell for the first time.

"We should join the army," Scalvia said, tugging on Arud's hand.

"I won't leave Lykke."

"You have to, or she will be lost. They need you to lead them. It's Lykke's best chance."

He stood torn for a moment, debating the value of his sister's life weighed against the future of mankind. What an unfair burden to be placed upon his shoulders. His mother's image flickered before him as a specter, though her eyes glinted with life. "Go, Arud," she whispered through closed lips. "Trust her." She faded, and Arud sprinted with Scalvia away from the creatures, away from Lykke, toward the impending army that neared the shore. He hoped Vang had reached the city in time to give the king the Bloodstone. He was counting on it.

Ψ FIFTY-THREE Ψ

The soldiers reached the valley and lined up, just as night fell. Led by King Dalgaard, several hundred armed men hovered, holding silver-tipped axes and maces, bolts and arrows. Cur women started their transformation, those who had chosen to side with man, regardless of King Ulfhednar's original intentions.

The ferine gathered into a loose formation, flanking both sides of the valley. Ahlgren stood in the center as the commander. Lykke stood beside her, teeth bared. Arud's heart sank. Somehow Ahlgren had convinced her to side with them. What lies had she spun to turn her against him?

Both sides faced off. The battle, predicted centuries past, was about to take place; Armageddon had arrived. Time slowed and Arud watched, as if a bystander at first, as Scalvia shifted into her Cur form and charged toward the creatures.

The echoes of the men crested through the valley as they followed her lead. Transformed Cur headed into battle. Arud marched forward, his focus on Lykke, desperately trying to speak to her with his mind to no avail.

They cleared half the valley. Tribal screams mingled with howls clogged the air. The soldier's pace quickened, then turned into a sprint. Cur running on all fours dug up snowy dirt with sickle-like claws. The full moon spread supernatural light across the battlefield as if it were daytime.

Suddenly, Ahlgren shifted. Her skin swapped with the whitest fur Arud had ever laid eyes upon. Her muscles rippled out, slicing through where her puny human muscles had once been. She grew in size, then doubled, then tripled, towering over the others as a massive beast balancing on brutish hind legs.

Arud gasped. He had never seen a creature so motley and intimidating in all his life. How were they ever going to defeat her?

Ahlgren howled a thunderous roar, and the ground shook beneath them. The ferine howled in response, then bounded toward the charging army. They would soon be upon each other. Arud stared ahead as he ran full force toward the beasts, never losing sight of Ahlgren, whose massive body stood like a fir tree among a glade of grass.

Lykke charged as a ferine. Arud couldn't help but wonder if it was of her own accord or if she still was influenced by the seer's magic. He fought back tears. He would not let the ferine take another person whom he loved. He would fight to save his sister.

In a great collision of fur and flesh, the two armies clashed. Screams and growls, slashes of sword and teeth, rang through the valley. Arud sliced his silver spear into the chest of a ferine leaping toward him as he rolled out of its path. He lifted to his feet as another charged. He released a bolt that caught in the creature's hind quarter, then sliced his knife through the wounded ferine's neck, taking off its head. Arud plowed forward, through the raging battle, toward Lykke.

He hacked at the creatures, dodged attacks, slipped

through claws, and caught a few strikes to his arms and back. They burned like fire, but he felt them healing as quickly as they came. His sights stayed upon Lykke. He heard nothing but the rumble of battle. He wondered where Scalvia was. He hoped she was all right.

Ahlgren sat atop a bolder at the base of the Sindri-Urd Range, where Lykke paced in anticipation. Arud was closing in, swimming through the sea of creatures and as he neared the base of the rock, Ahlgren leapt between him and Lykke.

Arud readied his bolt. "I don't fear you, Seer."

Ahlgren spoke with a human tongue through her ferine muzzle, a metallic discord resonating from the oddly shaped syllables. "You. Should."

She clawed at him, and Arud pulled back. Her razor sharp nails ran at least a foot long. Her padded paws spanned larger than Arud's head. He could not win. He shot off a bolt that struck her pelt then bounced off. Her skin was too thick to penetrate. What else could he do?

Lykke gnashed her teeth at the air with a hollow clicking, her eyes garnet with rage. Arud studied the valley. Soldiers and Cur and ferine fought for the cause they each believed in. For what? For one side to claim rule of the realm? For the other species to go extinct? Arud glanced heavenward at the diamonds sprinkled against black, a rare beauty, the constellations, seen only with the inky sky as a backdrop. This was everything; the Cur and ferine, and man.

Arud and Scalvia and Lykke.

He must save his sister before she was absorbed by

the darkness. He threw his bolt to the ground and grabbed a spear in one hand and his sword in the other. The metal glinted in the moonlight. Lykke stared at him from the rock, her pace slowing.

"I am coming for you, Lykke," Arud shouted.

She howled.

Ahlgren stood upright, her body now towering three times Arud's. Arud burst forward, cutting into her leg as Ahlgren backhanded him. He flew sideways through the air, smacking into the crescent base of the mountain. Pain shot through his entire body.

He lifted to his feet. His mind again shook as he charged toward her with his spear outstretched. Ahlgren charged back. Arud reached her and ran his spear into her chest with unnatural strength. It broke through fur and flesh, and she screamed, splaying her paw over the wound gushing out blood.

So she *could* be hurt.

Enraged, Ahlgren shot forward and pushed Arud to the ground, her large paw covering his neck, choking off his windpipe.

"You have failed, Arud. Lykke is mine, and soon I will have your blood as well to fulfill the prophecy."

His vision spotted as darkness edged, closing in all around him. He couldn't break free.

"Not if I can help it."

It was Scalvia.

Ahlgren lifted off Arud, who gulped air as he crawled off to the side. His neck hurt, and each swallow scraped his bruised throat. His tearing eyes blurred his vision as he tried to pull himself together.

"You?" Ahlgren said. "You would attack your own mother?"

"You are not my mother."

With a growl, Scalvia shifted into her ferine form, her body nowhere near the size of Ahlgren's. Arud knew she stood no chance against her. Unless he did something, Scalvia would be killed. He looked upon the boulder. Lykke stared down, her eyes changing, sad almost, her body still in ferine form.

"Lykke," Arud said hoarsely.

She fluttered her eyes, but did not move, still under the spell.

"Lykke...help us."

Her head moved.

Ahlgren and Scalvia circled each other, showing bloodied yellow teeth. Their hackles raised in high ridges down their spines.

"Lykke, please. Don't do this. Don't help Ahlgren. It's because of her that our mother is dead."

Lykke stared at Arud. Could she even understand him?

"She'll kill everyone we love."

Ahlgren pounced and Scalvia tumbled out of her way, but her timing was off and she caught a five-clawed rake down her back. She flew to the ground, her front claws catching in Ahlgren's leg. Her face contorted in rage, blotched with dark crimson blood, and she charged upon Scalvia.

"Lykke, please!" Arud pushed to his feet.

Ahlgren pounced on Scalvia. Deep piercing wails flooded the air as they wrestled in a tight circle trying to kill one another.

Arud stared at the surreal scene around him: bodies' bloodied and broken, creatures mauling humans, humans massacring creatures. He faced his sister, a frothing ferine, lost within herself, hidden behind the beast. If he wanted her back, he would have to kill Ahlgren.

And then, he remembered something Bane had told him: *"It is your love for her that strengthens you, that binds you together."*

"No matter what happens, I love you, Lykke" he called.

Her ear twitched. He hoped some part of her had heard him. With a readied bolt, Arud launched himself onto the rock, aiming his weapon at Ahlgren. But he could not shoot. She scrapped with Scalvia so furiously he could not risk shooting her by mistake. Blood covered Ahlgren's snow white fur. Scalvia was too black to differentiate.

She whimpered and dropped her hold on Ahlgren, who stood upright, blood dripping from teeth to her muzzle.

Arud ran over to Scalvia. She was breathing, but not moving, her wounds deep. Arud slowly stood, turned to face Ahlgren. "I'm going to kill you today. Do you hear me? I *will* kill you today."

Ahlgren bayed in laughter.

Arud felt black rage course through him, awakening places he never knew existed. His blood was hers. It was Vinter's. It was Toov's. He was not just a boy protecting his sister. He had become powerful. His blood was powerful. But what did that mean?

Ahlgren moved nearer to Lykke, her back facing Arud. She stretched out her huge paw and grabbed Lykke by the neck. Instantly, Lykke changed into her human form, appearing like a limp rag doll in

Ahlgren's massive grip. Her face turned purple. Her hands groped at the paw cutting off her air. With bulging eyes, she looked to Arud, whispering his name with her last breath.

Arud trembled. The ground quaked. The air swirled in torrents all around him. The whole world seemed to be shimmying as Lykke's life passed before his eyes. He screamed a chilling growl that echoed through the valley.

And he launched forward.

He no longer cared if he lived or died. His only thoughts were of killing the Seer. As he ran, he felt his skin stretch and peel. His bones shifted and his muscles tensed, pushing him faster toward the Great Mother. His eyes pressed closer together as his vision opened, the darkness barely noticeable. Now he was running on all fours, his breathing deeper, his pulse faster. He charged at Ahlgren, and she turned in time to see him flying at her.

And for the first time, it was her eyes that filled with terror.

Ψ FIFTY-FOUR Ψ

Arud slammed into Ahlgren, knocking her off her feet. Her grip slipped, and Lykke fell to the ground. Arud pinned Ahlgren, his own body somehow towering over hers. The hand he held against her chest was covered in silver fur. Thick silver blades had replaced his nails. His muscles had tripled in size.

He was a ferine.

He wrestled Ahlgren as Scalvia had. Each stab of his silver claws made her flesh sizzle. Each raging bite from his serrated silver teeth tore her apart. He attacked. For his mother, his sister, his life, his world. He used it all to power his onslaught.

Ahlgren fought back. Her claws dug into his pelt and skin. Her teeth ripped through his muscles, but his rage overpowered her hunger for dominance.

Out of the corner of his eyes, Arud saw Lykke stirring. She was alive. In that second of distraction, where his love was stronger than his hate, Ahlgren struck out and swatted him away. He landed hard on his back, the air knocked out of him, and Ahlgren wasted no time launching onto his chest.

"You discovered your power, I see," Ahlgren said, her claws slipping deeper into his neck. "Now can you understand why I sent Scalvia to collect you and your sister."

Arud felt his mind go numb.

"We were forced to live in the Dreadlands, to live off the degradation and filth of the world. We were painted as the enemy, but it isn't true. We are the victims. Can't you understand that? Your blood and Lykke's blood will make everything right again."

She raised her hackles, her flexed paw above her head. Her claws grew another few inches. Arud braced for his impending death. Lykke screamed. Scalvia stirred and Arud turned his head. They stared into each other's eyes as Ahlgren's claws pierced Arud in the heart.

He gasped.

The world disappeared for a moment.

Scalvia screamed.

Her beautiful body was human again, as dark hair fell across her shoulders in waves, and bright unwavering eyes filled with tears.

Suddenly, Ahlgren's face contorted, and she retracted her claws. Black blood oozed out of her mouth and stained her white muzzle. She clutched her stomach. Blood drenched her paws. Arud's claws had entered her, continued through her body, and out her back.

"What have you done?" Ahlgren stammered.

"Made everything right." Arud twisted his hands. His claws shredded through muscles and tissues, shattered bones and punctured organs before he yanked them out again. Slivers of her black heart dripped from his claws. She sucked in a jagged breath and staggered backward.

"I have fulfilled the prophecy," Arud said, as Ahlgren stumbled to her knees.

His eyelids went heavy. His breathing turned shallow. Pain seared in his chest. The taste of iron filled his mouth. He blinked, then forced his heavy eyelids open. Lykke was on Ahlgren's back tearing at her face with clawed hands.

Arud blinked again, opened his eyes.

Scalvia had latched on to Ahlgren's side, stabbing her in the head with her silver dagger. Blood spilled from the wounds, draining Ahlgren's life.

A death to sustain life.

Tears spilled from Arud's eyes and down the sides of his cheeks as he felt his own life slipping away. But he welcomed death, knowing the others were going to be all right. Knowing Lykke was going to live and grow up in a world without fear of the ferine, with Scalvia to love her as a sister, the way Arud always had. Just before his eyes closed for the last time, a brilliant red light shone through the air from Vithalia City, raining blood on the battlefield like rubies.

Vang had made it.

Ψ FIFTY-FIVE Ψ

Arud's eyes opened. He was surrounded by quiet, a stillness so eerie it took him awhile to remember what had happened. Images flooded his mind: the ferine army, silver weapons cutting fur and flesh, Scalvia and Lykke toppling off Ahlgren, his silver claws tearing out the Great Mother's heart.

He sat up in the cool darkness and swung his legs over the edge of the cot. The floor was cold marble, and it sent a shiver across his skin. Smooth walls glittered like a pearl, and Arud realized where he was.

Vithalia City.

He was draped in a soft cloth dress reaching mid-calf. The air smelled heavy of medicinal herbs, reminding him of his home. Of his mother.

On a nearby chair lay his pants and tunic. Gingerly, he stepped across the room and dressed. He hurt all over, but he was alive. How was it possible? He touched his chest. Only scar tissue and scabs remained from where Ahlgren had cut through him.

He opened the door on silent hinges and peered out. Men and women busily criss-crossed the halls, carrying out their business. Arud must be in the city's healing facility. He imagined there were many wounded and dead. He wouldn't allow himself to estimate the numbers. Closing the door, he sat back on the cot, winded. He checked his body in the glass attached to the wall for any additional wounds. His hair had been cut and washed. His cheek was emblazoned with a fresh scar. Tenderly, Arud touched the small of his back. It hurt, but he felt only a bump left over from where Ahlgren had sliced him.

The doorknob turned, and the door swung opened. Lykke poked her head full of golden curls into the room. Arud smiled.

"Arud, you're awake!" she said, running into the room. She fell into his arms where he held her tight.

"I thought I'd lost you," he said.

"You won't ever lose me."

A tall man with dark hair and broad shoulders stood behind her. He walked over to Arud and smiled. "Greetings, Arud. My name is Bodolf. I am your uncle."

Arud forced a smile, his face flinching. "Pleased to meet you, sir."

Bodolf nodded. "And I, you. Too many years have passed without knowing you and Lykke. She tells me you are a skilled hunter."

"Yes. My father taught me well."

"And who do you think taught him?" Bodolf laughed. "I look forward to your recovery. Wilderboar season begins in a few weeks. Think you will be ready for a hunt by then?"

"I hope so," Arud said.

"Get well, nephew. We have much to catch up on. Come, Lykke. Let your brother rest." Smiling, he turned and let himself out of the room.

Lykke kissed Arud's cheek. "I'm so happy you're better."

He smiled as she danced out of the room, closing the door behind her. No sooner had it shut then it reopened.

"Hey, you," Scalvia said, standing in the doorway. A dress clung to her figure from her bare shoulders to her bare feet.

"Scalvia."

She sat beside him, kissed his face. "How are you feeling?"

"Better now, knowing you and Lykke are safe." He stared into her eyes. The yellow rings had dissolved, returning her irises to a stormy gray hue.

"The war is over, Arud. We've won."

He pushed her hair back behind her ear and half-smiled. Was it really over? The ferine were defeated. Arud had destroyed their Great Mother. Peace was restored to the realm, and soon everyone would be safe to travel, even amidst a full moon. But in the back of his mind, like a splinter he couldn't reach, Arud wondered of the Prophecy of Myrkr, the one Bane had mentioned would come to pass now that the Prophecy of Ulfhednar had been fulfilled.

Scalvia lay beside him, holding his hand, and he sighed in the comfort of her skin; the scent of her hair. For now, he would mend and find peace.

Before he was forced to once again shift.

Before the ferine rose to seek vengeance.

Before Arud would have to fight another battle.

Ψ THE END Ψ

This page intentionally left blank.
To learn why, join the 1,000True Fans Club.
http://tinyurl.com/hup9xaq

If you enjoyed this book, please take a moment to review it on Amazon for other readers to discover it.

Become a fan

 @jaimiengleauthor  @jaimiengle

@jaimiengle

Jaimie is available for school visits & conferences. Visit jaimiengle.com for dates.

ACKNOWLEDGMENTS

This story wouldn't be complete without acknowledging several people who have helped along the way. First and foremost, to God for gifting me with a talent to write stories and the job to share them with others. To Matthew J. Kirby, one of my favorite authors, who read an early section of this story and encouraged me to develop the book. To the editors at Big 5 Houses who loved the manuscript and gave me the confidence I needed to indie publish. To my beta readers, especially Christine Edwards and Jim Knight, my muses, and Karen Dibbern for noticing the "frozen strawberries"; to Lucas Engle for developing the plot with me on dog walks and Jason Engle for explaining that "Nightcrawlers," the original title, were worms. To Philip Benjamin for crafting the most beautiful book cover imaginable and Debbie Johnson for your artistic touch in creating the mapped borders of my story world. And finally, to you, my faithful reader, for reading my stories and sharing them with friends; for being the reason I write. Without all of you, I never would have had the courage, pleasure, or reason to write and publish this book.

Jaimie Engle was once sucked into a storybook, where she decided she would become an author. She has modeled bikinis, managed a hip-hop band, and run a body shop. Her passion is talking to kids about writing and social issues because words have power. When not writing, she's probably editing or playing trivia. She lives in Florida with her awesome husband, hilarious children, and the world's best dog. Become a fan at jaimiengle.com.

INSPIRE. EMPOWER. EDUCATE
WWW.JAIMIENGLE.COM

54261395R00206

Made in the USA
Charleston, SC
31 March 2016